DUNCAN McGEARY'S
DEATH OF AN IMMORTAL
Vampire Evolution - Book 1

BOOKS of the DEAD

Duncan McGeary

Cover Design by Small Dog Design

Book Design by James Roy Daley
Edited by Lara Milton

**Death of an Immortal:
Vampire Evolution Trilogy #1**

Copyright 2014 by Duncan McGeary

For more information, contact: Besthorror@gmail.com
Visit us at: Booksofthedeadpress.com

Dedicated to Wes Hare, who was always encouraging, from the beginning.

Chapter 1

Terrill awoke to an empty mirror. Empty but for the bland motel décor: the disheveled bed, with its too many pillows and overstuffed bedspread; the innocuous framed picture of leaves on the wall. Empty, though the mirror was right in front of his face.

She probably thought he was dead. Sometimes when he slept, he forgot to mimic the motions of breathing. She was probably trying to see if his breath would fog the mirror. Oh, God. Why had she done this? The part of him that was human struggled to control the part of him that was immortal. *No!* he shouted at himself in his mind. *Leave her be!*

His vampiric instincts, the same instincts that had kept him alive for a millennium, were in full command. The small vessel of empathy he'd managed to fill, drip by drip, in recent years disappeared in an overpowering bloodlust. His fangs fully extended, dripping with the venom that would paralyze her.

The little white hand holding the mirror looked bloodless, though Terrill had yet to take her blood. The female was naked and pale with fright from head to toe. Her eyes were wide, her pupils dilated, her chest quivering. No predator could have passed up such a pure victim. Terrill instantly flushed with the thrill of the hunt, his sleepiness evaporating in a surge of hunger.

Again his mind fought against his overwhelming urges. *Don't do it! Let her go! Let her live, damn you!*

She screamed, dropping the mirror to the floor with a crash. It shattered: seven years of bad luck—or in Terrill's case, probably more like seven hundred years. In the girl's case, it wasn't even seven seconds. She made it halfway across the room before Terrill flew out of the bed and sank his fangs into her neck.

Don't… oh, God. It was so good. He had missed this so much. Why had she woken him? Why had she roused the monster inside him?

His mind was still screaming *Stop!*, but now it was too late. Once a vampire started feeding, he couldn't stop until he was finished.

She was dead in seconds.

Terrill saw himself in her dying eyes—the only way he could ever see his reflection. He hadn't seen himself in twenty years. It didn't matter; he still looked the same—sharp saturnine features, eyes glowing with bloodlust, frowning in his hunger, black hair immaculate even amid his wild feeding.

He laid the girl's lifeless body gently on the floor. Guilt wrapped around his shoulders like an old familiar shawl. He nearly staggered. Inside, he felt a savage rush, an exhilaration he hadn't felt in a very long time. But the thinking part of him, the part to which he'd sacrificed the past twenty years, was sickened. It was gone; all his effort had come to nothing. He was the same soulless creature he'd always been. Nothing could change that.

Joy. That was the name she'd given him. When she'd signed into the motel, she had used the name Jamie. She should have stuck to Jamie—a prettier name, a name that was real—just as she should've stuck to her hometown origins, gotten a job as a waitress, attended community college, met a nice, stupid boy—who knows where she would have ended up?

Not here. Not dead.

Her scream still hung in the air, and Terrill extended his hearing to the neighbors on either side and to the street outside. Nothing. The people who inhabited this seedy motel were no doubt used to screams in the night—and used to ignoring them.

Quiet as a tomb, Terrill thought.

He took a shower, got dressed, and left. Considerate of the people sleeping nearby, he closed the door quietly and walked softly down the rickety stairs and out into the empty street. He was always considerate.

* * *

Terrill made it to the end of the block. The streetlamp was at half strength, flickering. There was a false dawn on the horizon, but real dawn would follow within the hour: in thirty-four minutes, to be exact. Terrill could calculate sunrise nearly to the second.

He turned and walked back to the motel and made his way to the top of the landing. His senses were on full alert, but there was no one about, no one watching. He slipped back into the room.

The girl lay in an unnatural tangle, her arms flung overhead, her legs drawn up behind her. Terrill straightened her body, smoothed her hair. He took the heavy bedspread and tucked it around her. He closed her frightened eyes.

She was almost completely drained, but he was able to suck up one last mouthful of blood. He went to the bathroom and spit the blood into the bathtub drain.

At the last second, he took her necklace from the table by the bed. The crucifix burned into his hand before he put it into his pocket. Even there, he could feel its power.

Why had he taken it? He didn't know. He just knew that he needed some part of her to come with him, and the crucifix had been important to her.

He kissed her on the forehead and left the room in the same manner as before. Dawn glimmered in the east. The skin on Terrill's face felt taut, as if preparing for the pain the sunlight would bring.

His car was three blocks away.

He made it just in time.

The windows were tinted to just the right extent: he could see the light of dawn, he could even drive, but the burning—the hellfire—was held at bay. He crawled into the backseat and closed his eyes.

Chapter 2

"So what's your name?" the girl asked.

"Really? Do people really ever give you their real name?"

"No," she admitted. "But I can tell something about them by the name they do give me."

"Then... my name is Ted."

She looked sad. Genuinely sad. As if she actually cared about a stranger she'd met in a bar—a meal ticket, a John.

Curious, he asked, "What does that tell you?"

"You want to be ordinary. You want to stay home and watch TV, eat at McDonald's, gain fifty pounds and live out your life." She eyed his lean, tall frame, his impeccably tailored suit, his razor-sharp haircut, his manicured nails. He looked to be in his late twenties or early thirties, but he seemed so much older. "Everything you aren't..."

* * *

Terrill slept less than an hour: forty-five minutes, to be exact. He woke snarling, his jaw protruding, his fangs exposed, his claws extended.

There was knocking at the car window, and through it, he could see the outline of a head, wearing a hat he recognized as a policeman's cap. He calmed himself. For a thousand years, he had never been able to restrain that first impulse after discovery—the impulse to kill, to feed. It was only in the past few centuries that he'd been able to control it at all.

Terrill breathed deeply as the knocking increased in force and tempo. He gauged the height of the sun, the slant of its rays, the distance he needed to maintain. He positioned himself about halfway across the backseat from the window, and reached over and hit the button. He retracted his hand just in time as the window rolled down.

The light hit the first quarter of the seat full on; the next quarter was in the shade, but still burned. He slid over about an inch, and it was tolerable.

"This is a no-parking zone," the cop said. He was beefy, red-faced, and exactly the type of prey Terrill had always preferred: someone who could, on a good day and with immense luck, actually hurt him—although it hadn't happened yet.

"I was getting way too sleepy last night," Terrill said. "I decided it might be safer to pull over and get some rest."

The policeman radiated skepticism; he probably met every response from every citizen with the same attitude. It made the guilty squirm, no doubt. Terrill kept his face blank and the cop finally shrugged. *So far, so good,* Terrill thought.

"Well, that's a good idea, sir," the cop said. "I applaud you for it. But you need to move along."

"Thanks. I will." It was a rare sunny fall day in Portland. Terrill had gravitated to the coastal Northwest because such days were unusual. The rain and clouds, the fog and the mists—all were perfect for him.

Terrill didn't move. He *couldn't* move. Climbing into the front seat would necessitate moving into direct sunlight. So he busied himself with straightening his clothes, smoothing his hair, smiling at the cop.

"May I see your driver's license and registration?" The officer sounded exasperated.

While the policeman had been thinking about his next move, Terrill had reached into his pocket, taken out his gloves, and put them on. He angled himself over the seat, trying not to look too awkward. The angle was wrong and as he struggled with the latch of the glove compartment, his sleeve rode up his forearm and he felt the sharp pain of long-dead flesh exposed to sunlight. Finally, he snatched his registration and fell back into shadow, and the pain immediately subsided as his arm healed. He handed the documents over to the cop carefully, making sure every inch of skin was covered.

Meanwhile, he casually looked around at the neighborhood. Cops always attracted attention. There would be people watching this, from the corners of their eyes, glad it wasn't them who had been stopped. Terrill practiced the attack in his mind: reaching out and grabbing the cop's head, twisting his neck before the man could make a sound, leveraging the body swiftly through the window, closing the window, and scrambling over the seat and driving away.

He reached into the light and opened the window the last couple of inches. Again the sleeve rode up and exposed part of his arm, and he grimaced at the pain. The cop was still examining the papers.

Terrill waited for the words "Would you please step out of the car, sir?"

Ironically, fully opening the window seemed to reassure the cop, as if it had somehow made Terrill less of threat. The cop handed him back his papers, even going so far as to reach in enough for Terrill to take them without extending his arm into the light again.

"Have a good day," the cop said.

"Thank you. I will."

Terrill maneuvered himself over the center console and plopped into the driver's seat, but not before his right cheek was exposed to full sunlight for a second. It sizzled and smoked. He put his gloved hand to his face and looked at the policeman, who was looking at the traffic.

He started the car and put it into gear.

"One more thing," the cop said.

Terrill almost pulled away, because the officer had that warning tone in his voice again.

"You need to have your rearview mirror unobstructed."

The mirror was covered with one of Terrill's many hats, which he had casually hung there. Terrill reached up and removed it, hoping the cop wasn't looking directly in the mirror. But the officer had already lost interest and was waving him on.

Terrill eased into traffic. He headed east on Burnside Street, and when he looked in the rearview mirror, he saw that the cop was following him. He kept heading east, finally reaching the airport and turning into the parking lot. The police car kept going.

Terrill sat back and closed his eyes.

Time to leave town? He always left town after a kill.

He'd stayed in Portland longer than anywhere else. Twenty years of drinking cow's blood and that of an occasional stray dog. Twenty years of existing peacefully among humans.

Damn her. Why had she woken him like that? What had made her suspect him? And why couldn't he have had just a second to think, to pause, before he killed her?

"Jamie Howe," she had written on the motel registration form. A small-town girl, too honest to lie even for one evening, except to her John, and even then, she had caught him looking and shrugged at him with a wistful smile.

He pulled out his phone and looked her up. There was a Jamie Lee Howe from Bend, just on the other side of the Cascade mountain range. He pulled out of the parking lot and headed southeast, toward Mount Hood.

Terrill had sworn he would never kill again. But he had. He was still vampire, not human. All he could do now was try to make up for it somehow, to make amends to the girl's family and friends. To rebuild what little shreds of humanity he still contained by learning all he could about Jamie Lee Howe. Who was she, and how had she ended up in the bed of a vampire?

Chapter 3

Jamie had wanted him to find her, Carlan was sure of it. She had signed in with her own name. Had she suspected there was something wrong? Was it a cry for help?

"You knew her?" one of the techs asked. It was quiet in the motel room, except for the shuffling sound of the plastic shoe covers they wore and the occasional squeak of latex gloves.

She was exposed to the world, naked. There was little blood. She looked pale and lovely. *Peaceful,* Carlan thought. *Peaceful at last.*

"She was like this when you found her?" he asked the tech.

"We untangled her from the bedspread. We're thinking whoever killed her knew her, because they carefully covered her up. They crossed her arms across her chest."

Carlan shook his head. Jamie didn't know anyone in Portland. Why had she come here? What was she doing in a seedy motel? Why had she left him? He'd taken care of her for years—she had wanted for nothing. That last time, he'd even offered to marry her.

Damn her and her obstinacy. What had gotten into her?

He wanted to lie down beside her, lay his head on her chest. He struggled for a moment to contain his impulse, turning away from the tech.

Someone opened the curtains and the room flooded with light. Everyone in the room flinched. Carlan put his hand up, shielding his face from the light, and turned away. He looked down at Jamie again. Her eyes seemed to be staring at him. Accusing him. It was his fault she was here. His fault she was dead.

She looked tiny, deflated. He always called her "Short Stuff," but she had been a dynamo in a small package. Now she looked like she'd been soaked in bleach, all the color drained from her.

"Close the damn curtains." The voice was commanding, and as soon as the room dimmed again, Carlan saw a very large, very fat man in the doorway. The guy had a huge bald head and small, narrowed eyes that surveyed the motel room, landing on Carlan. "Who are you?"

"Richard Carlan. Bend Police."

"What's your interest in the case?"

"I dated her for a while. Her family asked me to find her."

"How long have you been in town?"

"I drove over the pass this morning."

The big cop stared at him. They both knew that in cases like this, the boyfriend or husband was always the primary suspect. Finally, a big beefy hand was extended. "Detective Brosterhouse."

Carlan shook the hand. His eyes went back to Jamie. "Why is there no blood?"

"Yeah, well, you're not going to believe this." The older cop leaned over and gently turned Jamie's head, revealing two deep punctures in her neck.

"So you're thinking?"

"The lab guys found some blood in the bathtub. I think he probably drained her there and then wanted us to think 'vampire.' Or he thought he was a vampire. Who knows what these nutcases think?"

Carlan was trying to act professional, like it was any other crime scene, any other murder he'd seen. But it was Jamie. His Jamie.

She looked utterly defenseless on the floor, her nakedness... he closed his eyes.

"Can't..." he faltered. "Can't you cover her up?"

Brosterhouse nodded to the tech, who flipped one of the corners of the blanket over her.

Just like that, she was gone. Forever.

Carlan would find the person who did this and kill him. She was his— no one else's. She'd run away from him, but it was all a misunderstanding. Things had gotten messy, complicated. He'd lashed out, but he hadn't meant any of it.

She hadn't given him a chance to explain, to apologize, to make up.

Brosterhouse was watching him. He struggled to keep his face impassive.

"The only real mystery here," the Portland cop said, "is why the vampire charade. Other than that... well, it's obvious she was a working girl."

Carlan's face flushed and his jaw clenched. He couldn't help it.

Brosterhouse nodded as if confirming something to himself. "I'm willing to let you help us," he said. "But you need to check with me before you do anything, got it? Meanwhile, give me the number to your station in Bend."

Carlan rattled off the number. They were going to check on him, he knew. They'd find out that she had had a restraining order on him. Once, that would've been embarrassing, but with Jamie dead, he didn't care.

He hadn't left Bend until six a.m., but he'd have to find a way to prove that. Forensics had already determined that she had died sometime between midnight and dawn.

With or without the help of the Portland cops, Carlan was going to find whoever had done this. He was going to make the killer pay. He wanted whoever had done this to feel the same despair, the same sense of loss, that he did.

Whoever had killed Jamie must have family, friends. He'd find the murderer. But more, he'd find whoever the murderer loved most and…

"We're ready to move her now," the forensics guy said to Brosterhouse.

The big cop waved Carlan out of the room. They stood to one side of the door, on the landing, as the body was loaded onto the gurney and wheeled from the motel room.

"Wait," Carlan said suddenly.

"What is it?" Brosterhouse asked. Something in his tone suggested that he was expecting Carlan to confess or something.

"Let me see her again."

"She's gone, pal. I don't think that's a good idea."

"No… I need to check something."

Brosterhouse hesitated, then went over to the gurney and unzipped the body bag. Carlan leaned over. He tried not to look at her face as he stared at her punctured neck.

"She's missing a necklace, a silver crucifix. Her mother gave it to her." Unbidden and unwanted, the image came to him of the last time he'd seen her: her battered face, her bloody fingers holding the crucifix as if it would protect her from his blows. He felt a moment of doubt; then his hunger for revenge returned.

"Whoever killed her took it."

Chapter 4

As he drove up the Mount Hood pass, the thick forests of the Cascade Mountains reminded Terrill of the old Black Forest of his youth. He was comfortable with the shadows, the darkness of the rocks and streams. Once, upon arriving in the Northwest, he had experimented by bundling up and walking the Pacific Crest Trail in daytime, just to see if he could do it. He had gone for miles, evading sunlit areas, hopping from shadow to shadow. He loved the rain and the thick growth of trees and vegetation.

He had never been east of the summit.

At the top of the pass, the trees changed—within seconds, it seemed— from thick fir forests with heavy underbrush to larger and more expansive ponderosa pines with little undergrowth.

The air became dry, fragrant with the smells of pine needles and bitterbrush. The sun seemed brighter and lower to the earth.

Terrill almost turned around. He could do nothing to bring the girl, Jamie, back. What would he accomplish by putting himself in danger? In the rearview mirror, he saw comfortably slate-gray skies with dotted trails of rain clouds overhanging the Willamette Valley. Ahead, he saw brightness and danger.

The High Desert, a part of the Great American Basin, was something he'd purposely avoided, flying over by airplane every time he needed to travel. East of Bend, he knew, were miles and miles of lava rock slopes, filled with low, scraggly juniper trees and dry, woody sagebrush. He felt exposed just thinking about it.

Vampires thrived in the visceral fluids of men and of the earth; in the darkness and the cover of the cities, in dark and rainy forests and mountains. They avoided the sparseness of small towns, where a local might be immediately missed and a stranger immediately suspected. Above all, vampires avoided the sun.

Terrill pulled over to the side of the road.

"What the hell are you doing?" he asked himself out loud.

He could turn around, head farther north, into Olympic National Park and on to the equally rainy Seattle area. It wasn't too late.

* * *

"Where are you from?" Jamie asked. It was after their first lovemaking session. She had started off stiff and uncomfortable, but his need had been great and he had ignored her discomfort at first. Then something had changed inside him, and he had slowed down and tried to bring her along with him. That had never happened before. He took what he needed and wanted from humans, without caring whether they liked it.

But he had to admit, it had been a more satisfying experience somehow when she had climaxed with him... or at least pretended to. She was a whore, he reminded himself.

"Nowhere and everywhere," he answered finally.

"That's too bad," she said. She frowned.

"Why?" he asked. Most people were intrigued by his answer, envious of his world-weary traveler pose, but she seemed almost to pity him.

"I love Bend, my hometown. It's the best of all worlds. It has everything I've ever wanted."

"Yet here you are, in Portland."

"Only for awhile. I'll go back as soon as..."

"As soon as what?"

"I have a couple of things I have to work out. There is... someone... I need distance from. But eventually, I'll go back. I know it."

He watched her face as she was speaking, and her enthusiasm was irresistible. He grabbed her and slid her underneath him while she laughed.

"You should visit sometime. I think you'd like it there!" she said.

"I like it right here, right now."

* * *

The summit of the Mount Hood pass was half in shadow and half in light. Terrill pulled out onto the highway and drove down into the light.

Half the trees he passed were orange, seemingly dead. *Pine beetle damage*, Terrill thought, thinking he'd read something about it in *The Oregonian*. The dryness didn't make him any more comfortable. The mountain lakes were bright blue and the roads to them paved with red cinders. He kept to the main highway and drove through the quaint tourist town of Sisters and on into Bend.

He'd become practiced at finding local motels where he could pass unnoticed. Not too fancy, not too seedy; not too new or too old; bland and slightly downhill of their peak: that's what Terrill preferred. Bend had several that fit the bill.

It was still hours until dark. This late in the year, he'd be able to venture out after about four p.m. as long as he wore his hat and gloves and a long scarf wrapped around his face. But he had a couple of hours to kill until then, so he drove around, exploring the town. It didn't take him more than hour to drive all the main roads.

Finally, he judged it dark enough to pull up to the office of one of the motels, park under the overhang there, and hop out. He rented a room with a queen-size bed, microwave, and refrigerator, and paid for a week.

Terrill checked into his room and then consulted the Yellow Pages for the nearest independent butcher. He got back in the car and drove to the butcher's, where he ordered several pounds of steak, and then drove back to the motel. He ate the meat raw, licking the butcher paper clean of blood.

The blandness of the blood brought back the memory of his feeding on Jamie. He hadn't wanted that. Especially not after trying for decades not to kill another human. Especially not her. He had really liked her, perhaps more than any other mortal woman in his long existence.

Terrill felt defeated, sick, and the raw meat did little to make him feel satiated. He wouldn't feel satiated ever again, not if he could help it. He would starve first.

Or so he told himself.

But the memory of waking up, staring into an empty mirror, and feeling the old bloodlust again was overpowering. Even as he'd sunk his teeth into her neck, he'd been aware of the wrongness of it. Even as he'd drained her, he had known he was killing her.

But he couldn't stop.

Never again would he trust himself to seek comfort in another human being. *Another human being?* No, that wasn't right. He wasn't human.

He was a monster. He had always been a monster. He would always be a monster.

Chapter 5

In London, England, Horsham awoke at the exact moment the sun went down. There was a soft sound in the other room, and his fangs immediately extended, his face elongated, and his claws dug into the mattress. He leapt off the bed and was at the door in moments. Then he stopped and took a breath. *No!* he thought. *Rule Three: Never feed where you live. Take hold of yourself!*

He was gripping the doorknob so hard that it had crumpled in his hand. Saliva dripped from his jaws to the floor, but he retracted his fangs. He rolled his shoulders, trying to relax them, and looked down at his claws and turned them back into human hands.

The servant girl in the next room turned when the door opened. Her fabled master, whom she had never seen in person before, came in wearing a thick bathrobe, his dark hair tousled and an even darker look on his face.

"You are never to be here when I awake," he growled. "Get out!"

She paled, as if realizing the danger she was in. "I'm sorry. The paperboy was late today, so…"

"Get out!"

"Yes, sir. Right away." She fled from the room, closing the door behind her.

Normally, the coffee and morning newspaper were waiting in the kitchen when Horsham woke up at dusk. The servants and guards who protected him throughout the day were gone—for their own protection. Sometimes he couldn't help himself when he first woke up. At that vulnerable moment, his hunger was always at its strongest and most instinctual.

He sat and drank the coffee in three gulps, glanced at the paper and threw it aside.

Horsham walked to his desk and turned on his laptop. The Internet was the wonder of the ages. He should know: although he was a little fuzzy about computers, he certainly knew about the ages.

For generations, Horsham had hired cadres of young women to scan the world's newspapers for specific types of stories. He'd spent hours every week reading the stories that had met his parameters. As the decades went by without Terrill being found, those parameters had widened. Sometimes it had seemed like reading the news was all he did.

Now all he had to do was turn on his computer. Through the magic of algorithms, he got a complete and accurate readout of the world's news, from which he gleaned only the most pertinent stories. But even now, he had to read for a steady half hour every morning because of all the bullshit people printed. *Garbage in, garbage out,* he thought.

He was eight minutes into his daily routine when an item caught his eye.

Portland, Oregon. A young woman had been found murdered in a motel, drained of blood, with two puncture wounds to the neck. A broken mirror had been found near the body, and police theorized that one of the fragments had been used to kill her. They didn't try to explain the missing blood.

There was a vampire story nearly every day, somewhere in the world. But in almost every case, at least one of the details was wrong. This, on the other hand, was a basic news item, with no inaccuracies about vampires, and that made it interesting to Horsham. Even the fact that the victim hadn't been consumed didn't rule out Terrill. He wasn't acting like a normal vampire anymore; killing this girl had probably been unintentional.

Portland was a place a vampire might gravitate to, just as Horsham migrated to different parts of the world depending on the rainy seasons.

He deleted the rest of the stories but left this one up, with a note to investigate further.

Then he got dressed and went out to feed.

* * *

Europe was by far the best hunting grounds for a vampire. There were multiple countries—meaning multiple jurisdictions—within a few hours of each other. In the U.S., with its Homeland Security measures, it was getting difficult to find prey without attracting notice.

Horsham employed a random location generator, and today the program had spit out Inverness, the de facto capital of the Scottish Highlands. It was about a 560-mile trip from London. He hesitated. He could overrule the random generator, but he preferred not to. He also preferred not to leave a record of where he traveled, or else he would have taken his private jet.

He only needed to feed once a month, so a two-day trip to the Scottish Highlands wasn't out of line. He needed a vacation. He certainly could afford it. Compound interest was a vampire's best friend.

He packed his overnight bag and took a cab down to the train station.

Horsham paid in cash for a private room in a luxury sleeping car on the express train from London to Inverness. He stayed out of the public gathering spots on the train for the first couple of hundred miles, ordering his meals delivered to his room: raw steak, as raw as the law would allow them to serve. His hunger for blood was growing with every second, and now that it was about to be satiated, the urgency seemed to grow exponentially.

He'd held off for months this time, trying to instill discipline in himself. But he didn't want to wait too long—he had a theory that the longer he waited, the weaker he became. Being discovered—and having to move, to reinvent himself yet again—was less of a danger than being weak. Weak got you killed.

That's why he'd been certain that he could track Terrill down. Terrill couldn't afford to be weak. At first, Horsham thought it would be a matter of days… then weeks, months, years, decades. Occasionally, his old enemy would slip up, but by the time Horsham would arrive on the scene, Terrill would have moved on.

And then, for the past two decades, nothing. No news. Other, lesser vampires were at work in the world, but Horsham could sense that they weren't Terrill. Sloppy and self-indulgent, these vampires were often caught and destroyed.

Terrill and Horsham were the last of the old breed.

Eventually, it would be only Horsham.

* * *

As night fell, he made his way to the dining car.

They all looked up when he entered the car—of course they did. He was a striking figure: six feet, four inches tall, with solid black hair, dark eyes, and a silvered goatee (he'd added the silver), dressed formally, almost archaically, in a suit complete with a vest and boutonniere—a rich man's affectations.

Most everyone else was in shorts and T-shirts, even the well-off among them. Horsham looked around for young and unattached people—men or women, it didn't matter to him as long as their blood was healthy. It was mere force of habit; he had no intention of feeding where he had been seen.

There was a gay couple in the car, and both men eyed him. There were three tables of older couples, and one young family. There was a single female, better dressed than the other women and far better looking than the matronly American tourists. A working girl, he guessed from long experience. She gave off that flavor.

Horsham sat down, ignoring his fellow passengers, waving away the menu offered by a server and ordering another raw steak, this time with a baked potato and green beans, which he wouldn't eat but would push around on the plate like a six-year-old child. The proximity of so much human blood was almost too much, but he didn't show his growing hunger.

He ate the steak slowly, though he wanted to eat it in one bite, grab the nearest diner, and feast on him or her and then the rest of them. Short work. No witnesses. He could leap off the train at speeds that would kill a human. It would be a mystery, just another mass murder in the headlines.

A shadow fell over him, and he wasn't surprised when he looked up to see the single female. She was new at the game; disease or drugs hadn't yet ravaged her blood. She smelled like the finest meal possible.

He didn't smile at her, but simply raised one eyebrow.

"May I join you?" she said, and her voice was low and seductive. She'd spent hours cultivating that voice, practicing in front of a mirror, he surmised.

Why not? He could smell her, if not taste her. She was beautiful as well, red-haired and heavily freckled, with deep green eyes, wearing a formal blue dress. *I could eat her up,* he thought, amused. *No, really: I could eat her up.*

He smiled to himself, and she took it as an invitation and swooshed into the seat opposite him.

He took his empty water glass, filled it from the wine carafe and handed it to her.

"Thank you, kind sir," she purred.

They talked about nothing of consequence: the weather, the idiot Americans—raising their voices slightly so that they could be overheard. It was fun, but Horsham's bloodlust was rising along with his horniness.

He knew himself. He wouldn't be able to satisfy one need without satisfying the other. There were just too many witnesses.

He paid for the meal, peeled off another hundred and laid it in front of her. "Thanks for the company."

"The night is young," she said suggestively.

Horsham was already shaking his head. "I have an early day tomorrow. Again, thanks for the company. Have a good night."

As he got up, her hand landed on his arm. "For what you just paid me, I could…"

He snarled at her. Like a dog—no, like a wolf. He couldn't help himself. He turned away at the last second as his fangs extended, so at least no one saw that. But everyone heard the snarl. Everyone's hair had probably stood on end at the primal sound.

He walked away without looking back.

He didn't sleep that night, expecting them to storm his cabin and put an end to him.

* * *

The next day, when the train arrived in the Highlands, Horsham was exhausted, hungry, and angry. He rented a car, headed away from Inverness and into the bright green slopes and valleys, and fell upon the first couple he saw: Americans, on bikes, wearing their ridiculous spandex. He took great satisfaction in devouring them, leaving only their broken bones.

After he had fed, Horsham felt newly alive, and strength surged through him. He expended some of this new energy by piling so many rocks on the bones that it would take an ambitious and curious person to dig down under them. These days, hardly anyone fit that description.

He drove the rented car back to London.

Last night had been too close. He'd almost given himself away.

Next time, he wouldn't wait so long to feed. It had been an experiment: *If Terrill could resist for decades,* Horsham had thought, *surely I can resist for a few months.*

Let Terrill be a fool. No doubt his decision had to do with his qualms about killing people. But it didn't show greater discipline: it showed weakness.

Horsham would feed when he wanted. A vampire was meant to prey on the weak. It was his nature.

Chapter 6

In the morning, Terrill looked up Howe in the phone book. There were no listings for that name. He went to the motel lobby and logged on to the computer there. That was a little more helpful, but when he called the Howes who were listed, none recognized the name Jamie Lee.

Had she written a false name in the motel register after all? No, he was certain from the easy, casual way she had written, and the way she had hesitated in the middle and then shrugged, as if catching herself in the mistake, that she had written her real name.

Terrill put the name "Jamie Lee" into the search field and added "Bend, Oregon." Up popped Jamie Lee Hardaway, Bend High School, Class of 2010. He looked up Hardaway, and there was only one family listed. He called the number and asked for Jamie, and an older man answered in a whiskey-drinking-and-cigarette-smoking voice, "She isn't here. Can I take a message?"

He hung up. They hadn't heard yet. He was going to have to wait. He didn't think he should be the one to break the news: "Hello. Your daughter is dead. I killed her."

Which just emphasized how insane this was.

What did he think he was going to accomplish? Was he just curious? Or did he want to make amends? How could he make up for what he'd done? Did he want forgiveness? Could he confess and still escape? What good would it do?

He didn't know. But he had to try.

* * *

"Do you have family? I mean, of course you have family, but do you keep in touch?"

"My family is all gone." Terrill's tone didn't invite further discussion, but the endearing thing about this girl was that she overrode such considerations. She went right for the emotional heart of things. Terrill found himself responding to her candidness despite himself.

"I'm sorry," Jamie said. *"I've got a really complicated family. My mom's been married five times. My last name is my father's; he was her fourth husband. I have four stepsisters and six stepbrothers. I grew up with too much family, too far away. My little sister from Mom's last marriage and I are close, though."*

Terrill didn't answer at first, though her silence invited a response. He barely remembered his human family. He'd taken to the vampire life immediately. It was the vampires who had truly created him; who had taught him their ways so that he wouldn't be found out the first time he fed; who had protected him and traveled with him, not out of the goodness of their hearts, but because they had learned that a clan of vampires survived better than a vampire who was alone.

Still, he'd come to know them and, if not to love them, at least to become familiar with their ways.

Either way, the answer was the same. They were all dead.

Except for one. One who was his... brother. Yes, "brother" was probably the best way to describe Horsham. A brother—and a mortal enemy. Mortal for one of them if ever they should meet again. Terrill didn't want that. He'd fled rather than kill his "brother."

Horsham was still out there. Still hunting for him. There had been hired humans over the years who had tracked Terrill down, and even though he had fed on them before they could report his whereabouts, the fact that they'd been sent after him was confirmation that Horsham had not forgotten nor forgiven.

"I have a brother," Terrill said grudgingly. *"But we are estranged."*

"Don't give up!" Jamie exclaimed. *"If he's still alive, you ought to get back together. Really!"*

"I don't think he'd like that."

"But you don't know that for sure. How long has it been?"

"Years and years," he answered. Fifty-three years, to be exact.

"See? Maybe things have changed."

She cuddled up to him, ran her fingers across his chest and then down his body. *"Again?"* he muttered.

"Yes, please," she said, kissing his neck.

This girl is an Earth Mother, *he thought.* Nurturing, loving. *What was she doing here? Why was she with a stranger? What was her real story?*

Maybe he should try to contact Horsham. Try to make peace.

Even as he thought it, even as he fell into Jamie's arms, he knew that the girl's spell was an illusion, that such a thought would never stand the light of day. That it would burst into flame when exposed to sunlight just as surely as his own body would.

He wished he had her naïveté again. Her innocence. But he was too old, too old by centuries, to fall for such foolishness.

Such a beautiful girl. She needed to go home to her family. He would make sure of it, he decided. In the morning, he would give her enough money to go home and choose a different lifestyle. Such a pure spirit must not be smothered by the sins of the big city.

Those were his last thoughts before falling asleep.

Before waking up to an empty mirror and that terrible, deadly hunger.

* * *

Terrill waited until nightfall before venturing out and reached the bank by 5:45. He made sure that his accounts were at a bank that was open until six every day, though he did most of his banking online. At the bank, he withdrew $500,000 as a cashier's check, causing a bit of stir. The manager tried to act like it was all in a day's business, but the young clerks stared at Terrill with interest.

It couldn't be helped.

Terrill had all the money he could ever need. Horsham had a saying: "Compound interest is a vampire's best friend." It was amazing how much money he'd accrued over the past few centuries.

He walked one block over and opened another account (again getting curious glances) and asked for some blank checks. He found a printer still open and had the name "Prestigious Insurance" printed on the tops of the blank checks. Then he went back to his motel and ordered a delivery from the butcher shop.

Out of curiosity, he called the Hardaways' number again. He got a busy signal. An hour later, it was still busy, and from that he deduced that Jamie's death had been reported and the Hardaways were busy dealing with the consequences.

Terrill tried to stay in the motel, but he wasn't the slightest bit sleepy. TV was all sitcoms and reality shows, and they bored him. He hadn't thought to bring a book.

At about midnight, he ventured out on foot.

There was a public park, Pioneer Park, along the Deschutes River, a few blocks from the motel. It was dark except for some the lights on one side of the bridge.

Despite the cold, there was a couple making love under some blankets down by the riverside. No one could have seen them, though a passerby might have heard the lovers' soft exclamations—no one human, that is.

Terrill could see them clearly. The night was brighter for him than day was for humans. He could see every blade of grass, every goose turd that littered the park, the individual hairs on the heads of the lovers. He could see under their skins to the blood beneath, running like the branches of a tree, flowing to ever-smaller capillaries.

The blood called to him. They couldn't see him or hear him, he knew. He was, for all intents and purposes, invisible to the human eye. He was a ghost, a monster of the dark—a vampire. He stood over them and watched their slow movements become frenzied, their blood racing.

Once, he would've waited for their climax and then fallen upon them and ripped them into small pieces, consuming their blood, their flesh. And then, as casually as a diner throwing away the remnants of his meal, he would have tossed the bloody bones into the river.

Terrill walked away.

Without consciously deciding to go there, he found himself back at the motel. He lay on the bed, staring into the bright darkness.

For a long time, he'd always been able to rationalize killing humans who he decided deserved to die. Then Mary had come along and changed him. Now another woman had entered his life for a short time, and again, he had killed without wanting to.

He would never kill again, no matter what.

Not now.

Not after Jamie. She hadn't deserved it—she was the last person who had deserved it, and because of that, because of her goodness, he was done killing, forever.

Chapter 7

"*Officer* Carlan." Brosterhouse's voice boomed across the lobby. He accentuated "Officer" as if to emphasize the distinction between a homicide detective and a lowly patrolman. Obviously, the Portland detective had uncovered the restraining order. "You left Bend at six a.m.?"

"Check with my sergeant," Carlan said. "But yeah."

Brosterhouse was carrying a manila folder, and now, as they stood in the lobby with everyone looking on, he opened it. It was filled with copies of paperwork from the ongoing dispute between Carlan and Jamie.

"Can't we take this somewhere private?" Carlan asked, his voice low and even.

Brosterhouse ignored him; he pulled one of the pages out of the file. "These letters make for interesting reading. Especially this one—and I quote: 'If I should be found dead, it will be Richard Carlan who killed me.'"

"That's bullshit," Carlan said, his face growing red as everyone in the lobby, civilian and cop, stared at him. "We just had a misunderstanding. We were working it out."

"So she ran to Portland and became a prostitute because you were working it out?"

"She was hysterical. Crazy! I was on my way here to pick her up."

Brosterhouse stared at him with an expression Carlan recognized. It was the hardnosed skepticism that cops automatically turned on anyone they considered guilty. "If that's true, I could've arrested you. The restraining order is pretty clear."

Carlan had always wondered what he would do if he was accused of a crime he didn't commit. Would he immediately clam up? Call a lawyer? The rational and experienced cop inside him knew without a doubt that was the best thing to do. But he fell back on the same protestations he'd heard a thousand times, from guilty and innocent alike. "I didn't do it. She was already dead when I got there."

"Your alibi is shaky," Brosterhouse said. "We know you were in Bend the night before, but that gave you plenty of time to drive over the pass."

"But I loved her!" God, how pathetic that sounded. How guilty! They always said that, murderers who stabbed the "one they loved" a hundred times, who slashed and slashed until the "one they loved" was obliterated.

"You are no longer allowed anywhere near this case, Carlan," Brosterhouse said. "Go back to Bend. We'll contact you."

"But I might be able to help!" Being shut out of the case was an even bigger fear than being suspected. He needed completion. Jamie had died before he could talk some sense into her, before she could remove the restraining order and those damning letters. He imagined her on her knees while he shoved the letters down her throat. *Damn her! Why did she have to die and leave me to deal with this shit?*

From now on, people would always look at him sideways, even in Bend, where they knew him. He'd pass them in the hallway and there would be whispers, and laughter, and shame. Jamie had done this to him, and now he couldn't change it. He was angry with her, rightfully so, but even more aggravating was that his anger had no outlet. Unless he turned it on the killer, the bastard who had taken her away before he could get to her and change her mind.

Brosterhouse leaned toward him. He was huge, probably twice Carlan's weight, though Carlan was just a little below average in size. "If you were a Portland cop, I'd have your badge," he growled. "We don't look the other way here, like they do in Bend. That small-town bullshit doesn't wash here. Get out of town before I throw you in jail for even *thinking* about breaking the restraining order."

Carlan felt a sudden calm. He was a cop. He knew the law. He wouldn't be bullied like the poor saps he arrested every day who didn't understand their rights. He stared Brosterhouse in the eye.

"I didn't do it," he said evenly. "Fuck you."

He walked away, feeling like he had regained a little of his pride. He knew other cops in Portland, cops who would be willing to help. Brosterhouse was wrong: the bullshit wasn't confined to small towns, it was everywhere, in big cities and small, from sophisticated capitals to tiny, isolated hamlets. Bastard wanted to pretend the system of favors and the protection of your brothers didn't apply in Portland? Who did he think he was talking to?

* * *

It turned out that Brosterhouse was almost right. Carlan called three of his "buddies" on the Portland police force and got turned down by all of them. The first two simply hung up; the third said, "I never much liked you, Carlan," and then hung up.

Time to pack up and go home? Use his contacts back in Bend?

There was one more guy he could try, but he hesitated. It was his emergency escape valve, the guy he planned to turn to when all else failed. But he was out of options.

"Hey, Funkadelic!"

"What do you want, Carlan?" John Funk's voice was so cold, Carlan almost backed off.

"I need a favor."

"No."

"I still have it, Funker. I still have the evidence. The statute of limitations on manslaughter is the same as murder. Hell, they might just charge you with murder. After all, the only witness who could testify that it was a crime of passion is me." He started singing: "Who's got the Funk? Bop… bop… bop. I got the Funk. Who's got the Funk? Bop… bop…"

"Shut up," his former partner said. "I'm thinking about turning myself in. I never did like the way that went down. I didn't mean to kill him."

Carlan felt the fish slipping off the hook. "I know that! If it ever goes down, I could totally testify to that. The guy deserved it—raping a five-year-old girl. Hell, if you hadn't killed him, I probably would have!"

There was a long silence. A sigh. "What do you want, Carlan?"

"I need the evidence on a current case. A girl found dead this morning in a motel room on the east side. Name of Jamie Lee Howe."

"Who's the lead?"

"Guy named Brosterhouse."

Another long silence. "Maybe I should just turn myself in now," John Funk said. "Get it over with."

"No, no! Don't do anything that will get you in trouble. Just… you know, help me out."

"All right. This one time. But don't ever ask me to help you again, Carlan. I'll fucking turn myself in."

Well, maybe he would, maybe he wouldn't. But Carlan certainly intended to test his former partner's resolve if he ever needed him again. "I promise," he said.

"Remember, you asshole, if I go down, you go down for withholding evidence."

"Sure, sure." Not the way Carlan had it planned, but if it made Funk feel secure to think so, than so be it.

"I'll call you back," Funk said, and hung up.

Carlan stayed in Portland for another day, hanging out near the phone, watching Judge Judy and the other judges and *Law and Order* marathons all day. He had enough time to think, to wonder why he was trying so hard. Jamie was gone. There was nothing he could do about it.

Truth was, he wasn't as crushed by it as he thought he would be. Still, he hated that he hadn't been able to change her mind. He'd been thinking about her for so long that something else needed to take her place. Revenge fit quite nicely.

The Portland police weren't moving very fast. Prostitute killings were notoriously difficult to solve, especially if it was stranger-on-stranger violence. If the killer used a condom and was careful, he could almost always get away with it unless they found him weaving down the road with a body in the back of the car.

It was going to be up to Carlan, not the self-righteous Brosterhouse, to solve this case.

"What do you care?" Funk asked later that evening. "From what I saw in the files, you were on the verge of killing her yourself."

"I loved her."

"You don't love anyone. I remember how you treated women, Carlan."

"Yeah, but I never killed anyone, Funky. Remember that."

"Only because you've been lucky." There was a rustle of papers over the line. "The DNA tests came back early. Kind of weird. The lab says not only can't they identify the perpetrator, they're not sure it's even human DNA. The sample was probably contaminated."

The two puncture wounds in Jamie's neck passed through Carlan's mind, but he dismissed the wild speculation instantly. Humans killed humans. Always had, always would.

Only one day and the case was already going cold. Carlan could sense that the Portland police were on the verge of giving up, putting it on the back burner. As a last resort, he asked for traffic citations in the surrounding area on the night of the murder. Even if it was the way they had caught the Son of Sam, most detectives considered it a Hail Mary pass, too time-consuming with too little reward to pursue in most cases.

But Carlan took the time, spending most of the night and early morning going through the citations, and just as he was about to give up, he came across it: a warning for parking in a no-parking zone on the morning after the murder, given to a "well-dressed" man in a late-model Cadillac Escalade, sleeping off a binge in the backseat. Carlan rang up Funk and had him plug the license plate number into the database, and it came back as being registered under the name Jonathan Evers at a motel in Bend on the night after the murder.

In Bend. *That's too much of a coincidence*, Carlan thought. The Portland cops had probably written it off, if they had even bothered to check it out. But as a resident of Bend, Carlan knew how much someone had to go out of his or her way to reach the High Desert city. It really wasn't on the road to anywhere important. It was mostly a destination.

Somehow, the owner of this SUV, this Jonathan Evers, had begun the morning a block from the scene of a murder and had ended up in the hometown of the murder victim the following evening.

Carlan hurriedly packed up to go home. It was three o'clock in the morning. He'd have to convince the motel not to charge him for the night, but flashing a badge usually did the trick.

One good thing had come out of the waiting. He'd been thinking about Jamie and her family. His mind kept returning to Jamie's younger sister, Sylvie. When Carlan had first started dating Jamie, the girl had been only a teenager. Now she was legal: twenty-one or twenty-two years old, something like that.

Sylvie was an even more beautiful woman than Jamie, with the same kind of purity that had drawn Carlan to Jamie. More purity, actually, since she was that much younger and less experienced. Jamie had been soiled by the time Carlan got to her—she'd lied to him, and it was only after slapping her in the face a few times for her lies that she'd told him the truth. She hadn't been a virgin for years.

Carlan had been willing to forgive her, before she ran off. But inside, he had recoiled.

The more he thought about Sylvie, the more certain he was that Jamie's death had kept him from making a big mistake. The younger girl was so much more appealing.

He'd solve this case and present it to her like a gift. She'd be grateful, he was sure. She wouldn't be like Jamie, who hadn't known when she had it good.

Yes, Sylvie had been the right one all along.

Chapter 8

The Hardaway residence was on the trendy west side of Bend, only a block from the Deschutes River. The house was small and had probably been owned by the family for generations. Updated bungalows surrounded it, but it still had its original plywood siding, warped by the infrequent rains.

Terrill cruised past the house. Through the window, he saw a big-screen TV that seemed to take up half the little living room, a couple of old couches, and an older couple on opposite sides of the room, ignoring each other. It was nearly midnight, too late to knock on the door. There was no sign of the daughter.

He felt restless. He drove out into the High Desert east of town, feeling vulnerable because of the lack of cover, trying to get used to the openness of the terrain in this part of the country. He got back to the motel room as dawn was breaking, the sunlight ready to stab down on him.

It was mid-October, but the sun was shining brightly. Terrill chose the queen-size bed farthest from the windows and tried to get some sleep. He'd be up at the break of dusk. His internal clock would wake him automatically, honed by centuries of needing to feed at first possible moment.

He turned onto his side, remembering Jamie.

* * *

They were naked on top of the bed, one of her legs and one of her arms draped over him.

She was languorous. Something about her had appealed to him. He had decided to please her, to make her want it. In return, she was confiding in him, and for some reason he was willing to listen to this girl who had almost no experience of the real world. She had a kind of wisdom, though, a perspective that came from some deep well of goodness.

Jamie talked glowingly about Bend, and especially about her younger sister.

"Sylvie will get the chances I didn't," she said. "She's incredibly bright—good at math and science and all that stuff that I never could understand. She just needs a break."

"That's why you're here?" he asked. It seemed more diplomatic than "That's why you're a whore?"

For the first time, Jamie seemed a little defensive. Until now, she had seemed, if not happy in her work, at least content… or if not content, at least resigned.

"I've already put five thousand bucks into her college fund," she said testily. "That never would've happened if I'd been working at Burger King."

She was so young, so unspoiled. He'd sensed right away that she was just a wide-eyed girl in the big city. That's what had attracted him.

"It's not too late for you, surely," he said.

"Yes," she said. "It is."

Terrill knew America was full of young people in dead-end existences. Most weren't aware of it, but for some reason, Jamie had already scoped out the future and decided it was hopeless. He wanted to object and to tell her anything was possible. But he knew that she hadn't even finished high school, that she had no practical skills and had to rely on her beauty. Even that was beginning to wear off, though she was in her early twenties. Where could she go? What could she do?

Her grammar and diction were adequate, nothing more. Her clothing sense was that of a girl playing at being a sophisticated woman. She would be limited even in her chosen profession; at best, forced to pick up strange men in bars, at worst... he shuddered.

Once he had fed on such dregs of civilization, knowing they wouldn't be missed. But that way of existence was behind him now. Maybe he could help this innocent girl, make up for some of his past. It would be a small step, but in an immortal life, such small steps could add up. Already, he had quietly used his wealth to help other humans in return for small kindnesses.

"Go home, get married, have a life," he said.

She shook her head. "I attract the wrong kind of guy. Always have. I'm not going to be like my mother, marrying five times, each guy worse than the last..."

Terrill said nothing. If she survived her dangerous and unhealthy profession, she would probably end up exactly like her mother—marrying the men who paid attention to her, not questioning their motives, excusing their bad behavior, secretly believing she didn't deserve any better.

"Sylvie doesn't have to end up like that," Jamie continued, as if reading his mind. "She can go to college, get a good job. Wait for the right man to come along."

He must have been frowning, because she playfully patted him. "I'm sorry. You don't need to hear all this. But if you ever met Sylvie, you'd know why I talk this way."

He didn't answer. It was the rare human who could pull themselves out of their designated fate. But something about this young woman's faith in her even younger sister was inspiring. He'd help make it happen, he decided. At least give them the chance.

Terrill lay in bed with Jamie in his arms, the warmth of her body waking memories long forgotten: of life, of love and family and everyday existence. It was strangely comforting. For once, his hunger left him. Or so he thought.

* * *

The windows glowed from sunlight one moment, then darkened the next. Terrill awoke instantly at the cusp of dusk as the ambient light shifted.

He got up, surrounded by empty mirrors. If ever he was tempted to forget his nature, he need only rent a motel room, in which mirrors often served as decor. An empty room surrounded him and empty mirrors reflected it; it was as if he wasn't even there. He only existed in the darkness and the shadows, which meant he was invisible, night or day.

In truth, he was unlikely to ever forget that. He woke every evening hungry for blood. For many decades, he had been prudent enough to wake alone. The one time he had forgotten—the one time he had felt comfortable enough to let the human stay with him—had ended badly.

Now he was on this strange trip to a part of the country he'd never intended to visit, with this crazy idea of approaching strangers, risking his life... all for a girl he'd barely known, with whom he'd planned a simple sex-for-money transaction.

But she had not treated him that way. She'd treated him like a human being. It was the first time in a long time that anyone had done that.

Terrill dressed in a conservative suit, something that hopefully wouldn't stand out too much in a small town where most people dressed informally. It was the best he could do. He'd never owned a flannel shirt, as far as he could remember, and had never even tried on a pair of jeans. In part, he dressed formally because old-fashioned, classic clothing offered him more cover. Hats, gloves, vests, coats, long-sleeved shirts and trousers: all gave him a small advantage over sunlight.

His wardrobe was also a result of his long existence. Clothing styles came and went, and he didn't even try to keep up with them.

Terrill stuck his hand in his pocket and felt a burning pain. He cried out and withdrew the stinging object. He dropped the crucifix but held onto the silver chain, which hurt him, but didn't burn like the cross did.

He stared at it curiously. He'd always been confused about why crosses had this effect. He had no opinion about religion. He didn't believe in an afterlife—well, other than the type he was experiencing, anyway. It was all mumbo jumbo to him. Why should a cross, or holy water, or silver, or any other of the many folk wards against vampires have any effect on him at all?

On the other hand, why question it? Were any of these superstitious talismans any less likely than the fact of his own existence?

Terrill touched the crucifix again, and though it hurt, he found that he could stand the pain. It burned a few centimeters of the surface of his skin, but went no further.

Without thinking, he swung the chain over his head. The cross bounced off his chest and then settled, and he staggered and cried out. The silver chain cut into the back of his neck, and he had an image of his head detaching and bursting into flames. He reached up and found that the chain had dug into the surface of his skin, but stopped there.

The cross burned into his chest and stuck, his skin fusing with it. The area continued to ache, but the initial sharp pain subsided. He could stand it, he decided. He removed the chain, because the wounds it was inflicting were visible. The crucifix remained fused to the skin of his chest.

He'd once fed upon a priest who, it was revealed when the outer layers of his clothing were removed, had been wearing a hair shirt. The mortal's skin had been mottled and covered with rashes, his back flayed by self-flagellation. As Terrill remembered it, the priest hadn't been a righteous man, but a vicious schemer who had used the Inquisition for his own benefit, so it had surprised Terrill to see that the man apparently had a genuine religious side.

Or perhaps a sadomasochistic side, since the sadism was more than manifest in his official duties. A torturer who tortured himself.

Terrill winced as he put on his shirt. He didn't ask himself why he left the crucifix burning into his chest.

He drove to the Hardaway house the minute it became fully dark. He'd probably catch them at dinner, but so be it. It was important that they all be home.

He still wasn't sure what he would say. Perhaps nothing. Perhaps he'd simply hand over the check and walk away. That's what he should do. Anything else wasn't safe, either for him or for them.

But as he sat in his car, staring at the house, he knew he wouldn't leave without talking to Sylvie.

Chapter 9

Vicky waited for the paperboy. He was late, as usual.

She would pretend to be impatient, but secretly she was delighted. The last time, she had seen how Mr. Horsham had looked her over, as if trying to see how she looked with her clothes off. She had just been waiting for another excuse to be alone with him.

She had read everything about him there was to read, had followed him to nightclubs, and had even snuck into a few of them, watching from a distance as he handed out tip money like it was water. He liked the girls, that was for certain. Tall, willowy blondes. Such as herself. Well, such as herself after going to the salon every two weeks to keep the blonde hue in her hair.

She checked herself out in the mirror of her compact. The Horsham estate had almost no mirrors—actually, none that she'd ever seen. She had a few too many dark roots to be perfect, but not bad: blonde and beautiful and young.

Mr. Horsham was older than his official biography, she'd decided. Not that he showed it. No, he had one of those tall, lean bodies that never got flabby, and dark, lustrous hair that never greyed or grew thin.

But the news stories went too far back for him to be only forty years old or so.

He had to be lonely, possibly even depressed. He never left the house until after dark, and he slept all day. It was time he had a woman take care of him full time.

The paperboy—actually a middle-aged man—finally showed up.

"The truck was late," he muttered, and she believed him because he'd obviously been running, sweat dripping off his fat face.

"It best not happen again if you want your bonus," she snapped. Mr. Horsham paid bonuses that were bigger than a month's wages if you pleased him. She planned to please him very much indeed.

He wasn't up when she got to the kitchen. His meal was laid out, but there was no light coming from under the bedroom door. Vicky looked around at the curtains. *Wouldn't it be nice if they were open when he got up, catching the last vestiges of the day's light?* she thought. She went to the window, but she couldn't see anything that would open the curtains. They seemed almost permanently attached. *How strange.*

"What are you doing?" The voice was guttural, unlike the smooth tone she was used to hearing from Mr. Horsham.

He was in the shadows, wearing a bathrobe. He seemed to have an erection. She flushed. Vicky had thought she was prepared for anything, but now that the moment had come, she felt uncertain. His silhouette wasn't quite right, as if he was wearing something on his face, something that protruded.

Nevertheless, she pirouetted prettily, a move she'd practiced a hundred times in the mirror at home. She had a great body, and she knew it.

"You have the perfect body."

She couldn't believe he'd said it. She'd dreamed of him saying that, but not like this.

"Why thank you, sir. It is at *your* service." There. She'd said it. A little more bluntly and crudely than she'd planned, but then again, she hadn't expected her boss to be already aroused.

He stepped into the light. He was wearing a mask, a fright mask of some kind. Not funny at all. He seemed to be running toward her; why would he be doing that? She tried to plaster a smile on her face and opened her arms.

As he got within a few feet, Vicky saw that he wasn't wearing a mask after all. She couldn't move. She couldn't scream. She felt herself being slammed against the dining table and falling to the floor.

Then he was on top of her, ripping her clothes off. Violating her. She had dreamed of this, of being ravished, but there was nothing sexy about it. He was grunting or something, nuzzling her neck. Biting her. She tried to push him off. She'd changed her mind. She didn't want sex after all. She didn't want to be here. She'd sue him for sexual harassment, she decided. Maybe even file charges.

But she could barely raise her arms. He continued to bite her, and she felt liquid flowing down her neck and chest. Had they spilled the orange juice? He was sloppy, disgusting.

He reared up as he came, and she saw his face one last time, the face of a monster leering down at her. He cupped her breast, then leaned over and took a bite out of it. The pain was somewhere in the distance, happening in another time and place, to someone else.

The light dimmed, and she could no longer see him, only feel him—eating, eating.

* * *

33

Vicky had the perfect body. Just the right proportions of meat and fat. Horsham tried to hire servants who were built that way, figuring it never hurt to have a walking pantry full of meat for emergencies. She also had no family and few friends. Otherwise, she wouldn't have been working for him.

When he was finished, he took what was left of her and stuffed her down the special disposal chute he'd installed in his kitchen, which went directly to an incinerator in the basement.

He'd warned her. She'd been skulking about for months, even stalking him on his nightly rounds. She'd almost been his meal several times, but he preferred not to kill anyone who could be connected to him.

But this had been necessary. She had broken one too many rules of the house. She'd dared to research his past. It had only been a matter of time before he disposed of her, one way or the other. This had been nice. It was a little early to feed again, only a few days since he'd returned from Scotland, but sometimes he needed a little booster.

It wouldn't cause any problems. It had been years since he'd eaten an employee. Didn't want to do too much of that; the other servants tended to notice. But no one would doubt he had fired Vicky, and no one would miss her; she had been a little bitch to everyone around her.

Horsham turned on his laptop, washing down the taste of her with orange juice. A red flag immediately popped up. He read it and picked up his cellphone.

"Sanders. Get Twilight ready for a trip to America. We'll stop in New York tomorrow and fly on to the West Coast the next day. That's right. No, not California. Portland, Oregon."

* * *

Less than an hour later, Horsham settled back in his seat in the private plane called Twilight. Its windows were permanently shuttered, since a jet could fly from darkness to light in minutes. *At long last, a hint of Terrill's location,* he thought with satisfaction. It was nothing more than a hint, but it was more than he'd found in decades.

It didn't matter how long it took. Terrill would pay for what he'd done.

* * *

"They are food, Horsham. Nothing else. Don't forget it."

They had waylaid a stagecoach, taking the money. That's all that would've happened if one of the men hadn't gotten foolish and taken a shot at them. The bullet hit Terrill in the shoulder, and they both fell upon the occupants of the coach in seconds, ripping them to shreds. It was a snack, nothing more, both of them having fed the night before.

One of the humans was a little girl, and Horsham hesitated, just for a second, remembering his own daughter at that age. Terrill tore into her, and she was dead in moments. By the time he was done with her, his bullet wound was completely healed.

"Don't you remember being human at all?" It was possible that Terrill didn't remember, since he was many hundreds of years older than Horsham. Since the disappearance of their Maker, Michael, he was perhaps the oldest vampire on Earth.

"I remember never having to answer to another human again."

"Even Michael?"

Terrill laughed. He never seemed to have any doubts. He reveled in his existence and did as he pleased, but had an eerie sense of how far to push it. Michael the Maker had advised Horsham to follow Terrill.

"The bastard is a survivor, I'll give him that," Terrill said, strangely subdued.

Michael had been quiet for years, eating only when he needed to, the rest of the time holed up in his library, reading book after book about human philosophy and religion. It was strangely disturbing to Horsham. To all vampires. What was he doing? they wondered. Why was he acting that way?

When Michael had simply disappeared one day, no one had been surprised. Perhaps he'd just grown weary, had walked out to greet the day's dawning. Or perhaps he had gone to ground, only to emerge centuries or millenniums later. He'd done it before.

Michael had been a kind of mentor to other vampires.

Terrill felt no such obligation. He led by example, and it was a bad example for most vampires who emulated his aggressiveness without having his uncanny sense of self-preservation.

"The fewer vampires, the less they notice us. The less they notice us, the better," Terrill said, when Horsham realized he was now the third-oldest—second-oldest?— vampire in existence. Horsham almost never felt fear, but when his traveling companion (he wouldn't say friend) said this, he felt a tinge of trepidation. Not only wasn't Terrill following the Michael's example and helping his kind, he was actively working for their doom.

Horsham almost broke away from Terrill at that moment.

He would always regret that he hadn't.

* * *

The Twilight landed in New York and refueled. Horsham had lost about four hours of night, which was too bad. They landed in Portland five hours later, losing another couple of hours of night. It was nearly midnight; there was time enough to get a late meal, but not to do any business.

He booked a room at the Benson and then went on the prowl, getting a sense of the town. He got back before dawn and slept until three p.m. It was a dark day, drizzling, so he bundled up and ventured out.

He got to the Portland Police Bureau's headquarters just as the day shift was ending.

Detective Brosterhouse was getting ready to go home when Horsham intercepted him. "Please, detective," he said. "I flew all the way from London just to talk to you about the Howe case."

The big detective sighed, took off his coat, and sat back down at his desk. "What's your interest in the case?"

"I've been following similar cases in England. I wanted to follow up, see if it matched the details."

"What do you want to know?"

There was a skeptical look in the human's eyes. Horsham realized he hadn't thought it through sufficiently. He'd expected a bored civil servant, going through the motions of solving the murder of a prostitute, but was obvious that this Detective Brosterhouse was fully engaged. Horsham had given him a false name, Mr. Harkins, private investigator, and showed him a false ID. But it wouldn't take long for a real detective to discover who had arrived in Portland from London on this day.

"I'd like the see the crime scene first, if I may."

Brosterhouse shrugged. "Sure. Room 221 at the Travelin' Inn. Costs thirty-five bucks a night, but watch out for the bedbugs. They bite."

"Could I perhaps entice you to walk me through it—everything you've found?"

"We've found almost nothing," the big detective admitted. "The only thing interesting about this case is how much interest there is in it. Normally, the murder of a prostitute only grieves the family, and half the time not even them. But this one? First that cop from Bend, and now you. So what is it about this case that interests you?"

"Cop from Bend?" Horsham's interest was piqued.

"The victim was an old girlfriend of his," Brosterhouse said. "If Carlan hadn't allegedly been in Bend when the murder occurred, I'd have bet anything it was him. I still think it might have been."

Bend was a nearby town, apparently. Horsham had a strange inkling that there was a connection there.

The mighty Terrill, terror of Europe for centuries, vicious and remorseless, had stopped killing many years before. He'd disappeared.

Why? What had changed? Horsham remembered how Michael had been at the end, seeming almost regretful. But most of all, he remembered how he himself had once begun to question the killing of humans. How Mary had changed him, until…

Horsham was aware of the irony. Once, Terrill had been a vampire's vampire, and it was Horsham who had had doubts, who had had regrets. Once, it was Terrill who had killed indiscriminately and cared for no one and nothing, and Horsham who had looked for villains, who had cared for the innocent and the weak.

With one act, Terrill had changed Horsham forever. Without Mary, Horsham had lost all interest in humans, except as food. It was perhaps ironic that Terrill had changed, that they both had changed—but it didn't matter. Terrill must die. Nobody, human or vampire, would stand in the way of that end.

* * *

So now, unexpectedly, it seemed that Terrill had fed on—and killed—a human again. If it was true that Terrill had somehow grown a conscience, what would he do next?

Horsham remembered his own response when the human he loved was murdered. Suddenly, he was certain what Terrill would do and where he would go.

"The girl was from Bend?" he asked.

"Newly arrived in the big city. A lamb to the slaughter."

"Let me buy you dinner, detective. You can tell me what you know."

Brosterhouse sat behind his desk like a statue, massive, ponderous. He nodded once. "It couldn't hurt. This is about as cold a case as it could be."

The policeman took him to a steak house, where Horsham picked at an overcooked hamburger while Brosterhouse gave him all the information they had. Which wasn't much. Which wasn't really anything at all. Except for one detail.

"She was untouched, except for the puncture wounds?" he asked.

"Yeah, it was weird. Someone laid her out and wrapped her up like he gave a damn. Drained her of blood and then treated her gently. Sickos, weirdos, creeps. There are all kinds, all kinds."

The detective didn't have much more information than that. It didn't matter. That wasn't the real reason Horsham had enticed him out of the police station. Horsham didn't leave witnesses. Where he went was nobody's business—especially not a cop who seemed a little too curious.

They headed back to Brosterhouse's car, and as they passed an alley, Horsham grabbed the huge detective and threw him into the filth and darkness of the alley as if he was a little child. The cop was fluorescent to Horsham's eyes. He saw the big man trying to see in the darkness, drawing his gun quicker than Horsham expected, firing a shot and getting lucky, hitting him right between the eyes.

Horsham stumbled away, running farther into the alley. He could survive almost any wound as long as he fed quickly, but a shot to the head was enough to weaken him, and he ran rather than continue the fight. He'd come back when it was all over.

A couple more bullets came his way, but both missed him.

At the end of the alley, Horsham found a homeless man leaning against the brick wall of one of the buildings and drank his blood in seconds. Then he kept going, not stopping to feed further. Staying in darkness, using every instinct developed over centuries of hunting, he made his way back to his motel room without anyone seeing his blood-splattered clothing and smeared face. He fell into bed, still weak. The bullet had fallen out during the nightmarish journey, but the wound to his head still made him dizzy. He'd need a few hours to recover.

After that, he'd get out of town. The detective would be looking for him. The whole Portland police department would be looking for him.

But when Horsham didn't want to be found, he was nearly impossible to track. He'd find out where Bend was and hope Brosterhouse didn't remember his curious questions about the town.

Chapter 10

Terrill waited in the car outside the Hardaway residence. The woman was cooking in the kitchen, the man had returned home in the last half hour, and there was a light on in a second-story window. Terrill saw the shadow of someone walking past that window. They were all home. What was keeping him rooted to the driver's seat?

He got out and slammed the door. The neighborhood was quiet: everyone in their place. Once, he would have found it an ideal place to feed, would have picked a house at random and slaughtered the occupants. It still amazed him that for hundreds of years he had never questioned that humans were food and vampires ruled the night.

A cat ran across the sidewalk in front of him, giving him a startled glance, as if it had only seen him at the last second. Terrill could stand there, still and quiet, and most people would walk right by him without seeing him. It had once been one of his favorite techniques—letting his meal come to him.

He took a deep breath, then walked up the sidewalk and the three concrete steps to the door. Then he hesitated and almost turned around.

He was a murderer. He was the cause of their grief. He hadn't wanted to do it, he was ashamed, but nonetheless, he was the reason their daughter would never come home. What right did he have to stand at their door, to enter their home, to talk to them, to offer them condolences?

The door opened before he could knock, and a young woman stood there staring at him.

"Can I help you?" she asked.

She looked like Jamie; but then again, she didn't look like Jamie at all. In fact, she looked like no one he'd seen since ancient days. Her nose was too long; it could accurately be described as a Roman nose. Her eyes were wide set and large. Her chin was slightly pointed, and she had high cheekbones, a wide, tall forehead, and thick raven hair.

She looks like she came off a Greek urn, he thought. Each individual feature was a little off, but the whole was stunning.

"I... I..." he stammered.

"What does he want?" The old man's voice was gruff. He appeared to be in his seventies, which meant he had already been near sixty when he'd fathered this girl. It was six in the evening, but Terrill could tell the man was already drunk. He pushed the girl out of the way. "What do you want, buddy?" he said belligerently.

Jamie and Sylvie's mother followed, dishrag in hand, looking as though she hadn't stopped crying in days. It was hard to see either daughter in this beaten-down woman, who was in her mid-fifties, with limp brown hair and heavy jowls.

"Is this the home of Jamie Lee Howe?" Terrill asked.

"Not anymore," the man muttered. "The slut is dead."

"Howard!" the woman pleaded. He turned and glared at her until she looked away.

"I'll take care of this, Mom," Sylvie said, and the woman moved away, drifting over to the sink and picking up a dish, taking a few swipes at it with the dishrag and then standing still, staring out the window.

Sylvie pushed her way to the door again, stopped next to Terrill and waved him down the steps. "We can talk out here," she said. "Mom's in no shape to talk about Jamie, and Howard doesn't have anything to say."

"Fuck you," Howard said. "I'm watching a show..." He stumbled away.

"He actually does care, in his own way," Sylvie said. "He did everything he could to keep Jamie in town, but she didn't want to stay and she was old enough to make her own decisions."

She didn't say anything else, just stood staring at Terrill frankly.

"I..." Again, his voice faltered.

"You knew her, didn't you?" Sylvie said. "I can see it in your eyes. You're sad."

"Yes," Terrill said, then realized he hadn't planned to admit it. "I mean, I met her a couple of times."

"'Met' her?" From her tone, Terrill realized Sylvie knew what Jamie had been doing in Portland.

"For business. She came to me for a life insurance policy. I represent Prestigious Insurance."

"Oh." She was obviously disappointed. Then she realized what he'd said. "Insurance?"

"She wanted to make sure that you were provided for—a college fund, as it happens."

"We've already got the five thousand from her savings account," the girl said. "It came in handy; we were late with the mortgage. Howard lost his job a couple years ago and the unemployment checks have stopped coming. His Social Security isn't enough."

"Well, that's just it," Terrill said, more and more sure he was doing the right thing. "This payment is contingent on your going to college. It can't be used for anything else."

Sylvie didn't look happy or unhappy. She just stared at the ground for a few moments. "That's too bad, because I'm not leaving Mom until she is in good shape," she said. "Which may be never."

"I'm sorry. The terms are quite specific. The money can only be accessed as long as you are in college."

She shrugged and gave him a lopsided smile. Her goofy demeanor and classic good looks were irresistible. Jamie was right. She needed to get out of this small town.

"You can't live their lives for them," he said.

"That's what Jamie always said. And yet, that's exactly what she did for me, despite me telling her not to."

Sylvie would have had every right to ask him what business of it was of his, but instead, she again got that curious look on her face. "You knew her for more than business, didn't you?"

He didn't say anything, but the answer must have been written on his face. Sylvie laughed, and it was as if she didn't have a care in the world: a delighted laugh. "I knew it! You're just her type, all doomed and gloomy."

He tried to think of what to say. *"Yes, I was screwing your sister. For money."* No, that wouldn't do.

"Don't worry," Sylvie continued. "I know what Jamie was doing—but knowing her, she was trying to be more than just… just a…"

"She was more," he said. "To me."

"Yeah, that's Jamie. Making every job the most important job in the world, whether it's babysitting or flipping hamburgers or being a… being a whore."

Terrill stared at her in bafflement.

"You're wondering how I can say that," Sylvie said. "You're wondering why I'm not crying, why I can still laugh. Well, mister, someday I'll cry. Maybe I'll never stop crying, but not now."

"She talked about you," he said.

"Oh, let me guess. Her brainy sister? Her amazing sister? Well, Jamie always was a little starry-eyed. I'm not like that. Jamie just got unlucky, that's all. She met the wrong guy at the wrong time. It happened, and now I have to take care of Mom. And Howard, even Howard. He isn't a bad guy, just sort of pathetic."

Terrill could see she wasn't going to change her mind. It was time for a change of plans. "She made me executor of the policy," he said. "It says that you have to stay in school, but doesn't say where or for how long. I'm sure we can find a way."

"You sure you can't just give me the money?"

If I have to, I will, Terrill thought. But having gotten a good look at her parents, he suspected that Sylvie would end up seeing very little of it.

"Why don't we meet for lunch tomorrow?" he suggested.

"OK. We can meet at the Black Bear restaurant at 1:30. That's my lunch break."

"I thought you were going to the community college?"

For the first time, she looked troubled. It was as if the frown didn't fit her face, as if she was pressing the lines into her perfect skin. The expression disappeared as quickly as it appeared. "I had to drop out. We can talk about that tomorrow."

"Yes," he said. "We will. I can't meet you until the evening, however. How about after your shift?"

"OK. Come by at five."

He nodded.

She stuck her hand out. "Thank you, Mister...?"

"Terrill," he said, amazed at the sound of his own name. He hadn't used it in hundreds of years.

He shook her hand. It was warm and dry, and a charge seemed to go up his arm. She was looking at him with wide eyes.

"Until tomorrow evening," he said, and walked away without another word, now certain he was doing the right thing.

Chapter 11

Carlan drove back to Bend, his mind churning. He wasn't going to accomplish anything in Portland, not with Brosterhouse in the way. Despite Jamie's restraining order, in his hometown he was still in pretty good standing with his colleagues, many of whom had their own problems with ex-wives and girlfriends.

He also had a trump card. The last time he'd been in trouble with his boss, Captain Anderson, he'd been relegated to deskwork. There, he'd come across a discrepancy in the inventory of guns. He'd known from the moment that he reported the missing rifles that his boss had sold them for cash, and his boss had known that he knew.

Carlan was careful not to overuse this useful piece of information. He was satisfied staying a patrolman, where the possibility of bribes for moving violations and other misdemeanors was available. Being a detective entailed more oversight, not to mention that the brass tended to be harsher about any hanky-panky involving felonies.

Still, he'd saved the information for a rainy day.

He pulled into the police station parking lot and checked the captain's parking space. Empty. Damn. He'd forgotten that Anderson took Mondays off. He'd have to wait until tomorrow.

He pulled back out onto the highway and headed downtown, to Room 23 of the Badlands Motel. The Cadillac Escalade was there, despite it being midafternoon. He thought about knocking on the door, but decided his first plan was still the best plan. When he took this bastard down, he didn't want there to be any questions.

When he pulled out again, the car seemed to make its way to the Hardaway house without any conscious thought on his part. He'd spent a lot of time parked out in front of that house, hoping to get a glimpse of Jamie, hoping she would talk to him, let him explain. The restraining order should have kept him away, but who was going to arrest him?

He'd been patiently waiting for hours every day. Then, one afternoon, Sylvie had come out of the house and marched directly over to his car.

"She isn't here," she said flatly.

"What?"

"Jamie isn't here, so there's no sense stalking her."

"I'm not stalking anyone. I just want to talk to her. After that, I'll leave her alone."

Sylvie didn't argue with him, just turned around and walked back into the house. It was only weeks later that the arrest in Portland of one Jamie Lee Howe on charges of prostitution had been picked up by his search engine. After weeks of seething resentment and anger, it turned out she hadn't even been home. He didn't mind her yelling at him; he didn't even mind the restraining order. But leaving without telling him?

He'd headed for Portland the very same day.

She should have stayed in Bend, let him take care of her. It made no sense for her to go the Valley, and it especially boggled his mind that she had resorted to selling her body. Hell, it had taken him months to get a little, and even then he'd had to be insistent about it.

If she had stayed with him, she would never have had to worry about anything ever again. All because he'd slapped her, just that once. Hell, Dad had slapped his mom a hundred times, and they had been perfectly happy.

Carlan got out of the car and adjusted his belt, the gun, as usual, making him feel powerful and secure. He walked up to the door, trying to remember that first date with Jamie, the coy little kiss at the end. But instead, his mind wandered to Sylvie's form—the way her slender body had sashayed a little when she was walking away from him. Was she trying to give him a message? That he'd chosen the wrong sister?

The old man answered the door.

"Hey, Howard," Carlan said casually. "Just coming by to check and see how you're doin'."

Howard stared at him with blurry eyes, as if trying to remember who he was. Then he broke into a grin. "Officer Carlan, how good to see you!"

Jamie's parents had always liked him. Because he was a cop, they had thought he would be a good catch for Jamie. Apparently, Howard either hadn't known about the restraining order or had forgotten. When Jamie's mother came out of the kitchen, he could see from her hard eyes that she had known and hadn't forgotten.

But Howard had already invited him in, and Carlan quickly sat down on one of the couches. He smiled at Jamie's mother—Jennifer? Jean? Best not to guess.

"Please don't make any special effort on my part," he said. "I just wanted to come by and express my sorrow at Jamie's... passing. I wish I could have been there. I would have kept her safe."

"Bend is a lot safer," Howard agreed. "I can't figure it out. Why she did it. Why go to Portland, with all those lowlifes?"

Jamie's mom almost said something, then decided against it.

"One good thing came out of Jamie's death," Howard said. There was a strangled sound from the other couch, and he blanched. "I mean... no, honey... nothing good came out of it. I didn't mean it that way. I'm just talking about the insurance, you know..." His eyes pleaded with his wife, but she wouldn't look at him.

"Insurance?" Carlan asked sharply.

"Turns out, Jamie bought an insurance policy for Sylvie's education. A big amount, too, unless I'm mistaken."

"That was quick," Carlan said. Better and better. Unlike with Jamie, where he'd had to pay for everything, Sylvie could pay her own way. "I've never heard of a policy that only pays for school."

"That's what I said," Howard exclaimed, looking to his wife for confirmation. "But the guy said that there was some flexibility there: like, if Sylvie was living at home, she could use it for expenses."

"He actually came to your door?" Now Carlan had heard everything. Usually you had to track down the insurance companies and hold their feet to the fire to get anything out of them.

"I'm pretty sure he's good for it, too. He was driving a big Cadillac Escalade."

Carlan froze. The smile fell off his face.

"What?" Howard said, looking alarmed. "What's wrong?"

"Oh, nothing... hey, listen. I forgot an appointment," Carlan said, getting up. "Again, my condolences to both of you. Be sure to give Sylvie my best."

As he made his way to the door, Jamie's mother spoke for the first time. She had a whiskey-and-cigarette voice, too, deeper and more alarming than her husband's. "Stay away from Sylvie."

"Honey!" Howard exclaimed. "What are you talking about?"

Jean—that was her name, Carlan suddenly remembered—got up and pushed Carlan toward the door and then through it. "What are you talking about?" he protested, echoing Howard. But he didn't resist.

"Jeanie! That was really rude!" Howard said.

As the door began to close behind him, Carlan heard the woman say, "Howard. Sometimes you're so blind."

* * *

Carlan sat in the car for ten minutes, trying to wrap his brain around what he'd just learned.

Why would the killer be offering Sylvie money for school? Guilt? Remorse? Was it a trap to lure another girl to her death? What was his game? Who was this guy, and why was he targeting a single family like this?

For a moment, he wondered if he should wait for the guy to deliver the "insurance payment" before taking him down. The money would come in handy. But he quickly discarded the idea. It was ridiculous to believe that the guy was going to hand over money to a girl he'd never met.

No, this was a cold-blooded murderer, and he was trying to entice Sylvie into his trap.

Carlan decided he couldn't wait until tomorrow to take this "Jonathan Evers" down. He'd track down Captain Anderson on his day off, call in his favor. He had been to his superior's house once for a Halloween party; it was somewhere in the lower West Hills, on a steep road—Roanoke Avenue, that was the name of the street. He'd get an arrest warrant for the man in Room 23 of the Badlands Motel and search the room for evidence.

Even if he couldn't make the charges stick, he could at least warn the guy away from Sylvie. The Hardaways didn't know what a good friend they had in him.

He'd lost Jamie, but he wasn't going to lose Sylvie.

Chapter 12

Terrill arrived at the Black Bear restaurant a few minutes late. The skies had cleared in the late afternoon and he'd had to wait for the sun to sink behind the Cascade Mountains before venturing out.

He'd thought all day about how much to give to Sylvie. Too much money and she might wonder: too little, and she might just spend it all on other things. He decided on an amount and wrote out a check with the

Prestigious Insurance heading. If it turned out not to be enough, he could always send more later.

Chainsaw carvings of black bears surrounded the restaurant, and paw prints were stenciled onto the sidewalk. The entrance was enclosed within a gift shop selling kitschy plates and statues. It was dinnertime, and the place was packed.

Sylvie was talking to some friends near the front counter, still wearing her waitress smock. She saw Terrill and waved. She finished her conversation and went into the back, emerging seconds later as a civilian.

She nodded toward the inside of the restaurant and led him to a small table in the corner, near the swinging doors to the kitchen.

"You hungry?" she asked. "We make some pretty good hamburgers here."

"No," he said. He wanted to hand the check over as soon as possible. He wanted to get out of this High Desert land, with its bright sun and scant shade. He needed to get back to a city, where he could blend in, where his behavior wouldn't be observed by the same people every day. The local butcher was already looking at him askance, and if he stayed much longer, he'd have to track down another source for raw meat.

Terrill handed over the check.

Sylvie didn't look at it. She put it face down on the table and stared at him. "Why are you doing this?"

"Doing what? I'm just delivering an insurance settlement."

"Why are you delivering it? I wouldn't have even known about it until you wrote me a letter. If you'd put up enough roadblocks, I probably wouldn't have even fought it. You could have sent it looking like junk mail and I would've thrown it away. Why didn't you?"

"At Prestigious Insurance, we don't do things that way."

"That's another thing. I spent half an hour on Google looking for a Prestigious Insurance and couldn't find it."

"We fly under the radar," he said.

"No kidding. But why? Why would an insurance company not want to be known?"

Terrill took a drink of water, trying to cover up his consternation. Why the hell was she questioning her windfall?

The swinging doors opened and a waitress came out, trying to balance an overloaded tray. She didn't quite make it out the door; one of the plates landed upside down, mashed potatoes squirting out onto Terrill's shoes.

There was some sarcastic clapping, but Terrill rose and reassured the young waitress that it was all right, waving her away from wiping off his shoes.

"That was nice of you," Sylvie said after the flustered waitress had left. "She's new. You could've really wrecked her confidence if you'd made a scene." She was looking at him with raw appraisal, and for the first time, she didn't seem suspicious of him.

"Pick up the check," he urged.

She put her hand on the check where it lay on the table. She hesitated, then flipped it over and looked down. "Holy shit!"

"Yes, your sister was quite generous."

"I could live on this for ten years. Hell, I don't need to go to school."

"Yes, and then what? Besides, as I've said, the insurance is predicated on your continuing your education."

"Well, Central Oregon Community College doesn't cost all that much," she said. "I'm not leaving Bend. I can't leave my mom and dad right now. They need my help."

"I understand they have a new four-year program here," Terrill said.

"Yeah, if you want to be in the hospitality industry, or a chef, or something like that. Hard sciences are still over in the Valley."

The restaurant was getting more crowded with the dinner rush, the swinging doors were opening more and more often, and the clanking of dishes and the shouts of cooks washing over their conversation was making it more and more difficult for them to hear each other.

Four guys wearing soiled baseball uniforms came in and sat at the next table over. They weren't lowering their voices from the playing field level.

"There's a nightclub next door," Sylvie said. "It should be quieter over there this early in the evening."

The other waitresses waved to her on her way out, and the desk clerk smiled brightly. It was obvious Sylvie was popular around here. They checked him out, too. A well-dressed guy in his thirties—an obvious catch. Then again, a girl like Sylvie probably had plenty of guys sniffing around.

* * *

The nightclub was mostly empty, it being too early for the nighttime crowd. They found a quiet table near the bar and ordered a couple of Deschutes Ales to pay for their table.

"You old enough?" Terrill asked belatedly.

Sylvie smiled brightly. "Turned twenty-one a month ago."

After they had both taken a deep swig of their beers, Terrill cleared his throat. "You were saying that there weren't any hard science programs here, but with enough money, the programs will come to you. Believe me, with your grades, no school will turn you down, especially if you pay full tuition."

"How the hell do you know about my grades?"

"Well, I assumed. I'm right, aren't I?"

Sylvie looked away. She had stuffed the check in her pocket, and it seemed to him that she didn't even want to think about it.

"Why are you fighting this?" he asked softly.

Tears came to her eyes and she looked down. "Jamie died. It seems all wrong that I should benefit from that."

"It's not your fault," Terrill said reassuringly. "You had nothing to do with it."

"But I still feel guilty. Like I caused it, or something."

"What you said last night at your house—she got unlucky, that's all. She met the wrong guy. It could have happened here, or anywhere, believe me."

"But she might not have been over there in Portland at all if it wasn't for me." Sylvie put her face into her hands and sobbed. "She wouldn't have been doing… what she was doing."

"Sylvie. Listen to me." Terrill stared at her until she looked up and met his eyes. "Your sister was thinking of you, and you will honor her memory by taking this money and making something of your life."

"I will?" She smiled sadly.

"Yes. You will. It's what Jamie wanted."

* * *

They drank their beers and ordered another round, and settled into a companionable conversation about schools. Sylvie seemed to know a lot about which colleges had the best programs, and Terrill encouraged her to look into them. She was easy to talk to, just as Jamie had been. But whereas Jamie had had a slightly defeated manner, Sylvie was still optimistic, still hopeful the world would come through for her.

They didn't notice when the four baseball players from the restaurant came in, or when two of them walked over to their table.

"Sylvie? Is that you?" one of them said.

The two men stood over them with big grins.

"Yeah?" she said in a neutral voice.

"It's Peter Saunders. I dated your sister in high school."

"I remember you," she said. She obviously didn't like the guy, but was trying to be polite.

"Hey, I heard about what happened to Jamie. I'm sorry."

Sylvie softened a little and her eyes grew moist. "Thank you, Peter."

He sat down in the booth next to her, and she had to scrunch closer to the window to make room.

The other man loomed over Terrill. "Scoot over, man," he said, and pushed his way onto the seat. Terrill gave way reluctantly. They both smelled of sweat, of healthy young male. Once, Terrill would have torn them to pieces for their rudeness, but now he stayed silent.

"Yeah, I was sorry she moved to Portland," Peter said. "She was the best piece of ass in Bend."

Sylvie stiffened. Peter looked over at Terrill challengingly, as if to ask, "What are you going to do about it?" Terrill stared back, but still didn't say anything. It wasn't the reaction Peter was looking for. He seemed a little disconcerted.

The guy next to Terrill spoke up. "She never would put out for me."

"No?" Peter said. "Well, you are one ugly son of a bitch."

"Not even on the second date."

"Well, I heard she was selling herself over in Portland. Once those bastards over there hollowed her out, maybe you could've afforded her."

"Come on, you guys," Sylvie said. "Get out of here." She didn't sound as much angry as sad.

"Why? Jim here was wondering if you put out for free. Or do you cost money too?"

"That's enough," Terrill said. The tone in his voice froze both men. They stared at each other, as if challenging each other to say something. Peter looked Terrill up and down and seemed to decide he wasn't much of a threat. Both men were huge, steroid-inflated jocks. Terrill was as tall as they were, but nowhere near as muscled.

"I like your duds, man," Peter said. "Obviously, you can afford her. Jamie always was a skank, ever since middle school. Sylvie probably costs more, being that she's so much fresher."

"Stand up," Terrill said.

The two jocks looked at each other, grinning. They were about to get what they came for. No doubt they didn't expect Terrill to put up much of fight. They stood up and waited for him.

He took his time, wondering what he was going to do. If he fought these two men, he doubted he would be able to control himself. Any other time, any other place, he would have taken the chance. But not here, not in front of Jamie's little sister.

He tried to stare them down, and they backed away a step in response. If there had just been one of them, it probably would've been over. But each of them was egging the other one on.

Peter took a swing at him, which he easily evaded. But Jim came in low, from the other side, and Terrill was slammed against the edge of the table. The air went out of his lungs and he collapsed to the floor.

Both men started kicking him, and he put his hands over his head to protect it. He wasn't afraid. Under the cover of his hands, he was trying to minimize the damage, taking notice of what part of his body was being struck. He hoped that was enough to satisfy the young men's bloodlust.

He fought the urge to tear them apart. His fangs started to extend, but he kept his face down. He thought he heard a gasp from Sylvie but didn't dare look at her. A kick to his neck left him gasping for breath, and his fangs and claws retracted. That had never happened before in the face of danger. He wondered about it as he continued to take the blows without resistance.

It's the girl, he thought. He didn't want to turn into a monster in front of her. He didn't want her to know that he was her sister's murderer. He wanted desperately to look like a good man to her.

The guys were beginning to tire. It wasn't any fun if their prey wasn't going to fight back.

But Peter wasn't satisfied. He picked Terrill up and slammed his head down on his knee.

That was the last thing Terrill remembered.

Chapter 13

Captain Anderson wasn't happy with the interruption of his weekly bowling night, but agreed to give Judge Parrish a call. An hour later, Carlan had a search warrant in hand.

He drove by himself to the Badlands Motel and watched the suspect's room for an hour, until it became obvious that no one was home. He considered calling for backup. Without another officer as a witness, whatever evidence he found would be in doubt, possibly not even allowed in a court case. Then again, he didn't plan to ever let it get that far. He'd already decided to take this suspect down by himself. A little "resistance" and maybe the problem could be taken care of here and now. It was always easier to explain after the fact, especially if there weren't any witnesses who might second-guess his actions.

I probably should wait until the suspect returns, Carlan thought, but he was nervous. Parrish had signed the warrant with great reluctance.

"This is the flimsiest excuse I've ever seen for a search," the old judge had said. "A traffic ticket a block away from the scene of a crime is hardly evidence, or we'd all be guilty. Still, I trust Captain Anderson's instincts on these kinds of cases, and if he thinks there is something here, then I'll go along."

"Thank you, your honor," Carlan had said.

"But I warn you, you'd better find better evidence than this if you intend to arrest this man," Parrish had said.

"Yes, sir. That's why we need the warrant."

If the suspect showed and refused to answer questions, Carlan might never have a chance to confront him. He decided to go ahead with the search. Better to find something incriminating now.

He entered the motel lobby and flashed the warrant. He asked the young clerk, who looked barely out of high school, for the key. The clerk didn't volunteer to go open the door, just handed him the key.

"I'm not surprised you're here," the clerk said, swallowing nervously. "The guy is spooky. He's gone every night, gets back just before dawn, and then stays in his room all day."

"So?"

"Hey, this ain't the Ritz. Hell, he doesn't even turn on the TV!"

"Good to know," Carlan said.

He had no doubt he'd find something, or at least that he'd be able to concoct a story based on something he found. There was always guilty stuff hanging around; it was just how you interpreted it. Anything sharp? It could be a weapon. Porn? Evidence of a dirty mind. Bounced checks? A dishonest character. Alcohol? An out-of-control drunk.

The evidence might be flimsy, but it would be more than he had now. He didn't need much—just enough to justify more digging, and more digging always exposed more guilty secrets.

* * *

An hour later, Carlan had found nothing. The guy was a ghost. There was nothing personal at all in his room. He had a single change of clothing. The clerk had said he wouldn't allow maid service, but the room was spotless. The bed was made. Who the hell made their own motel bed? Who took out their own motel trash?

The more Carlan thought about it, the more suspicious it seemed. But it was hardly the kind of thing he could use for an arrest.

"What's your evidence?" Parrish would ask in that dry tone of his.

"That's just it, your honor. The guy is spotless—it's suspicious, I tell you!"

In desperation, Carlan searched the suitcase one last time, and then he found it.

The chain was curled up in one of the side pockets. He recognized it right away. The last time he'd seen it, it had been tight against Jamie's neck as he pulled on it, choking her, screaming at her.

She'd pushed him too far that time. What did she expect? How could she lead him on like that and then just drop him? He had a right to be upset.

The chain was missing the silver crucifix, but had something even better on it: blood. The links were encrusted with the dried brown stuff.

Carlan put the chain back where he'd found it and looked around the room. Was there anything there to betray his presence? He was glad now that the suspect was so tidy and minimalist in his habits. The place looked untouched.

He slipped out the door and walked quickly to the lobby. He saw the clerk's face pressed against the window as if he'd been watching.

"I decided to call for backup before I go in," Carlan explained.

The kid looked surprised, and Carlan knew he'd seen him enter the room. He walked over to the counter and then around it, stopping only inches away from the clerk. "I poked my head in, that's all," he said evenly. "You don't need to tell anyone that."

"Of course not," the kid said, backing up as far as he could in the narrow space between the counter and the mail slots.

* * *

Carlan waited outside the motel in his unmarked car.

He hadn't really expected to find anything—maybe just enough to satisfy himself. It didn't take much to turn the criminal justice system against someone. Sometimes just a suspicion was enough to get the ball rolling; an actual accusation was enough to get you halfway to guilty in the eyes of the public; and an indictment, more often than not, was all you really needed for a conviction.

To find slam-dunk evidence? Well, he was willing to let the system grind this guy down. He'd seen it often enough. It was very satisfying.

He could always take further revenge sometime down the road.

Officer Patterson showed up, lights flashing and sirens blaring. Carlan winced. He'd still been hoping he could catch the killer when he returned. Then again, Patterson was the perfect cover. The rookie was completely by the book, and was unlikely to catch on to Carlan's earlier snooping. Hell, he wouldn't even suspect it. Patterson still believed that all cops were the good guys.

The suspect was all but caught. As soon as the chain was found, Carlan would put out an alert for the Cadillac.

He made sure the rookie had put on his gloves, and then proceeded into the room. He went into the bathroom, knowing Patterson would probably make a beeline to the suitcase. It wasn't more than a few minutes before he heard the exclamation. Impressive. Carlan had almost missed it, but the rookie had found it right away. Carlan could barely remember ever being so conscientious and diligent.

"Hey, Officer Carlan?" the young man said in an even tone, which only revealed how excited he really was. "Didn't the crime scene reports mention a missing necklace?"

"Yeah. Miss Howe had a silver chain and crucifix."

"Well, I think I found the chain, at least. And it looks to me like there's blood on it!"

"Bag it up!" Carlan said, having no problem showing excitement. *Game, set, and match.* "Careful. We don't want to contaminate anything."

"Yes, sir," Patterson said, sliding the chain into an evidence bag and sealing it. They went over to the desk, and both of them signed the bag and dated it.

"Call it in," Carlan instructed. "The guy is driving around Bend right now. The license number is in the report."

"You want me to do it?" The young man could barely restrain his excitement. Carlan smiled. He felt calm, and he knew that he radiated a veteran's coolness that the rookie would try to emulate.

"Sure," Carlan said. "You earned it. In fact, why don't you take lead in this? I'll just tag along." His past relationship was bound to come up in the trial. Best make it seem like he was just along for the ride.

He glanced around the room one last time and shuddered. Such neatness was unnatural. The guy was a real freak. He looked forward to looking the murderer in the eye, making sure that he understood that Officer Richard Carlan was responsible for his downfall.

Then he'd make sure that Sylvie knew it, too. She'd forget all about their little disagreement. He'd be the hero.

Chapter 14

Terrill awoke with his head on the lap of angel, looking up into her glowing face. Angel. An angel. He hadn't thought of angels for centuries, certain of his damnation. She was looking out the car window, worried.

He groaned, and her gaze transferred the full power of her caring down upon him, and he squirmed in response. He didn't deserve her concern; she would spit on him if she knew what he'd done to her sister. It was too much.

He groaned again, not from the pain, but from the memory of Jamie. Kind, hopeful Jamie, whom he'd killed in a moment of hunger, without restraint. He didn't deserve this girl's pity.

"Let me up," he said.

He managed to prop himself upright, but the lights shining through the car windows made him dizzy. He was in the backseat of a taxi.

"Where are you taking me?"

"We're headed for the hospital," Sylvie said.

"What about the others?"

"They ran away. They thought they killed you. So did I."

"No hospital," Terrill said, slurring his words. He said it louder, trying to be clear. "No hospital. Take me to my motel."

"But they really hurt you," Sylvie protested.

"I'll pay you!" he shouted at the taxi driver. "Badlands Motel. Forget the hospital!"

The driver shifted subtly in his seat, slowed down slightly, then turned into the left lane. Terrill was sure he'd gotten through to the guy. He nearly dropped his head back into Sylvie's lap, but instead pushed her away.

"I'm fine. I just need some sleep."

"They beat the crap out of you! I don't know how you can still be conscious."

"I'm tough," he said. "Tougher than you can imagine." There was a packet of raw steaks in the refrigerator back in his room. That's all he needed, at least for the moment.

They drove for a few minutes in silence. Then Sylvie said quietly, "Why didn't you fight back? I could see you wanted to."

"There were two of them. I didn't have a chance."

"I heard you snarl at them, as if you wanted to tear their heads off. They heard you, too. If you had gotten up, put up a fight, I think they would've backed off. Instead, you... just quit."

How much did I give myself away? Terrill wondered. "I didn't want to hurt them," he muttered.

"My hero," Sylvie said softly. He couldn't tell what she meant by that.

* * *

The flashing red and blue lights bounced off the windows of the motel, the metal of the cars, and the wet pavement, seeming to suffuse the air around them.

Through the pounding in his head and the rhythmic pulse of the lights striking his eyes, Terrill understood what it meant.

"Take me to my car," he said. "Back to the restaurant... the bar..."

The cabbie ignored him, pulling into the parking lot. A few more yards and they'd be visible to the assembled cops.

"Turn around, now!" Terrill shouted.

"Look, buddy," said the cabbie, "if you're in trouble, I don't want any part of it."

"A hundred dollars if you turn around right now!"

The cabbie slammed on the brakes. He backed out of the driveway with a vertiginous swoosh and accelerated away down the street.

"What's going on?" Sylvie asked.

"Don't worry about it." Terrill had been about to say "It has nothing to do with you," but of course it had everything to do with her.

She and the cabbie were looking at each other as if wondering what kind of man they were sharing a cab with.

"Look, I fell a little behind on my motel bill, that's all," Terrill said, sounding insincere to his own ears. "My money is in the car—if I show up without it, they might throw me in jail."

"You got no money?" the cabbie asked, sounding outraged, slowing down as if he was going to toss them both out onto the street.

"Like I said, it's in my car—plenty of money."

"Better be," the cabbie growled.

* * *

They were silent on the way back. Terrill didn't know what to say without lying, so he didn't say anything at all. Sylvie apparently didn't want to hear him lying either, so she didn't press him.

They got to the Cadillac, which was the only car in the Black Bear parking lot. Terrill retrieved his secret stash of emergency cash from under one of the back floor mats and paid the cabbie off. He'd have to go to the bank first thing in the morning, because he was down to his last few hundred bucks.

"Do you need a ride home?" he asked Sylvie.

"If you don't mind," she said quietly.

It was probably obvious to her that he was taking a less busy route to her house. If the police were searching his motel room, they had his license plate number and the information that he was driving a black Escalade.

I should tell her now, he thought. She'd find out soon enough. By tomorrow, it would be all over the news. He'd been thinking about how he would explain himself ever since the morning it happened, but no explanation seemed strong enough. Because no explanation *was* strong enough, or ever could be. Was it possible she could ever forgive him?

* * *

He'd asked Jamie to take off her crucifix before having sex.

"I take it you aren't religious?" she said.

"You could say that."

"I'm not either. My sister, Sylvie, gave it to me, and I wear it for her. She's sweetly religious—completely nonjudgmental and loving."

"She'll grow out of it," Terrill said, only half joking.

Jamie was naked except for the chain around her neck. She removed it, kissed the cross and laid it on the nightstand.

"I don't think she'll change," she said. "It was weird. My family isn't religious at all, so we were really alarmed when Sylvie got involved with one of the local charismatic preachers. It was almost a cult. But Sylvie walked away from that. She kept her belief in God and the goodness of man and the possibility of redemption. She dropped all the rest of the claptrap.

"Funny thing is, she was always kind of... kind of holy, even before she got religion. It just gave her the terminology, the structure she needed. But she already understood forgiveness and understanding. If I went home today, she'd never say a word of condemnation. That's not her way."

Terrill was almost tempted to talk more about it, except that the sight of Jamie's perfectly naked and perfectly beautiful body knocked the thoughts right out of him.

Later, as he nuzzled her neck, he noticed the small imprint of the cross on Jamie's chest, right between her breasts, as if she'd recently tanned without removing her jewelry.

"The possibility of redemption," she'd said.

Terrill had long wondered if such a thing was possible. Sometimes, like now, when he was in the presence of someone good, he could almost believe it...

* * *

"I need to tell you something," he said as they pulled up in front of Sylvie's house. "You're going to hear a lot of things about me in the next few days. I just want you to know... I'm sorry it happened. I wish it had never happened. If I could change it, I would."

"What did you do?" But he could tell she'd already figured it out, if not consciously, then at some level of her subconscious. What else could he have done that would cause such an uproar? What else might have caused him to show up on her doorstep with blood money in hand?

"I've tried to change, but my nature won't allow it," he said. "I can't help being what I am."

Sylvie was looking at him with fear in her eyes, as if suddenly conscious that she was in a strange car with a strange man she'd only known for a day. She fumbled with the door latch, and he reached over and pushed the door open, accidentally brushing against her. She nearly cried out, and then she was out of the car and halfway up the sidewalk.

"Forgive me," he called after her, but he wasn't sure if she heard him.

* * *

Leave town, Terrill told himself. *You've done what you came for.*

But he drove only a few blocks before he found a quiet cul-de-sac and parked. He got into the backseat and closed his eyes. He hurt all over, but he barely noticed. The look in Sylvie's eyes as she began to suspect what he'd done would never leave him.

In all his years of hunting, he had never cared, never given a second thought to how the families and friends of his victims were affected.

Until the day he'd tried to prove a point to Horsham, and instead had changed his own life forever.

Chapter 15

It had been a long time since Horsham had felt the thrill, the danger of the hunt. Now, as he was chauffeured over the mountains, he felt more and more certain his quarry was close.

He had bought a small motor home in Portland, straight off the lot, astonishing the salesman by not negotiating. He had only one condition. "I want curtains on the windows or no deal."

"No problem!" the salesman had said, unable to hide his excitement. Horsham saw him summon one of the carwash monkeys and send him out to the local Bed Bath & Beyond. They'd quickly outfitted the motor home to his specifications. He casually mentioned removing the mirrors, and they readily agreed. A cash sale, full price... he could've asked them to kiss his ass and they would've done it gladly.

The pilot of his private jet, Shepard, agreed to be his driver, and they headed over the pass.

The vastness of the American West had always intrigued Horsham. A vampire could get lost out here. He'd contemplated moving here from Europe a century ago, but realized that vastness didn't mean anonymity. The settlers tended to know each other and to notice strangers.

Now it was different, obviously. The average Westerner was no different than any other city dweller—many of them lived in cities. They pulled up to their suburban houses, hit the garage door opener and entered their houses without ever interacting with their neighbors. They went to giant Walmarts and wandered the aisles, not knowing anyone. They interacted over the Internet and avoided each other in person.

When this is all over, Horsham thought, *I will look at the possibility of moving to the Northwest.* It was rainy and gloomy and dark and moist—everything he needed.

Daylight was breaking by the time they left Portland. Horsham retreated to the dark womb of the curtained back of the motor home. He curled up in bed, dreaming of revenge.

He felt rather than saw the switchover from the Valley to the eastern part of Oregon. He awoke, feeling as though danger was pressing down on him. It was as if the sun was trying to beat down the curtains.

"Where are we?" he shouted to his driver.

"We just hit the summit of the pass, sir. It's a beautiful day, blue skies, not a cloud in sight."

Horsham shivered. No vampire would voluntarily travel to such a place. What was Terrill doing? Why was he here?

He couldn't sleep after that. The sun seemed to be prying through the walls and curtains of his enclosure, as if seeking him out. He moved to the center of the bed and brooded. Damn Terrill for making him do this. Damn Terrill for putting him in danger. The older vampire, who had once been Horsham's mentor, was breaking all the rules, most of which Terrill himself had developed.

Did he have a death wish? It wouldn't be the first time a vampire had become careless and foolhardy because he didn't care anymore. If so, Horsham would see to it that Terrill's death wish was fulfilled.

A couple of hours later, the motor home slowed down and Horsham heard heavy traffic on both sides.

"We need to find a place to stay," he shouted to his driver. "To park..."

"I've got just the place," Shepard said.

A few minutes later, they stopped. Horsham went to the side of the motor home that was in the shade and peeked out. There were two other motor homes in a vast expanse of parking lot. In the distance, he saw a huge sign for Walmart.

"They let you park here for free," Shepard said.

How utterly charming, Horsham thought. *How nice of Walmart to provide me with a traveling buffet. People who won't be missed right away. Right there, next door.*

In a few days or a week, someone would find a few empty RVs and one RV full of the gore and bones of the missing. Horsham was looking forward to it. It had been ages since he'd lived among the visceral remnants of his meals. He'd been living the sterile life of a rich man for way too long. He began to salivate over the thought of it; his fangs started to extend.

"I'm going to stay here," Horsham said. "But we need to find a nearby hotel for you, Shepard."

"That's not necessary, sir. I know about your... peculiarities."

"You know? What do you know?"

"I know that you need to avoid daylight. That you need to feed. You can trust me, Mr. Horsham. I can help."

Horsham had dozens of employees, none of whom he allowed in his proximity for long periods of time. It wasn't that hard to figure out what Horsham was if they were paying attention. He hired people who didn't pay attention, people who had the capacity to be blind to what they needed to be blind to. It appeared that Shepard had spent a little too much time with Horsham, had gotten a little too curious.

"I see," he said calmly. "Still, I'd like my privacy. Come back here and I'll give you the money for a nice hotel."

Shepard came into the back, and Horsham could see that despite his bold words, the man was frightened to death, but also determined to get what he could for his forbidden knowledge. He was just inside the curtained back area and was obviously ready to jump back into the light at the first sign of danger.

Horsham handed him a couple of hundred dollars and told him to book two nights.

"Can't get a very good hotel room for a hundred bucks a night," Shepard said. "I think if I'm really going to help you, I need to get a good rest, the kind a really nice hotel would give me. Five hundred dollars would be better."

"I doubt they have five-hundred-dollar motel rooms here," Horsham said.

"Well, if I save you money, I can keep the rest, right?" Shepard was trying hard to make the extortion seem only reasonable.

Horsham decided to test him. He peeled another hundred dollars off his roll. "Rent a nice car and come back tonight at dusk."

"I think three hundred dollars more for the car would be better," his driver said, unable to keep the greed out of his voice.

So that's going to be the way of it, Horsham thought. He didn't mind the expenditure; it was the control the human thought he had that bothered him. He took out $500 and held it out. But this time, he kept it close to his body, and the human was forced to step a couple of more feet into the darkness.

"Do you know why I'm here, in this godforsaken, dried-up part of the country?" Horsham asked.

"No, sir. None of my business."

"Well, you've made it your business, whether you intended to or not. I'm hunting my mentor. A very dangerous… man. He taught me everything I know. You know what he told me?"

Shepard seemed to sense something was wrong and edged back toward the front of the motor home. He swallowed and shook his head.

"Never trust a human."

The man was quicker than Horsham expected and was opening the curtains as Horsham landed on his back. They both fell into the light. Horsham felt the pain of the sunlight, but even as he burned, he sucked up the blood of his victim and healed. He burned and healed, burned and healed.

Then he dragged the dead man into the back and feasted on the rest of him.

* * *

"Rule number one," Terrill said.

They were in Paris, right after the Nazis had marched in. It was a glorious time to be a vampire, death all around them, their own murdering ways completely unnoticed.

Terrill was working out the Rules of Vampire and using Horsham as his sounding board.

"Rule number one," he repeated. "Never trust a human."

"You'll have a hard time with that," Horsham said. *"We've gotten accustomed to our human lackeys."*

"That's exactly why it must be changed," Terrill insisted. *"Humans have too often betrayed us. We must disappear from the world in order to survive the world. Kill any and every human who discovers us."*

"But won't the humans notice the murders?"

Terrill went on without acknowledging his question, thereby answering it.

"Rule number two. Never leave the remains of a kill, or if you must, disguise the cause of death.

"Rule number three. Never feed where you live.

"Rule number four. Never create a pattern. Kill at random.

"Rule number five. Never kill for the thrill. Feed only when necessary to eat."

"Good luck with rule number five!" Horsham laughed. *"Vampires kill because we like it, and only secondarily to feed."*

Terrill shrugged. *"Those vampires who don't follow the rules will be discovered and destroyed. The fewer foolish vampires, the better for the rest of us."*

"I thought you were trying to avoid our extinction?"

Terrill frowned. *"Yes, but we don't need more vampires, we need smarter vampires."*

He continued. *"Rule number six. Never steal in the short term; create wealth for the long term."* Terrill turned to Horsham and smiled. *"As you're fond of saying, 'Compound interest is a vampire's best friend.'"*

"Yes, but you must have wealth to start with."

Terrill shrugged. *"So we make a one-time exception."*

"What else?" Horsham asked, curious despite himself. Vampires didn't follow rules; it was one of the things that separated them from humans. They did what they wanted when they wanted. But he had to admit, it was becoming rarer and rarer to come across other vampires. Alarmingly so.

"That's as far as I've gotten. I'm sure there should be more."

"No doubt there should be thousands of rules," Horsham said dryly. *"But maybe you should stop there."*

* * *

And so he had. Horsham, for one, had lived by these rules ever since. And so had Terrill, which was what had made him so difficult to find. Until now.

Chapter 16

Terrill woke with a start, his internal alarm going off at the very moment the sun dropped behind the mountains.

He'd slept fitfully through the day. Some kids had circled the car in the late afternoon, trying to peer inside the darkly tinted windows, curious at the strange vehicle in their neighborhood. He had had a few tense moments, but they'd gone away and he'd dropped back into a feverish sleep.

His eyes seemed glued shut. His mouth was dry and parched. He was shivering, though it was a warm evening and a blanket covered him. It required dredging up a distant memory from when he had been human to diagnose what was wrong with him.

It was as if he was running a fever... which should have been impossible. Above all, he was feeling pain in his chest. He unbuttoned his shirt and looked down at the cross, which had burned another half inch into his skin. The skin around it was red and inflamed.

What was he doing? Was he trying to kill himself? All he knew was that enduring the crucifix felt like the right thing, that he needed to suffer for his redemption. It was a constant reminder of what he'd done, not only to Jamie but to the countless humans he'd killed through the centuries.

* * *

"I don't believe in the supernatural," Terrill said.

"You realize the irony of that, don't you?" Horsham replied. He was dating a human woman named Mary, who was a saint by day and a sex demon by night.

Terrill had had a long time to contemplate religion, but he hadn't come to any conclusions. He was completely nonreligious.

"What irony?"

"Well, you say you don't believe in the supernatural, and yet here we are, vampires! The stuff of legend."

"But we're completely natural," Terrill said, certain that he was right. "We just haven't been studied yet. We're as real as the Neanderthals once were. We just haven't gone extinct."

"Yet."

"What?"

"We haven't gone extinct yet."

"Maybe," Terrill conceded. As humans became ever more numerous, vampires were being forced out of the shadows and into the light, where they were being systematically

destroyed. *With Michael the Maker's blessing, Terrill had created the six Rules of Vampire for the remaining vampires to live by. They seemed to be working.*

"So we're completely natural, like penguins or dolphins or guinea pigs. Except... why does holy water burn us, why can't we stand on consecrated ground, and why do we flee the cross?"

That was the flaw in Terrill's skepticism, all right. Why should the symbols of Christianity affect them so if there was no such thing as God?

"Because some part of us believes the old wives' tales," he said, not sounding completely confident in his argument. "Some part of our nature is susceptible to these symbols, whether we understand them or not."

That was what he told his brethren, but inside, he had his doubts. Once, he'd thrown holy water on a condemned vampire who had no reason to believe it was anything other than just water. It was alarming when the vampire burst into flames and disintegrated in moments.

Terrill often wondered if vampires who were Muslims or Hindus or Jews had their own vulnerabilities, but he'd never found a vampire who had originated in any of those cultures. Vampires seemed to be a European Christian phenomenon.

He also wondered if these weaknesses had existed longer than two thousand years. Michael was the oldest of all vampires, and he was twelve hundred years old. Michael never talked about the past, but he did hint that vampires had always existed.

"Maybe we're working for the devil," Horsham said.

He made it sound like a joke, but Terrill realized at that moment that the woman Mary was having a deleterious effect on his old friend.

Horsham was breaking Rule 1: Never trust a human.

Mary was becoming an inconvenience. No, she was becoming a danger.

Terrill had a simple solution for such dangers.

* * *

Mary. That had been the start of his damnation. Or perhaps, because he'd always been damned but just hadn't realized it, the beginning of his redemption. Or so he had thought for a long time. He'd tried so hard. He'd suffered physically the only way a vampire could, by refusing to feed for as long as possible. He'd thought he was succeeding. He was beginning to feel confident enough to seek human comfort.

If only Jamie hadn't woken him like that. If only she hadn't trusted him.

Terrill had broken half of the rules of his own devising. He'd trusted a human long enough to fall asleep with her. He hadn't disposed of her remains. He had killed in his own backyard.

He probably deserved to be caught.

He put his fingers to the cross, and they burned. Unlike any other wound, it wouldn't heal. He was feeling true *enduring* pain for the first time in centuries: pain he couldn't fix by simply feeding.

He was weak, weaker than he'd ever been. He needed sustenance as soon as possible. His ribs were bruised from the beating at the nightclub, and he suspected his face was black and blue as well. Those were injuries that could and should be healed if he intended to survive.

If not, he could just wait for Horsham to find him. It wouldn't take long. In Terrill's weakened state, Horsham would make short work of him. He wouldn't fight back. For Mary's sake; for Jamie, and for all the other innocent victims.

But Terrill found he wasn't quite ready to give up. Not yet.

The butcher closed at 5:30, so he needed to get going if he was going to get there in time.

* * *

He tried taking the back roads, but there was no way to get past the railroad tracks without taking one of the main arteries. He hadn't gone more than half a mile before he heard a siren.

Terrill didn't hesitate. He took off, turning back onto the darkened side streets. He ran a red light, then another, and the cops backed off.

He slowed down, taking right turns so he didn't have to run any more lights.

They were ready for him. He turned another corner and saw three police cars arrayed on the road ahead of him, blocking it. As he slowed, three more came whooping up on him from behind.

Terrill was boxed in. He jumped out of the car and ran into the nearest yard and down the side of the house.

All thoughts of giving up, all meditations on redemption, left him. He was vampire, pursued by his mortal enemy, mankind. He headed into darkness, his keen vampire senses finding tiny gradations in the level of light. He found himself at the end of an alley with a rocky hillside above him.

He could see the paths on the hillside clearly. The darker it was, the more clearly he could see. It was the obvious escape route.

But he turned aside and ducked through a hole in the side of an old standalone garage that was being used as a storage shed. He made his way to the darkest corner and crouched there.

He could hear search dogs barking and howling nearby. They wouldn't know what to make of him; his scent would have no meaning to them. They would whine to their masters, wondering what they were supposed to do.

But the dogs could see well in the darkness, better than their handlers. It was inevitable that they would make their way down this alley. It was an obvious escape route.

He heard the cops a few minutes later. The humans, too, had sensed that he would run into darkness. They, too, made it to the end of the alley and looked up at the hillside.

Terrill saw the flashlights going by, and heard the trudging and tripping of the humans as they made their way up the rocky slope with exclamations and curses.

But one light remained. Terrill heard a growl, and he kept absolutely still.

A vampire in darkness cannot be seen unless he moves. Humans can often sense the danger and will search for the cause, but rarely see it in time. Terrill blended in with the dark wood behind him, as solid and as unmoving as it was. The dog poked his head through the hole in the side of the garage and growled, and the human squeezed in after, running the beam of his flashlight around the dark interior.

Terrill closed his eyes. The light went directly past him.

Then the cop muttered something about wishing he was eating dinner at home and dragged the reluctant dog out of the garage. The dog hadn't seen or smelled Terrill either, but it trusted its primitive instincts more.

* * *

Terrill held still for what seemed hours, until suddenly, he started shaking. Once he started shaking, he couldn't stop. That had never happened to him before.

He hadn't eaten for over a day. His wounds were unhealed. But most of all, the cross was burning into him. He could almost feel the shape of it, could almost feel it glowing, consuming him.

For the first time since he'd been Turned, he had no food, no shelter, and no friends.

The cost of redemption is always high, he thought. *Otherwise it wouldn't mean anything.*

Pain alone was not enough. It meant nothing unless he helped others. Unless he helped Sylvie.

Chapter 17

Late in the afternoon, someone knocked on the RV's door. Horsham pulled one of the curtains aside an inch. The sun was still burning brightly. Still... the door was in the shade. He threw it open and stepped back from the daylight.

"Hey, neighbor!" It was the young couple from Rhode Island, Bill and Peggy, who were taking a yearlong sabbatical in a rundown VW minivan and blogging about it. Horsham had already decided he'd feed on them last, since people were bound to notice the disappearance of a blog. Then again, maybe not. Out of curiosity, he'd looked them up online, and while the blog had started out strong and enthusiastic, it was petering out with each wearying mile. They'd already spent most of their reserves, and they had the whole second leg of the trip to go. Horsham smelled defeat.

"Hi," he said, friendly, but not too friendly. He couldn't invite them in. Pieces of the driver, Shepard, were still scattered around the floor. Fortunately, he hadn't begun to stink yet.

"Have you seen Brenda and Dave?" Peggy asked. "We were going to go to a movie."

"No, haven't seen them. Can't have gone far."

Brenda and Dave were tied up and unconscious on the lower tier of Horsham's bunk bed. He planned to feed on them before heading out after dark.

"Weird," Bill said. "They usually take their RV when they go anywhere. Well, if you see them, let them know we were looking for them."

"You bet," Horsham said. He'd automatically picked up the American accent and idioms, and now sounded like he was from the Midwest somewhere. Such mimicking was a talent most successful vampires had. They blended in innocuously or they were discovered: there wasn't much in between. Horsham was wearing Shepard's clothes, cheap duds that had probably been bought right there at Walmart, rather than his own tailored outfit.

He closed the door and went back to his laptop. He'd been online all day with his computer experts back in London, asking them to do a search of all major financial transactions in Bend. He'd also had them hack into the local police database.

It appeared that Terrill was already on the run. A search warrant had been served on the motel room where he'd been staying. Apparently, from the police chatter, some damning evidence was found. They were looking for his car.

That was inconvenient. Horsham didn't want Terrill found by the police first. Then again, as crazy as Terrill had been acting, he was probably still capable of outfoxing the local constabulary. And the pressure was useful. It would force Terrill into the open.

Horsham had tried to put himself in his old mentor's place. Why was he here? What was he hoping to accomplish?

It had to do with the dead girl. Terrill had managed not to feed on humans for a couple of decades. Undoubtedly, he was feeling remorse, just like the last time Horsham had seen him.

* * *

One in a thousand victims of vampires became vampires themselves. There was no way of knowing in advance if it would happen. It almost wasn't worth worrying about. Most vampires feasted on their victims, ensuring there would be no reanimation. Occasionally, they'd leave a corpse undisturbed to see if it would Turn, out of curiosity, or loneliness, or because they somehow felt sympathetic toward their victim. Almost all these corpses remained cold. Wasted meat.

Mary was still in her wedding dress, but it had changed in color from virgin white to blood red. She looked peaceful, only a couple of punctures in her neck, almost delicately placed to do the least damage possible.

"I couldn't let you go through with it," Terrill was saying. "I'm sorry."

Horsham fell to his knees beside her. The anger didn't come at first. The thirst for revenge that would sustain the rest of his existence was still buried under the numb realization that she was gone.

He even let Terrill rest a hand comfortingly on his shoulder. She had died, and somehow Horsham still hadn't made the emotional connection about who had killed her.

"If she is meant for you, she'll come back," Terrill said. "I couldn't let you marry a human, Horsham. Never trust a human."

The old rule barely penetrated Horsham's consciousness. He'd heard it a million times, and yet somehow he'd never thought it applied to him. It never applied to Mary.

He had revealed himself to her only the week before, showing her his true nature. She stood naked next to the bed, staring down at him in shock. Then she made the sign of the cross.

He cringed, and she turned white at his reaction. She fled, half clothed, back to her room. For the next two days, she spent every moment in the local church, unwilling to even look at him.

On the third day, she reemerged, a determined look on her face.

"You shall never kill again," she said.

"Very well," he agreed, uncertain that he could succeed, but intending to expend every ounce of willpower trying.

"I will save you from damnation," she said. It was her new goal, her reason for being. Horsham didn't care, as long as she stayed with him.

Now, Terrill was saying something about being sorry, about wishing he hadn't done it. The hypocrisy of it suddenly bloomed in Horsham's mind. He stood and pushed Terrill away, fangs and claws fully extended.

Terrill lowered his head and left.

He returned that night, and they sat at opposite ends of the room, staring at Mary's corpse. She didn't rise that first night, or the next. But on the third night, as both of them drowsed, the corpse sighed.

She rose up and looked around her, confused. She looked down at her freshly washed white wedding dress and stared at the backs of her hands. At that moment, the hands became claws.

She'd be ravenous, Horsham knew. He'd killed a calf each morning of the vigil and now he rose to bring the freshest one to her. She started to eat, and then stopped. She threw the meat onto the floor and looked at the blood on her hands and started to keen. The loud, high, mournful lament froze both vampires where they stood.

Dawn was breaking; the light came in through a small crack in the curtains and landed on Mary's feet, which started to smoke.

"You must get away from the light!" Horsham shouted.

She looked at him, confused.

Then it was as if she suddenly understood everything. Horsham would always remember that look, a look that said she knew exactly what had happened and why, and yet accepted it.

"I love you," she said. He started to move toward her, but she turned her gaze away, and it was as if the light had gone out for him. He stopped.

She was looking at Terrill in pity. "I forgive you. I must be your last."

She rose up from the bed gracefully. She walked to window and threw open the blinds.

Terrill and Horsham instinctively jumped to the darkened corners of the room. But Mary stood in direct sunlight. She turned and looked at them, and gave them a beatific smile as she began to flicker. She opened her arms as the flames began to rise from her body, starting at her feet and moving upward.

She didn't move as she burned, and the last thing Horsham saw was her smile, enclosed in fire.

* * *

Terrill begged for forgiveness. For days and weeks, he was beside himself with guilt. At first, Horsham was so stunned he didn't react. And then, the more Terrill pleaded, the more Horsham's anger grew.

The day came when he whirled on his mentor and attacked, with everything he had ever learned. But Terrill was stronger and more experienced. He warded off the attack, but maddeningly, he didn't fight back.

Horsham finally gave up, collapsing to the floor, sobbing.

"I'm leaving, my old friend," was the last thing Terrill said to him. "I hope someday you can forgive me. I, for one, shall never kill again."

* * *

If Terrill had stuck to his principles, it was possible Horsham might one day have forgiven him. But to kill Mary, and then abandon the very reason he'd killed her! It was too much for Horsham to take.

He'd grown powerful over the last decades, honing his hunting skills even as Terrill became weak and his skills deteriorated. Next time they met, the outcome would be different.

The laptop was flashing a message from London. A $100,000 check had recently been submitted from a Prestigious Insurance company to a Sylvie Hardaway. There was no record of Prestigious Insurance existing, and it turned out that the beneficiary was the sister of Jamie Lee Howe.

The check was being held for confirmation of funds.

"Cancel the check," he typed. He had spent the past few years infiltrating every corner of the Internet, preparing for just such a day. "Refuse all access to funds in this account and follow any thread to any other account opened by the same person, no matter what name was used."

He closed the laptop with satisfaction. Terrill was without shelter, hunted, and now he was broke. The trap was closing.

Dusk was just beginning. There was time for a snack, and then it was on to the hunt. His two meals were awake now and screaming into their gags, squirming and staring at each other, bug-eyed with fear. Horsham decided to keep the meat fresh as long as possible.

He started on the legs and worked his way up.

Chapter 18

Terrill was curled in the corner when he heard scratching at the side of the garage facing the house. A small dog was worrying the ground just outside, unable to smell the vampire but sensing his presence.

"What are you doing, Tyson?" Terrill heard a voice call from the house.

The dog yelped and ran halfway across the lawn before turning suddenly and running back to the garage, almost slamming against the wooden slats.

"What's in there, boy? A rat? Raccoon?"

The dog yelped in agreement to both queries.

"Come back in the house. We'll check in the morning."

Terrill got to his feet, painfully. He needed to feed, but even more importantly, he had to get out of this garage before dawn, which he sensed was only an hour and a few minutes away. He scanned the cluttered junk with his night vision, his gaze landing on a curled-up tarp, stiffened by dried paint. He pulled it off the table and shook the dust off it. It would have to serve.

He left through the same the opening he had entered by. It had been at least eight hours since the search party had passed by. He started climbing up the hillside, looking for somewhere to hide. It was covered with bare rocks and short juniper trees, but on the other side there was a vacant lot, which connected at one corner with another.

Terrill made his way farther and farther away from the density of houses, his vision picking up the slightest variations of darkness and light. He was in a subdivision that bordered undeveloped land. He could make out some taller trees on the horizon. It would be close, but he thought he could make it there before sunrise.

When he finally limped up to them, he discovered that the trees weren't as tall or dense as he'd hoped. There was a small overhang in the nearby rocks with a large ponderosa leaning against it. He squeezed in between the tree and the cliff. It wouldn't be enough shade, he knew. He threw the tarp over himself and waited.

As the sun rose and the light finally hit Terrill's hiding spot, he realized that the tarp had tiny holes all over its surface. No matter how he positioned himself, at least one of the holes let in light that hit an exposed part of his skin. He tried covering the holes with twigs and leaves, but his efforts seemed to only widen the tears. Finally, he managed to contort his body in such a way that his skin was protected.

He'd been running for decades, always staying well ahead of Horsham's hunt. But trying to help Sylvie was probably going to be the end of him.

Appropriate that a saintly woman would be the reason he ended his exile, because it had been just such a woman who had begun it.

* * *

"Don't marry him," Terrill said.

Mary was in her wedding dress. Horsham had been shooed away, the groom denied the vision of his bride for now: tradition held that if he saw her in her wedding dress before the ceremony, it would bring bad luck. Terrill had escaped unseen from the rest of the wedding party.

"Oh? Should I marry you instead?" she asked.

He flushed. He'd been attracted to her from the first time he saw her, but he'd never said a word. He'd always watched her from the corner of his eye as she and Horsham walked hand in hand. He was envious, but he admitted it only to himself.

"That's not why I'm saying it," he said. "He is vampire and you are human. You believe in God; he is godless, soulless."

"I don't believe that," Mary said, turning toward him. She was tall, nearly as tall as he was, thin and raven-haired. With an oval face, a warm olive complexion, and dark brown eyes, she looked as if there was a Moor somewhere in her Spanish heritage. She was Catholic, and as devout as any human Terrill had ever met. "You have souls, you struggle with right and wrong, just as we humans do," she continued.

"You're wrong," Terrill said. But he wondered if that was true. Why did he care? Was it for her sake, or Horsham's? Or his own? What meaning did right and wrong have for a vampire? What did it matter, anyway?

And yet, if it didn't matter, why was he talking to her? Why didn't he just kill her now and be done with it? It would save Horsham the trouble later, when he got tired of her.

So he told himself. But he simply stared at her as she walked toward him. Such grace and beauty, *he thought. He'd been attracted to humans before, but always for carnal reasons, for sex or for food. Never had he hungered for their minds or their souls.*

Mary stood very close to him, and lifted her long, slender hand and caressed his cheek. "You and Horsham know you have done evil, but God will forgive you if you but surrender to Him," she said softly.

Terrill turned away before he gave in to the temptation to take her in his arms, lift her up and carry her to his bed. He wanted her, in every way. His fangs extended. Once he started feeding, he would not be able to stop. No vampire could. Did she understand what danger she was flirting with here?

Someday Horsham would give in to his desire; he would consume her, and she would be gone.

Terrill couldn't bear that thought.

"I do not need your God," he said. "I have everlasting life just the way I am."

"By killing others," she said. "Your soul is damned, but you do have a soul. It can still be redeemed. It is never too late, if you turn away from sin."

"No... I have done too much evil. It is impossible."

Her eyes turned soft. Again she approached him, and again she tempted him. This time he didn't resist. He kissed her and pressed his body to hers.

"I will save you both," she whispered in his ear.

They made love that night, and Terrill discovered, to his amazement, that she was a virgin. He'd assumed that she and Horsham had consummated their love. Instead, she had given herself to him.

She wanted to save him. She already was well on the way to changing Horsham. But she was greedy in her desire to convert them both.

As he climaxed, he knew what he had to do. He had to save her from certain destruction, and for that, he needed to kill her.

Terrill sank his fangs into her neck. She let out a whimper.

"No!" she said pleadingly. "Not this way."

It was too late. He'd begun feeding. He drained more and more of her blood, and it tasted sweeter than any blood he'd ever tasted.

"Terrill," she whispered. "I must be your last. You must never kill again. You must turn to God."

And then she was still, and he was crying. A vampire who cried. Such a thing had never happened before. Guilt washed through him. What had he done?

She will come back, he told himself. *And when she did, she would see how wonderful it was to be a vampire. She would be one of them, and they would live forever.*

He was sure of it.

Chapter 19

Terrill awoke beneath the musty tarp, his festering body covered by insects. Half of the bugs were dead from trying to feed on him; the other half were eating the bugs that had already died. Vampires were not part of the natural food cycle.

He was in intense pain, which was a rare sensation for him. The solution was meat, but he was too weak to hunt. He threw the tarp aside and shook himself free of insects, living or desiccated. He had bug bites all over him, none of them healed.

It showed what bad shape he was in. He needed sustenance soon or he would begin to rot like a long-dead corpse.

Still, he waited until well past midnight before he left his hideout. He had a few hundred dollars in his pocket, enough to buy food, but first he wanted to make sure he had more money in hand. He followed his path back through the vacant lots, having noticed a small neighborhood commercial center with a couple of banks during last night's journey to his hiding place.

He was in luck. The first ATM he tried would take his brand of card. There was no one in sight, not even any cars passing on the major road nearby. It was cold and dark and everyone was home, asleep.

The machine slurped up the card and he tapped in his PIN. The screen blinked for a few moments and then spit the card back out. He tried again––and again. On the fourth attempt, the machine kept the card. "Illegal transaction," the screen read.

A pickup drove by, then circled back around. It roared up next to Terrill and screeched to a stop. Two young men wearing scarves over their faces jumped out and approached him. There was nowhere to run. Once upon a time, these would have been the perfect victims; the kind of men society wouldn't miss and wouldn't search for. But Terrill wasn't looking for victims anymore.

"What're you doing, old man?" jeered one of them. "You trying to tell me a bum like you has money in the bank?"

Old man? Is that how I appear? Terrill wondered. He looked down at himself. His once-fine clothes were filthy and stained. His hands looked dried up. He was shaking.

"It took my card," he mumbled.

The one who had spoken got closer and wrinkled his nose at Terrill's smell. "You have to have the PIN, dumbshit." He turned to the other man. "Search his pockets."

"Come on, man!" the second one protested. "The guy is filthy. And what's the point? He's a homeless dude!"

"You'd be surprised, Barry. Some of these old bums have rolls of cash like you wouldn't believe."

"Oh, good. Tell him my name. That's just great." Despite his grousing, Barry walked over and gingerly began searching Terrill's pockets. The blood flowing through the veins of his neck was only inches away from Terrill. Despite himself, his fangs began to extend.

"Jesus. The guy is drooling," Barry said, disgusted. "Next time we roll a bum, you do the honors. Wait... I think I got something." He withdrew three crisp hundred-dollar bills from the inner pocket of Terrill's suit jacket. "I'll be damned—look at this!"

"Told you!" said the first guy. Then he turned to Terrill. "Listen, old man. Forget about us. Forget about Barry—uh, his real name is... Poindexter. Got that? His name is Poindexter."

"Yeah, John, that really ought to work," Barry said, but he was too excited by the three hundred dollars to be too peeved.

"He called me Murgatroyd," the first guy said, laughing. "That's my real name! Let's go, Poindexter, you fuckin' idiot!"

They jumped into the truck and roared away, swerving onto the street with a squeal of tires.

* * *

Terrill sank against the wall, unable to stay on his feet. He'd been sure the men were going to attack him.

Once, he would have torn Poindexter and Murgatroyd limb from limb, or at the very least, he would have easily evaded them. But now, he had no strength, no quickness in him. More importantly, he had no desire to kill men over mere money.

The machine had eaten his card. It was clear that Horsham had found him; no one else could have or would have frozen his bank accounts. The check to Sylvie had probably been all the opening Horsham had needed. It was only a matter of time before Terrill's nemesis tracked him down.

Why did he keep trying? Why continue?

He remembered Mary's forgiveness. Could he just give up and fall into the embrace of that kindness?

No, he wasn't done, he sensed. He still had to help Sylvie; he still had to honor Jamie's memory. *Jamie.* All the long years he'd denied himself, gone in a moment of weakness. He wouldn't simply quit now.

Terrill staggered to his feet.

He had stumbled only a few blocks before he saw a very fat house cat cross in front of him. He called out to it in a soft voice. It turned and stared at him, its eyes glowing in the darkness. It let him get within a few feet before it sprang away, running as if a pack of dogs was after it.

How pathetic he'd become, to resort to hunting pets and even then to fail.

A small Chinese restaurant was the last of the commercial buildings on his way out of the neighborhood. He smelled the discarded meat and vegetables in the Dumpster from half a block away. Before he realized it, he had thrown open the lid and was leaning in, grabbing handfuls of the mushy food. Some of it was meat; much of it was vegetables, which his body would reject.

Terrill walked away, his stomach full and yet somehow unsatisfied. He stumbled back to his hideaway and crawled under the tarp for the little warmth it provided. Ten minutes later, he was on his knees in the soft volcanic dust, throwing his guts up. Nothing stayed down, not the vegetable matter, not the moldy noodles, not even the spoiled meat. His body could retain nothing.

He needed blood or nothing at all.

Too miserable, too weak to do anything else, Terrill crawled back under the tarp. Never before had he hidden during the night. The darkness was his friend and ally, and he was master of it.

It wasn't too late, even now. He could still stalk an unsuspecting human, catch them by surprise, drain them before they could begin to resist—and it would almost immediately lend him strength, which would give him more power over his victim, and the next, and the next, until he was healed.

Terrill had been injured before, had been homeless and friendless before, but he'd never been so weak, and had never been without recourse to blood.

The only thing denying him escape from his plight was himself, and his promise to Mary and Jamie.

Something was biting his thigh. He reached down into his pants and pulled out a big, black beetle.

He brought it to his mouth and retched, unable to consume it. He tried a second time, and again he retched. Finally, he swallowed the insect whole, feeling its legs and antennae in his throat as it went down. He expected to throw up again, but to his surprise, it stayed down.

It was live flesh, after all. He started hungrily eating more of the wriggling insects, and in return—as if in compensation for his disgusting act—his bite marks began to heal. He put his hand to his face and found that the open wound over his eyes had closed.

If Horsham could see him now, he'd have his revenge. Reduced to eating bugs to survive, hiding under a canvas tarp, less than a man or a vampire. Stripped down to his essential carnivorous nature.

What would Mary think of his "soul" now? Would she recoil in disgust?

And yet, he thought maybe she'd smile at him. Mary would understand, as would Jamie. He had been brought so low because he had refused to give in to his vampire instincts.

As his lesser pains began to diminish, the steady thrumming of the pain in Terrill's chest returned in full force. He unbuttoned his shirt. The crucifix was sinking ever deeper into his flesh, and now it must be only centimeters away from his heart. What would happen when it crossed that final divide? Would he burst into flames?

He found it difficult to care. At least the pain would end.

He was about to drift off to sleep when he saw the flickering light of a campfire in the copse of trees at the edge of the rock outcropping.

He stumbled to his feet, dragging the tarp behind him.

For once in his long existence, when in danger and pain, he headed toward the light instead of the darkness.

Chapter 20

Brosterhouse managed to stumble out of the alley where the stranger had tossed him. He was covered in mud and God only knew what other kinds of disgusting fluids that had coated the asphalt. He reached the sidewalk before collapsing.

When he came back to consciousness, he was being loaded onto a gurney. The EMTs were having trouble lifting him.

He managed to sit up, provoking shouts of surprise. They were even more amazed when he managed to stand.

He avoided the hospital only because he personally knew one of the emergency medics. The young man owed him a favor for having screwed up some crime scene evidence.

"I'd really advise you to see a doctor," the EMT said. "You might have a fractured shoulder, and you almost certainly have a concussion."

"I'm fine," Brosterhouse said. He hurt like hell, but he wasn't going to admit it. He did a self-assessment based on his four years of college football and decided he'd live. He had kept playing after suffering worse injuries.

He was more shaken psychologically. He'd never been picked up and thrown like that, even by linemen bigger than him. Yet this scrawny guy with the posh accent, this Mr. Harkins, PI, had lifted him as if he was a child and thrown him an impossible distance.

But worse, Brosterhouse was certain he'd shot his attacker right between the eyes—just before the man had taken off running and disappeared down the other end of the alley. Either his senses were all screwed up, or… well, "or" nothing. *It had to be the concussion, right?* he told himself.

* * *

Brosterhouse went to work the next day with a headache, trying not to move his left arm too much. He'd swallowed some out-of-date pain pills and was feeling a little fuzzy, but murders usually didn't get solved if they weren't pursued immediately, and Brosterhouse had no intention of letting the Jamie Lee Howe case go cold without finding out why so many people were interested in it.

He turned on his computer and somehow managed to locate Google, which for him was an accomplishment.

As he thought, there was no evidence that a Mr. Harkins, PI, of London, England, even existed. Brosterhouse was slightly abashed that he hadn't checked that out before talking to the man. Then again, there hadn't seemed to be anything amiss at the time.

He got up to grab his first cup of coffee of the day. He'd probably drain the machine before the day was done, and the coffee would get progressively blacker and stronger, just the way he liked it. He returned to his desk, intending to plan out his investigation of the Howe murder.

He'd been sitting there for only a few moments when he got a call from the morgue.

"What do you mean, the body is gone?" he shouted. His head seemed to split in two. Each of the nearby detectives staring at him seemed to have a fuzzy-looking double. He waved them off and lowered his voice.

"When?"

Turned out the morgue guys didn't know when Jamie Lee Howe's remains had disappeared; it could have been any time between the delivery of the body and an hour ago, when the body was about to be autopsied.

Brosterhouse hung up and sat back in his chair. It was his fourth chair since he'd become a detective, and he'd bought it with his own money especially for his oversized body, so it wouldn't collapse like the others. Even so, it let out a metallic groan.

What the hell was going on with this case? Once again, his memory flashed to the two neat puncture holes in the victim's neck—and just as quickly, he dismissed it. No matter what, he wasn't going there.

He searched the squad room. He was lucky; the officer he wanted to talk to was still on duty: John Funk, a cop who was just marking time until early retirement.

"Hey, Officer Funk," Brosterhouse yelled out.

Funk looked up from his desk, startled. Probably watching porn on his computer or something. He saw who was yelling at him and winced. *A guilty wince*, Brosterhouse thought. *What is that about?*

Funk didn't shout back, but got up and made his way over to Broster-house, his carefully nonchalant manner radiating the message to his fellow cops that there was nothing unusual going on, that they should go back to their own business. It seemed to work; by the time he crossed the room, the usual murmur had started up again.

"What can I do for you, Detective Brosterhouse?" he asked softly.

"You know this Richard Carlan guy, right? Went to school with him or something?"

Again, Funk looked guilty. Brosterhouse didn't have the patience for that. "Look, I really don't care what you've been up to. I just want to know when Carlan left Portland."

"He stayed a couple of days," Funk said.

"Yeah, and somehow he got access to the traffic reports. Did you ever think that information might be useful to me?'

Funk didn't answer.

"Never mind," Brosterhouse said. "My own fault for not checking my-self. That's all, Officer Funk."

The other cop walked back to his desk, trying to act like nothing had happened, but it was obvious he'd been dressed down by his superior. *Not much damage done,* Brosterhouse thought. Just about every junior cop had been on the receiving end after he'd been disappointed.

He lifted the phone. "Henry? Get me the phone number of Officer Richard Carlan, Bend Police Department. Should I call back? No? You got it? Thanks."

Brosterhouse hung up, feeling a little embarrassed. These younger cops might be lazy, but they knew how to use the technology. He was becoming a bit of a dinosaur in the department. Then again, his solve rate was twice as high as anyone else's, so no one said anything.

* * *

He decided to be blunt, to try to catch Richard Carlan off guard.

"What did you do with her, Officer Carlan?"

Carlan sounded confused. "Her? I just visited her, is all."

"When?" Brosterhouse asked. This might be all he needed to make Car-lan the prime suspect, and all the just cause he needed to pursue the case.

"As soon as I got home. Sylvie needed to be told what happened."

"Sylvie? Who's Sylvie?"

"Wait, who are you talking about? I assumed when you asked about 'her,' you were talking about Jamie's sister."

Brosterhouse paused. The man sounded genuinely mystified. But who else would have taken the corpse? Nothing else made sense.

"Someone took Ms. Howe's body from the morgue," he said.

There was a long silence on the other end of the line. Finally, Carlan said in a quiet voice, "There's something weird about this whole thing. I'm glad you called, detective. There's been a break in the case. I served a search warrant at a local motel. We found evidence which ties in to Jamie's—that is, Miss Howe's murder."

"You have a suspect in custody?"

"Well… no. He got away. He was stopped at a roadblock and ran. What's weird is the trail went cold right away, even with the K-9 units. Not a trace of him."

"How did you arrive at this suspect?" Brosterhouse was furious. This was his case; the murder had happened in his town, on his watch. It appeared that Carlan had withheld evidence, which was a breach of professional courtesy, to say the least.

"I found a traffic ticket issued the same day on the same street as the crime scene. When I realized the suspect had driven to Bend, the hometown of the victim, I obtained a search warrant."

Truly amazing, Brosterhouse thought. How was it possible that such a flimsy connection was enough to obtain a legal search warrant? Still, maybe it would break open the case.

"This is my case, Officer Carlan," he said coldly.

"I realize that. I didn't want the suspect to get away."

"And yet he did. I'm coming over to Bend. I'll be there in a few hours. Assemble all the evidence and write a status report before I get there."

"But…"

Brosterhouse hung up before he said something he couldn't take back.

* * *

He drove over the pass in three hours, which was a personal record. The winter snows hadn't started falling yet, and the traffic was light. He pulled up to the Badlands Motel at 2:30 in the afternoon. He'd called ahead, making sure that Carlan was there waiting for him.

Carlan was hanging out in the lobby along with a young patrolman, Cam Patterson. They showed him the motel room and what they'd found.

"You shouldn't even be involved with this case," Brosterhouse said to Carlan when they were done. Patterson had done most of the talking, but Brosterhouse had heard Carlan's words being spoken in the cop's voice.

"Which is why I turned it over to Patterson," Carlan said defensively.

No doubt manipulating the younger officer every step of the way, Brosterhouse thought. "It doesn't matter. I'm taking over the case, as of now. I need you to hand over all the evidence. We'll have our own labs do the analysis."

"But we'd be quicker," Carlan argued. "You guys in Portland are backed up for weeks, from what I've heard."

"They've shortened that to mere days," Brosterhouse said. Well, more like a week and a half, but he was tired of this small-town cop's obstructionism. "How's the search for the suspect?"

"We think he's still in town somewhere."

"Oh? What's to keep him from leaving?"

"We're a small town," Carlan said, sounding confident. "There's an APB out for him, and he's been all over the local news, so there's no way he can rent a car or get on a plane or bus without being ID'd. Unless he steals a car, the only other way out of here would be by hitchhiking—and it's more than a hundred and thirty miles in every direction before he'd get anywhere. I'm betting he's still here, hiding."

Brosterhouse groaned inwardly. He wanted to get back to Portland, but as long as there was a chance of catching this guy, he needed to stick around the sticks.

He walked back into the lobby and booked a room.

Chapter 21

With his night vision, Terrill could clearly see the path to the camp, though it had been covered by loose brush in an obvious attempt at concealment. The fire probably couldn't be seen from the road, because it was behind a lava outcropping beneath some old junipers.

Cans and bottles littered the area, but the camp itself was tidy, almost as if it was a nice outdoor retreat for tourists. Five raggedy men who were passing around a bottle of whiskey surrounded the campfire. They weren't on guard, so they didn't realize Terrill was there until he was almost on top of them.

If he had remained in the dark, they never would have seen him, but in the flickering firelight, his shape probably came in and out of focus, much as his consciousness did. The short hike to the light of the campfire had taken all he had.

"What the hell!" one of the men shouted upon seeing him. The others jumped to their feet, reaching for clubs and knives. One of them even had a gun.

"I'm sorry," Terrill said. "I didn't mean to intrude." The fire was like sunlight to his eyes. He wanted to run away into the darkness, but he was in no shape to move. He tried to sit down, to get the spinning in his head under control, but somewhere between standing and sitting, he started falling. He hit the ground with a splat of soft dust.

One of the men came closer. Terrill could grab him, get just a taste, nothing more—just a taste. But despite his hunger, he remembered: a vampire never stopped feeding once he'd begun. He was in such bad shape that all five of the men were danger of being drained once he started.

"Don't come near me," he tried to say. He was uncertain whether any words actually emerged.

And then he fell into welcome darkness, a blackness that was comforting and familiar.

* * *

Jamie didn't believe him. They never did.

"No, really," he insisted. "I am a vampire."

"Well," she said, looking at him with an amused expression. "It takes all kinds."

Obviously, he'd been too sane and convivial the rest of the evening for her to believe this outrageous assertion. Nevertheless, he tried again.

"I am a vampire, and you must be out of this motel room in the morning."

He'd woken with a start in the middle of the night, surprised to find she was still there.

He'd woke her up and paid her, giving her twice as much as she'd asked, and told her, in as firm a tone as he could summon in his lassitude, to leave at once.

She had objected. "Let me stay a little longer. I like you; I like your touch. I haven't been cuddled like this in months, and I miss it."

That's when he'd told her, "I'm a vampire."

Her laugh was delightful. He wanted to hear it again.

"No, really," he said again. "It's important that you believe me."

He thought about extending his fangs for a moment, but he was too tired. If she fled screaming, he'd have to get up and disappear. That seemed like such an effort—and it was probably unnecessary. She was a professional. Surely she understood his instructions, even if she didn't quite believe his reasons for them.

She laughed again. "OK, Terrill," she agreed. "I'll be gone by the time you wake up, I promise."

He stopped smiling and looked her in the eye. "I mean it. I want you gone in the morning." He said it as coldly as he could manage. And yet, he too had enjoyed the cuddling—not just the sex, not just the conversation, but the touch and feel of someone he liked.

Her own smile fell away. For a few moments, he could see her debating with herself about getting up, getting dressed, and leaving. He wouldn't have stopped her.

But he was secretly glad when she moved closer to him and put her head on his chest. He was still smiling as he fell asleep.

* * *

Terrill awoke with fangs and claws fully extended.

There was no one in the tent. He quickly came to himself. Something had changed in the night. He felt a little stronger, a little more lucid.

It was midafternoon, he sensed—a cloudy day, dangerous but not lethal.

He was in a neat and tidy tent. His sleeping bag, while musty, smelled relatively clean. There was another sleeping bag matching his on the other side of the enclosure. He could hear voices outside, having what sounded like an everyday conversation, as if they were talking about the weather or the traffic or lunch.

It was strangely comforting, though it shouldn't have been. He was in the camp of five armed and dangerous humans, who probably wouldn't have any compunction about killing or at least running off anyone they considered a threat.

Terrill closed his eyes and assessed himself. He felt strangely healed. No doubt there were cuts and bruises and sores all over his body, but they weren't getting worse, they were stabilizing.

Why? He hadn't had any raw meat, and certainly no blood. Was it the insects he'd eaten? That didn't seem likely.

He had a vague memory of waking up several times in the night and being fed some sort of broth. Something in the soup had helped him, he sensed. He was amazed. Most human food did nothing for him; indeed, more often than not, his body rejected most of what humans ate.

He listened to the soft murmurs of the voices for a while, and then drifted back off to sleep.

* * *

Terrill snapped awake at dusk, as he always did. He crawled out of the sleeping bag, surprised that he could move so freely. He opened his shirt to check the cross on his chest, which was a dull ache. To his amazement, the skin around the crucifix seemed to be healing; at the least, it was no longer festering.

"What the hell is that?" he heard a voice say.

The man sitting next to his sleeping bag sounded curious, not confrontational. He was stocky and appeared to be in his mid-forties, with a shaved head and the beginnings of a beard, each with about the same amount of black stubble. He had watery blue eyes and creases all across his face, as though he spent most of the time in the sun. His clothes were old and worn, but not too filthy.

Terrill closed his shirt quickly and buttoned it up.

"At first I thought it was a very ornate tattoo," the man continued, "3-D, like. But then I felt it. Embedded in your skin. Never seen nothing like it."

Terrill tried to say something, but it came out as a croak.

He tried again. "Thank you."

"No worries," the man said, smiling. "The cross is kinda cool. I'd like one like that."

Terrill didn't want to discuss the cross. "Thank you for helping me," he repeated.

"Hey, what's mine is yours." The man looked down at Terrill, obviously curious. But he didn't say anything else about the cross.

"What did you feed me?"

"We had some squirrel soup, with some carrots and broccoli." He saw the look on Terrill's face and misinterpreted the confusion he saw there. He laughed. "Don't worry. It wasn't really squirrel, just some lunchmeat we diced up."

Terrill's bewilderment had come from the description of vegetables in the broth. By now, he should have been sick and throwing up. But he felt fine, and he had no memory of upchucking.

"You sure? It wasn't all meat?"

"Sadly little meat. Meat is expensive. Why, what's the problem? You a vegetarian or something?"

Somehow that struck Terrill as immensely funny. He started laughing, and once he started, he couldn't stop. He had never thought the day would come when he'd be suspected of being a vegetarian.

"So the old guy's awake?" he heard another voice say. A second man entered the tent. He was younger than the first, in his late twenties, heavily tattooed on his neck and hands and probably the rest of his body, with giant black plugs in his earlobes. He was wearing a black T-shirt and camouflage pants, covered incongruously with a bright blue parka.

He stood over Terrill, but the look on his face wasn't kindly.

"He's a little woozy," the first man said.

"He looks awake to me. I think he should take off, but if you insist on letting him stay, he needs to know the rules."

"Yeah, sure. The damn rules."

The tattooed man frowned but seemed to decide there was no point in arguing. "Perry here has agreed to let you stay in his tent, but you still have to contribute your fair share, understand?" he said.

"I'll try," Terrill replied. He took stock of himself. He felt better, and surely he could venture into the darkness tonight and contribute to the common good. "Yeah, no problem."

"Better not be. This camp is getting crowded." The tattooed guy left the tent, scowling.

"Mark's a little overbearing," Perry said. "But don't worry. He can't kick you out unless we all agree. This was my camp first, and Grime and Damien still owe me, though Harve might follow Mark's lead."

"I'll try to help," Terrill said. He stood up and shook the man's hand. "Again, thank you for helping me."

"Sure. You scared the daylights out of us," Perry said. "We thought you were gonna die!"

Terrill smiled at the word "daylights."

"You have no idea," was all he said.

Chapter 22

The life insurance check for $100,000 bounced. Sylvie wasn't really surprised. She'd never believed it was real; she'd just been curious to see if it would actually clear.

She'd woken up with the radio blaring and her parents excitedly telling her about the fugitive who had killed her sister—the same man who had been in this very house only the day before!

It disappointed her, more than anything. She was disappointed in herself that she'd been fooled, that she hadn't sensed his evil. He had seemed so nice, so honest—so caring. He hadn't seemed like the violent type; he'd even refused to fight back when those two rednecks in the bar attacked him.

Apparently the murderer felt guilty. Or was pretending to feel guilty. "I'm sorry," he'd said, though Sylvie hadn't known what he was referring to at the time. He'd sounded so sincere. *How nice.*

The check bouncing probably meant that he'd been up to no good, no doubt trying to seduce her with his soft talk about education and opportunities and all those will-o'-the-wisps that she'd already given up on before he came along.

Somehow, until that moment at the teller's window, Sylvie had managed not to think about what had happened to Jamie. It was as if Jamie was still alive, just over the mountains, and might walk through the front door any day. The teller saying "insufficient funds" had triggered a wave of grief.

Insufficient everything. Jamie was gone, and Sylvie was alone.

She came back home from the bank, went to bed and stared at the ceiling. Most of the day passed before she looked at the clock again. Was this what depression felt like? Grief? She didn't want to move, or to think. She wanted to close her eyes and block it all out.

It got darker in the bedroom as the sun stopped slanting through the windows. Sylvie didn't turn on the lights, just stared into the shadows.

She took off her crucifix and held it up, swinging it on its silver chain. She'd given an exact duplicate to her sister. A lot of good that had done. She put it on the nightstand. But a few minutes later, without really thinking about it, she picked it up again and put it around her neck.

She reached over to the nightstand and opened the drawer. She took out a small purple book. It was her sister's diary.

Sylvie had known something was going on with Richard, but Jamie had refused to talk about it. So one night she had taken the diary, intending to read it. Then, little flibbertigibbet that she used to be—a young girl who now seemed so innocent, so naïve, even though it had only been a month ago—she had gotten busy with some silly project or another.

It was only after Jamie left that she read the diary.

The entries had started out with Jamie's usual cheerful voice, and then had become euphoric as she fell in love with the strong and handsome Officer Carlan. Then, one day, he'd struck her over some minor complaint.

Jamie had tried to excuse the man, to see it as a one-time event.

Then he'd done it again—and again.

Reading the diary, Sylvie could see where Jamie had come to the reluctant conclusion that she needed to stop seeing Richard, and then her growing dread as the man wouldn't take no for an answer.

It was the final entry that haunted Sylvie:

"Richard insists that we go through with it. But I can't imagine myself living my life with that man. I'm going to do something I never thought I would do. No one must know—especially Sylvie, my sweet sister who loves God. But it must be done."

Sylvie put the diary back into the drawer, stared at the ceiling, and tried to imagine what Jamie had been running away from.

Her mother yelled from downstairs, sounding worried. "Dinner is ready, Sylvie. Come and get it before it gets cold!"

Sylvie didn't move.

A few minutes later, the doorbell rang. Still she didn't move. She heard a man's voice downstairs, and somehow she knew it was Richard Carlan. Who else could it be? She turned her head into the pillow and hummed, trying to drown out the baritone drone of his voice.

"You have to come down and talk to him." Her father was standing in the doorway. "It's only polite."

"I have nothing to say to him."

"Come on, Sylvie. He's a policeman—a good man. Jamie and he were going to get hitched someday, I'll bet, if Jamie hadn't..." He let the rest of the thought trail off.

Sylvie got up and walked to the door. Her hair was all over the place, her clothing wrinkled and disheveled, and she didn't give a damn. She marched down the steps and into the kitchen.

"What do you want?" she said in a flat tone.

"Uh... I have to talk to you." Carlan said.

"So talk."

Carlan looked at her parents, who were obviously listening to every word but were trying to look preoccupied with other things, Mom doing the dishes and Dad picking up a day-old newspaper.

Sylvie walked into the living room and turned around. "What do you want?"

Her abruptness seemed to rattle the police officer, who was always so sure of himself. She took some small satisfaction in that, but really, she didn't care. She never wanted to see this man again, this man who had been so horrible to Jamie that she'd run away.

The living room was dark. Sylvie, in her gloom, realized how tattered and sad it was. Even the bright light from the kitchen seemed faded and dimmed. The whole world seemed awash in tan tones: the green in the sofa, the awful red color Mom had insisted on painting the walls—all were beige and brown and dingy.

"You heard I found Jamie's killer?" He didn't say "we" or "the police," she noticed. No, "he" had found the murderer. He sounded so proud, so excited, as if it was some kind of great career achievement, forgetting, probably, that the murder he'd just solved was of someone he had supposedly loved. Proof, not that Sylvie needed it, that Jamie had never really meant anything to him. She'd been a good-looking trophy, no more.

"Good for you," she said.

Again he seemed nonplussed. "Why don't you like me?" he blurted.

"You can seriously ask me that? You forget, I was home waiting for her when she walked in the door with a black eye and a cut lip. More than once."

"We had some heated arguments. She hit me too, you know. You know how angry she could get!"

"What about that last time? You beat her."

"I had a good reason," he said.

"I found her diary, Richard. I know exactly what kind of bastard you are."

"You think I hurt her because I wanted to?"

"You beat her. It doesn't matter what you wanted to do. The fact is, you hurt her. She ran away because of you."

"Your sister wasn't who you thought she was."

"Now you're going to tell me what my own sister was like? There isn't anything you could tell me that I don't already know."

He looked smug. "Yes, there is."

Her heart fell. She was going to hear Jamie's secret. Whatever he was going to tell her, it was bad. But at the last second, she admitted to herself that she already knew.

"We were going to have a baby, Sylvie. She was pregnant."

She turned away, suddenly uncertain. A moment before, everything had been so clear. Her life was a mess, but she was damned if she'd let a snake like Richard Carlan get near her.

"She had an abortion, Sylvie. I know you're religious, like me. It was a mortal sin! But even then, I would have forgiven her. I was ready to take her back!"

"She made a mistake," Sylvie heard herself saying. "But it would have been an even bigger mistake to marry you." No doubt she was damning her soul in defending her sister, but if she had to condemn Jamie, she'd rather be damned. Jamie had been a good person who had made mistakes. The biggest mistake was ever going out with this awful man.

"Look, Sylvie," Carlan said. "I won't hold what Jamie did against you. I'd like us to be friends. Maybe go out sometime."

She couldn't quite take in his words. Had he heard a word she said? Hadn't he heard the anger in her voice? She laughed, a dull, disbelieving laugh. "I'd rather run away to Portland and become a prostitute."

He turned white, and for a moment, she took great satisfaction in the fact that her words had hit home. But then she noticed that he was looking over her shoulder at the sliding doors that led to the back porch. She turned around and caught a glimpse of something moving away, but couldn't make out what it was.

When she turned around again, Richard was already opening the front door and nearly running down the sidewalk to his police car.

Good. Whatever it was that had scared him away, she hoped it was permanent.

Chapter 23

All afternoon, Jamie watched her little sister lying in her bed. Her vivacious, wonderful, funny sister looked defeated, staring up at the ceiling with sightless eyes.

Jamie had learned that as long as she stayed out of the light, people couldn't see her. In just the last night, making her way across the mountains in the back of a truck, she'd already learned a lot about her new condition.

She wanted to open the window and give Sylvie a hug. Tell her everything was all right.

But everything wasn't all right. Even through the glass, it was as if Jamie could see the red blood coursing through her dear sister's neck. Since she'd awakened to this new, strange existence, the hunger hadn't left her.

* * *

Jamie had woken up in a cold metal box. She sensed it was dark, and yet she could see every contour of her prison. There was stainless steel on all sides, smelling of death.

Why she didn't panic was a mystery. She'd always been a little claustrophobic while she was alive, preferring to take stairs rather than elevators whenever she could. But she lay there and thought about her situation with a logic she had never before possessed. Instead of darkness and enclosed spaces scaring her, she realized they were her friends.

She was dead. It was knowledge that she'd been "born" with, just as she knew instinctively that it had turned dark outside. She sensed she was surrounded by the dead, in their own cold containers, but unlike her, they weren't reanimated.

The nice client had said "I'm a vampire," and she had laughed.

She remembered the last thing she'd seen as a mortal: a man transforming into something else, something bestial and frightening. She hadn't had long to think about it, he had drained her so quickly and efficiently.

Yet—strangely, because she must have already been dead—she remembered him standing over her, looking human and horrified, laying her out gently and crossing her arms over her chest, and saying over and over again, "I'm sorry. I'm sorry…"

"I'm a vampire," she said out loud, and in the little space, it sounded very loud and very ludicrous. But there was no denying it.

How long she lay there, she never knew. She waited patiently, remembering her past life as if it had happened to someone else. She was aware that she was getting hungry, and that her hunger looked red—red as blood.

In some ways, it was as if she hadn't changed. She still had the same thoughts, the same memories. But they somehow took on different meanings. Everything felt different.

She'd always been a little naive. She laughed to herself at the thought. She'd ended up dead because she'd trusted the wrong man. It had always only been a matter of time before she trusted the wrong man.

But was the wrong man the vampire who had bitten her? In all fairness, he had warned her, though he couldn't have expected that she would believe him. But what had really put her in that motel room that fateful night?

Officer Richard Carlan, the bastard. It was funny that she'd ever had mixed feelings about him, that she could ever have thought there was a bond between them. Now that she was no longer human, she could understand human motivations better than she ever could before. She saw through the pretenses, the defenses, the masks and the lies.

As she lay in that stainless steel drawer, she decided that she'd go back to Bend, track down Richard, and settle the score. She understood that the old Jamie would have been horrified by the thought of revenge, but the new Jamie knew it was exactly right for her.

She heard a couple of voices through the metal walls, and the sound of approaching footsteps. She got ready to jump out.

That's when she first felt the transformation of her fangs extruding, her face protruding outward as if in search of blood, her hands turning into claws with which to grasp her prey. Even from a few feet away, even through the barrier of steel, she could sense the living flesh approaching.

The drawer started to open. The light stabbed into her eyes and she nearly cried out. She closed them for a moment, and when she opened again, they had adjusted to the new ambiance. She was ready to feed.

But something drew the two men away. Their voices receded.

The drawer remained ajar. Jamie reached up and pulled against the opening, rolling the drawer all the way out. She jumped down onto the cold tiles. She felt a little weak, but not too bad. *Not too bad at all, considering I'm dead.*

She was naked. There were some lab coats hanging from hooks near the door, and she grabbed one and headed out of the room.

She had to get out of this place, preferably without running into anyone. It was late at night, and the lights were dimmed in the hallways, the rooms black. She made her way out of the hospital, flitting from darkness to darkness.

Once, hearing someone approach, she slipped into a dark room, and a nurse stuck her head in the door, looking around but somehow not seeing Jamie. The nurse closed the door and walked away. Jamie continued on, feeling invisible.

As soon as she got outside, everything was easier. There was more darkness to exploit, and it seemed easy to avoid humans. For one thing, her hunger warned her of the approach of any living thing.

She needed to feed. She understood that. But something told her that her first feeding was important. She decided that Richard Carlan deserved that honor.

She spent the next day in the back of a semi, hiding in the corner when the driver checked his cargo.

When the truck stopped for gas in Bend, she jumped out and ran into the woods nearby.

The stealth, the danger, was exciting. Later that night, she broke into a local thrift shop and got dressed, choosing dark clothing to match her mood.

Until then, the closest she'd gotten to a human was the two morgue attendants and the nurse in the hospital. Outside the thrift store, she'd turned a corner, and for once her instincts had failed her. There was an old man, a homeless guy, a few feet away, staring at her in alarm.

Jamie was on him before she had time to think, her fangs sinking into his neck as he let out a forlorn cry. It was a resigned cry, as if the man had always known he'd end in a bad way. She tried to pull away once she had gotten a taste, but found she couldn't stop until the man was drained.

She discarded him with disgust. *So much for Richard Carlan being my first meal,* she thought. *So much for it being important.* The old man tasted foul— he'd been dying already. She crouched over him, lifted one of his arms, and started to eat it.

It felt natural. *I should feel guilty,* she thought. *I should be repulsed.* But the rules had changed. Her old values were for humans. She was vampire, and that was something completely different. She ate a few more parts of the old man, but left the rest, even though she was still hungry. Better to find some healthy flesh next time.

Jamie got up, went back into the thrift store, washed up in the bathroom, and picked out a new wardrobe. There was $20 in the cash drawer, and she took that, too.

From there, she made her way back to her old home.

* * *

Mom and Howard were in the kitchen. Jamie climbed up on the roof, unafraid. Nothing seemed to scare her anymore except light, and she was beginning to understand that artificial light was only dangerous in that it revealed her presence. The fear of bright light was simply an old vampiric instinct that had yet to adjust to modern times.

She could fall off the roof and break her neck, and it wouldn't matter. She would immediately heal, as long as there was blood to drink and flesh to eat.

She watched her sister, who lay unmoving. Watched as Sylvie took off her crucifix and then put it back on. Watched as she reached into the nightstand and pulled out a purple book.

So that's where her diary had gone! Jamie had wanted to take it with her. What had she written? How much had she revealed? She couldn't remember.

Poor Sylvie. Inside her vampire heart, it seemed to Jamie that she still felt love for her sister. But it wasn't as strong as it had once been, and it was fading with every minute that passed. All her old feelings were fading. Soon, she sensed, she would be giving very little thought to her old life.

But for now, she wished she could comfort her sister. As Sylvie lay on the bed, it seemed to Jamie that she could see the red blood in her sister's veins throb and pulse outward, bending Jamie's willpower in a direction she didn't want to go. Love was fighting with hunger.

It was probably a good thing that Howard showed up at Sylvie's bedroom door. Her sister finally got up off the bed, looking as though she didn't care about her appearance. Sylvie had always been a little vain—it was her only apparent vice. Now, even that was gone. Sylvie left the room.

Jamie climbed down the tree to the back porch and stared through the screen door.

The visitor was Richard Carlan, she saw, and though Jamie couldn't hear the words, she knew that the bastard was trying to impress Sylvie. Her sister, to her credit, was obviously not buying it.

Jamie moved back into the darkness and removed her clothes. She went back to the screen door, and this time, she stood within the reach of the light. She stood there, stock-still, her eyes boring into Richard, willing him to look her way.

When he finally looked up, he staggered as if struck and turned perfectly white.

Jamie raised one hand and beckoned to him. Then, with vampiric speed, she moved back into the shadows as her sister began to turn around.

As she got dressed, she felt pleased with herself. She could have gone after Richard. It wouldn't have taken much. She knew that she was faster and stronger than he was, that she could be on top of him long before he reached his car.

But she had plenty of time for revenge.

All the time in the world.

Chapter 24

The RV was starting to reek, even to Horsham. He'd enjoyed his little nostalgic foray into his primitive past; it had brought back memories of his savage feedings before Terrill had found him and taught him how to behave. Pretty soon it would be time to move on.

He'd enjoyed sitting there, listening to the police scanner, letting the cops roust his prey into the open. Despite their excitement, the police were overconfident about catching Terrill, unless the old vampire had lost all his skills.

Even Horsham would have a hard time tracking him down if he didn't want to be seen.

No, better to lie in wait, somewhere Terrill was likely to turn up. Unless he was mistaken, that would be the home of his last victim's family. Terrill would be trying to make amends, to apologize. In his weakness, he would break every Rule of Vampire.

Horsham had watched the dead girl's house for the past two nights, but had either just missed Terrill or the other vampire hadn't shown up yet. Horsham would give it another couple of nights before he tried something different.

As he got ready to leave the RV, one of the corpses belched gas, and Horsham wrinkled his nose in disgust.

There was a reason he had lived in such luxury over the last few centuries, after all. He'd begun to enjoy it.

No, he decided, it was time to leave now. He'd abandon the motor home where it was and book a room somewhere, take a long, scented bath, have a glass of wine.

There were no witnesses. He'd taken care of that.

He packed a bag, unhooking the police scanner and shoving it among the underwear and socks. He grabbed his laptop and left, locking the door behind him. As he walked away, he left a little ghost town of RVs of all shapes, sizes and ages.

All of them empty of life.

* * *

Horsham walked to the nearest decent-looking motel. He didn't have to go far: the corporate chains lined the highway near the Walmart. He booked a room, dropped his computer, scanner, and single suitcase onto the bed and left.

He decided to walk to his stakeout (he hated that word), assuming that Terrill was unlikely to show up until full dark.

Twice, cops slowed down to look at him. He wasn't trying to hide. No doubt he looked a little like Terrill, though he appeared older and was several inches taller. He smiled at the cops and they sped off.

He became stealthier as he approached the Hardaways' neighborhood. Terrill could show up at any time, and he'd instantly spot anything out of the ordinary. Horsham discovered a little vacant lot behind the home's backyard; he could see pretty much everything he needed to see from there.

He sat down on a flat rock and became still. To any mortal creature, he was all but invisible.

The female vampire walked right by him, which no self-respecting vampire would have done.

How delightful! Horsham thought. *A baby vampire!* He hadn't observed one of those in years. They usually didn't last long. While they were born with the knowledge of how to be a vampire, they weren't born with the self-control needed in this age, when humans overflowed every available corner of the world and were possessed of high-tech imagery devices and weapons.

He watched her clumsily climb a tree, then clamber onto the roof of the home's first story and peer into a second-story window.

It was that girl from Portland, Jamie Lee Howe: a one-in-a-thousand unintentional vampire. Did Terrill know she'd Turned? That he was a Maker? Unlikely, even though he'd left a pristine corpse. It was such a rare occurrence, it had probably never occurred to him. It certainly hadn't occurred to Horsham.

The girl had to be starving. When Horsham had first Turned, he couldn't stop feeding for days. He'd taken so many victims that the entire town was searching for him when Terrill came along and saved his ass. Just the proximity of live flesh had triggered his feeding frenzy, yet here this new vampire was, mere feet away from a human, and she was holding back.

Sure, it was her family—but it wasn't, really, not anymore. Vampires became emotionally detached the minute they Turned. They were no longer part of their old lives. Indeed, it was unusual for any vampire to seek out anyone or anything from their past life.

Except for revenge. That was quite normal. They'd discover their newborn powers and realize they no longer had any qualms about taking human life, and the combination was deadly to any former enemy of a new vampire.

Was that why she was here? It wasn't uncommon for parents to be the first victims.

The cop in Portland had said something about the murder victim having a restraining order out on someone. A boyfriend?

The baby vampire was admirably motionless while she watched her sister. Horsham was impressed. He started to get up, but at that moment, the girl turned and began climbing down the tree. She looked through the sliding door into the living room, displaying a vampire's uncanny sense of exactly how close they could get to the light. Then she retreated and started taking off her clothes.

That was interesting! Horsham settled back to watch. She stood at the glass door and waved for someone inside to come out.

Well done. That would scare whoever was inside half to death. Meat always tasted better seasoned with a little adrenaline.

As she turned around to get dressed, he slipped away into the shadows and quickly made his way to the front of the house. There was a police car parked there and an officer walking quickly toward it. Horsham sped through the shadows, ending up only a few feet from the fleeing cop.

"Pardon me," he said politely.

The man couldn't restrain a yelp of surprise. Then he scowled, embarrassed. "Where'd you come from?"

"I didn't mean to startle you," Horsham said in as soothing a voice as he could, which, considering that seducing prey was one of a vampire's main weapons, was very soothing indeed. "Is this the Hardaway residence? I heard what happened. Tragic."

"Yeah, it is—very tragic. That's why they don't need to be bothered by strangers, Mister...?"

"Harkins. And you are?"

"Officer Richard Carlan. I'm investigating the case. What's your interest?"

"Oh, I'm new to town. Just moved into the neighborhood, and wondered if I should drop by with some food or something, give them my condolences."

"Not necessary," Carlan said. He seemed impatient to be off, looking over Horsham's shoulder worriedly.

"Well, I won't keep you, officer. Thanks for the information."

The cop dropped into the front seat of his cruiser and sped away without looking back.

Horsham quickly went to the back of the house again. The vampire girl was gone, but she couldn't have gone far.

Unless he missed his bet, she was out hunting.

She was doomed unless she found a mentor, and Horsham was feeling the need for some company. He'd teach her the Rules, and she would help him take vengeance on the vampire who had created her.

He found her a couple of lots over, hunting a dog that was whining because it sensed something approaching that didn't have a smell. Horsham came up behind her and tapped her on the shoulder.

She whirled with admirable speed, her fangs and claws fully extended, but she couldn't see him. He'd frozen into the darkness of the bark of the tree next to them. She stomped around the yard for a few moments, very unladylike, and then shook her head in confusion. He waited until she began stalking the dog again and then tapped her on the other shoulder.

"What the...?" she hissed.

He let her see him this time, standing far enough back that he could evade her if she reacted by lashing out, but again, she showed unusual restraint.

"Who are you? *What* are you?" She stared at him with dawning realization. "Are you what I think you are?"

He laughed. "I don't know. What do you think I am?"

"What I am: a vampire. I don't smell the blood in you. You must be. And if you're here, then you must know the vampire who Turned me."

"Indeed I do. Would you like to meet him?"

She was silent for a few moments. Maybe he had guessed wrong. Maybe she wasn't looking for revenge against her Maker. Maybe it was the opposite. Maybe she wanted to thank him. Either way, she could be used as a weapon against Terrill.

"I think you need some help," Horsham said soothingly. Her fangs and claws retracted about halfway. He continued talking. "New vampires need to be shown the veins, so to speak. There are rules that we live by, and you need to learn them if you wish to survive."

She nodded her head. "I wondered... it couldn't be this wild, this chaotic for everyone. We'd never survive."

"Precisely," he said, sounding pleased. *This is indeed a one-in-a-thousand vampire,* he thought. For the first time, he warmed up to the thought of being a true Mentor. He'd never been one before: he'd always been a little too selfish, a little too obsessive in his hunt for Terrill.

"Rule number one," he said. "Never trust a human."

Chapter 25

When Terrill emerged from the tent, Mark and another man, a fat, scruffy fellow with a full gray beard, were trying to start a campfire, and not having much success, from the sound of all the cursing.

Mark looked over at Terrill. "Hey, newbie. We could use some firewood," he called.

"No problem," Terrill answered. The dark was gathering beneath the rocks and trees, but he could easily see the ground. It was picked clean of loose wood for hundreds of feet around the camp. He looked around.

There were three large tents, a tarp slanting down from the lava outcropping with supplies beneath it, and some large, white water bottles, and cases of Top Ramen, beans, and rice. There were a couple of tables and chairs built from rough wood, and some tree stumps being used as stools. There was even a clothesline, with laundry flapping in the early evening wind. Fifty feet away, on the other side of the camp, was a latrine, a big hole in the ground with a couple of logs separated just enough to sit on and get your business done.

It was quite homey, as if they were all on vacation.

Terrill finally found a downed juniper a couple of hundred yards beyond the outskirts of the camp. He loaded up, carrying the smaller limbs in one arm and dragging the trunk with the other. He dumped the wood beside the now-raging fire without a word and went back and got more.

"That should be enough for tonight," Perry said when Terrill returned for the second time. "Sit yourself down."

All the available spots were taken, so Terrill dragged the trunk of the downed juniper over next to Perry and sat on one end of it.

"That's Harve," Perry said, nodding to the fat, bearded man. "The little squirt is Damien, and the dirty guy is Grime."

Damien was younger than the others, skinny, and he wore what looked like the remnants of a business suit. He'd obviously once had a short haircut that was only now growing out. Apparently, he was the next newest member of the camp, having arrived only the week before. The last man,

Grime, lived up to his name. He was filthy, and Terrill could smell his stink even through the smoke.

They were all looking at him, and he realized that he was supposed to be supplying a name. He was flustered. He hadn't given out his real name in hundreds of years, except to Jamie, and look how that had turned out. But he was also tired of lying.

Perry bailed him out. "With that big honking cross on your chest, I'm calling you Christian."

Terrill was surprised. That was the last name he had ever expected to be called. The last name he would have ever called himself. And yet…

He nodded. "Sure."

Mark was looking at him with raised eyebrows, but obviously it was traditional among these men not to ask too many questions.

"I'll drink to that," Harve said, producing a full bottle of whiskey.

"Here's the rules," Mark said after they had all taken a swig. "You have to bring in your own water and your share of the food. If you're a drinker, you have to bring in your share of the booze. And I mean, if you drink a lot, you bring a lot. Got it?"

Terrill nodded, his face impassive.

"As the newbie, you have to get the firewood and dig the new latrine when we need one." Mark smiled without much humor. "Little Damien here is glad as hell you showed up, 'cause we need a new hole."

"All right," Terrill said. He looked at Perry, who gave no reaction one way or the other.

Grime muttered something, though Terrill couldn't quite make it out.

"What's that, Stinky?" Mark demanded.

"He said, 'You sure love rules,'" Perry said.

"Yeah, well, someone has to make this place livable."

Grime's answer was a very loud fart.

Mark made a face and looked at Grime. "Jesus! I'll give you my share of the water if you'll just wash yourself, for God's sake! Otherwise, I wish to hell you'd just get the hell out of here."

Grime said something that was indecipherable.

"Old Grime and I were here first," Perry said reasonably.

"Yeah, and it was a shithole," Mark said. "I fixed this place up; that ought to count for something."

"Yeah," Perry said. "It's real comfortable now. Almost like one of them state-approved places. Oh, wait. I hate them state-approved places. You know why? Because there's always some asshole in charge who thinks he can boss you around."

Mark shut up, but the tension remained in the air.

"You want to take a vote?" Perry asked after a few minutes of silent drinking.

"What's the point?" Mark muttered. "Mister New Guy doesn't get a vote, but you got Grime and Damien wrapped around your little finger."

Perry just smiled. He looked around the campfire, his eyes landing on Terrill last. He seemed to be appraising the newcomer. "You're right about that. I have the votes. As a matter of fact, I'm thinking it's *you* who ought to be the one who leaves."

Mark sat in silence for a few moments, brooding, staring into the fire. He exchanged a look with Harve, who nodded. Then he stood up and pulled a big bowie knife out of his pocket.

"Listen, you old fart. This whole 'vote' thing is just bullshit if you can't enforce it. You got Grime here, who's pathetic, and Damien, who I'm betting is a little wimp who's been kicked out of his mommy's house, and you got New Guy, who's as weak as a kitten."

He turned to Harve, who stood up and reached behind himself to bring out a baseball bat. "I think you're right, boss. I'm tired of these useless freeloaders," Harve said.

Terrill saw the alarm in Perry's face. He'd probably deliberately maneuvered the discussion in this direction, but it was obvious it had all come to a head faster than he had expected. Damien and Grime were both backing away from the campfire. Perry started to fumble for something in the pack beside his chair. Terrill saw the barrel of a pistol.

But Mark was ready for him. He'd probably only been kept in line until now because of the gun, but now he ran toward Perry, the big knife raised. Perry fumbled with the gun and dropped it. He reached down for it, but he was going to be too late.

Terrill moved faster than he thought he still could, faster than any human could, and stepped between Perry and his attacker.

The knife sank into the left side of his chest, slipping between his ribs.

He fell backward, the knife still lodged in his heart.

It was a grave wound, even for a vampire. If he had been stabbed with wood instead of metal, that would have been the end of him. Even so, for a few moments, he felt paralyzed.

"Oh, my God!" It was a high voice, one Terrill hadn't heard yet, so it must have been Damien. "Don't worry, I'll go get help." The voice receded toward the end and Terrill guessed the young man was running away.

He felt rather than saw Perry hovering over him. The knife was removed with a slurp, and Terrill's body began to feel again. What he was feeling was tremendous pain, but at least he was feeling something.

There was a scuffle of some kind, and then he heard Mark say, "You and your gun; that's the only thing that kept you in charge. Now I've got it. You and Grime take the dead guy and get him out of here. Bury him, whatever. The knife you got in your hand—you know, the one with your fingerprints all over it? Keep it."

"There were witnesses," Perry said, but he sounded defeated.

"Grime? Good luck with that. I also doubt you'll ever see Damien again, and I doubt that was his name. He was embarrassed every minute he was here; I doubt he's going to advertise it now. So what do you got? It's your word against Harve and me. So my advice? Bury the guy. No one will ever miss him."

"This isn't the end of it," Perry said.

"It better be," Mark said, sounding cheerful.

Terrill felt himself being lifted by the arms and legs. From the smell, Grime had his arms, so Perry must have had his legs. They stumbled away, dropping him several times in the process. Terrill thought maybe he could move, but when he tried, he found that he couldn't. After another few hundred steps, he tried again. Nothing.

They were well away from the light of campfire before his leg twitched.

"Holy shit!" Perry exclaimed, dropping Terrill's legs. "Did you feel that?"

"...idn't ...eel... othing," Grime answered. Terrill could suddenly understand him, as if he'd been given a Rosetta stone. The man mumbled his first letters, but if you made allowances for that, he was clear enough.

Terrill groaned. Grime dropped his arms and Terrill slammed into the ground, his head hitting a rock, which made it hard for him to speak for a moment.

"...hat's ...mpossible," Grime said.

Terrill sat up and both men sprang backward with shouts of alarm.

"That can't be," Perry said. He looked frightened.

In answer, Terrill opened his shirt. Where the knife had gone in, there was only a red mark, but the crucifix seemed to blaze in the moonlight. He tapped the cross with his fingernail and it made a metallic sound.

"Must have hit the cross," Terrill said.

Perry wasn't buying it, Terrill could tell. But the cross seemed to reassure him somehow, and he grasped at the explanation, willing to believe it——outwardly, at least.

"Can you walk?" he asked.

Terrill got to his feet. Grime backed away, his eyes wide. He kept his distance, but thankfully didn't run away.

Perry regained his composure. He shook his head. "There's something really strange about you, fella. But... it is what it is. Since we've lost our home, we'll have to seek shelter somewhere else. Don't have much time to do anything but go to the homeless shelter. You up for that?"

Terrill nodded. He didn't want to go back to the tarp with the holes in it if he could help it, but going into town was going to be dangerous. However, a trio of homeless men was less suspicious than one homeless man. And it wasn't like he had any other choice.

They started walking toward the road. Both of the other men walked behind him, at a distance, talking quietly between themselves. Terrill didn't mind. For some reason, he trusted Perry. If his instincts were wrong, then he was probably finished anyway.

He was at peace. It was as if he'd hit bottom and was on his way back up. Something had changed inside him. He was feeling emotions and thinking thoughts he hadn't experienced in centuries.

He was feeling almost human.

He didn't see the young man they called Damien hiding in the bushes, a cellphone to his ear, his mouth open in disbelief at the resurrection he'd just witnessed.

Chapter 26

Brosterhouse found Officer Carlan at his desk in the main squad room.

The Bend Police Department had assigned Brosterhouse a room in another part of the building, somewhere out of the way—a minimal courtesy on the part of the local police. It was obvious that behind the scenes, Carlan had made an issue of an outside cop taking over the case.

Brosterhouse was carrying a couple of coffees in white Styrofoam cups. He sat down without being invited and tried to give Carlan one of the cups. Carlan scowled and shook his head. Brosterhouse opened the lid and drank half of it down. Foo-foo coffee, with some kind of added flavor. It was hard to get plain old black coffee these days. Still, he polished off the cup and took the lid off the second one.

"You like this Hardaway family, don't you?" he said.

"What do you mean?" Carlan sounded defensive.

"I mean, you seem to hang around their home a lot. The way the Hardaways described you, you might be their son-in-law or something."

"Of course. I dated their daughter for over a year. What's that got to do with anything?" Carlan was filing papers, not looking up from his desk. *I'm busy,* his manner said. *You're interrupting my work.*

"The two sisters look a lot alike, don't they?" Brosterhouse was keeping his voice casual, as if he was just making conversation.

Carlan flushed, and Brosterhouse knew he'd hit on something.

"Not really. They don't look anything alike. Besides, Sylvie's too young for me."

"That's not what *she* says." Brosterhouse let some of his skepticism creep into voice.

"What?" Carlan stopped shuffling papers and looked up. "What's going on here? Why all the questions?"

"The Hardaway residence was broken into last night."

Carlan looked puzzled, and unless he was a hell of an actor, Broster-house thought he really was confused. But there was something going on with this officer. He was dirty, Brosterhouse could feel it: the kind of po-liceman who thought his authority gave him power over others, and who used that power over women most of all.

"What's missing?" Carlan asked.

"I can't divulge that," Brosterhouse said briskly. In reality, the Har-daways hadn't found anything missing. Carlan seemed shaken, and now was the time to apply some pressure. Maybe the guy would spill something by mistake. Brosterhouse's voice became hard. "Ms. Hardaway says you were there yesterday evening."

"Yes, and she probably also told you I left. I didn't have any of their valuables in my hands, either."

"No… not that she noticed. But she also didn't see you drive away. Who's to say you didn't come back?"

"Oh, hell. This is ridiculous. I left the scene right then and there." Car-lan paused, and then he smiled. "Wait a minute. I just realized—I have a witness. As I was leaving, I talked to some new neighbor. A Mister Hark-ins."

Brosterhouse didn't breathe for a second. That couldn't be a coinci-dence. But if it was the same guy, what did he have to do with the case? Could he be the killer? It took some real brass to question the lead detective on a murder you yourself had committed—not to mention hurling that same detective into an alley—but it also fit the psychological profile of most serial killers. "Describe this guy."

"Oh, tall—maybe six feet, three inches. Nicely groomed and dressed, slender, in his late forties. Dark hair."

"Did he have an accent?"

Carlan had been confused by the questioning, shaken, even. But this question seemed to let him off the hook, and he took on an interested ex-pression. "Yes, as a matter of fact he did. He sounded British. Highbrow. You think he has something to do with this? Hanging around the scene of the crime? That kind of guy?"

"Maybe," Brosterhouse conceded reluctantly. *Dammit.* The whole dy-namics of the conversation were changing. The pressure was easing off of Carlan. He'd been near breaking, near to spilling out the truth. Now he had a nice red herring to divert attention.

"I'm going to send some officers over to canvass the neighborhood," Carlan said, sounding rejuvenated. "Find this Mister Harkins. Shouldn't be too hard; he said he just moved in."

"You do that," Brosterhouse said tiredly. It was unlikely that Mr. Hark-ins would be found so easily.

He rubbed his eyes. He was tired, and the coffee wasn't doing anything but giving him a sour stomach. He wanted to go home, but he was pretty sure he had the murderer sitting here right in front of him. They hadn't found any of Carlan's suspect's fingerprints in either the motel room or the car, which Brosterhouse had to admit was pretty strange—as if the guy had worn gloves to bed and in the bathroom. But as far as he was concerned, until the DNA evidence came back, Carlan was still the prime suspect.

He would focus on trying to trip up Carlan, on getting him to confess.

Still, there was the nagging question of this Mr. Harkins, with his... unusual strength. He'd been about to think "supernatural strength," but Brosterhouse refused to let his thoughts go there. In fact, he'd been trying not to think at all about what had happened in the alley.

How did the Englishman fit into all this? Most murders were about love or money. Unless he was completely wrong, this murder had all the signs of being about love.

But there was another kind of murderer: the kind who killed strangers, and who then hung around to watch all the emotion and drama that surrounded the crime—the kind who tried to get close to the authorities so he could soak it all in. A serial killer.

Brosterhouse had been relieved to find that the sketch of Jonathan Evers didn't look like Harkins. There were some similarities, but it was obviously a different man.

The name was a coincidence. It had to be.

Chapter 27

Richard Carlan was innocent and he knew it, but he'd been a cop long enough to know that wasn't any guarantee you'd stay out of jail, not if a determined cop came after you.

Brosterhouse was coming after the wrong guy, but Carlan had no way of proving it. It was frustrating that there hadn't been any fingerprints. The Portland lab was taking forever with the DNA, just as he'd feared.

He had a good sketch of the missing "Mr. Evers," at least. The motel clerk had been very observant. But the killer seemed to have disappeared into the darkness without a trace. Though the dogs had been at the scene of the abandoned Escalade within minutes, they hadn't been able to pick up a scent... which should have been impossible. Carlan had driven back to the motel room and grabbed some of the fugitive's clothing, but even that didn't help.

Brosterhouse seemed determined to stick around, and it was making Carlan nervous. His relationship with Jamie had been complicated and messy, and who knew what the Portland cop might turn up if he looked long enough?

Carlan was kicking himself for having uploaded the video he'd taken to a site that paid him a thousand bucks—one of those "boyfriend revenge" sites. It hadn't even really been about the money. The thousand bucks looked pretty paltry now, especially since it was all spent. But the video was still one of the top ten most downloaded whenever he visited the site. Jamie had been a good-looking girl, and even sexier with her clothes off. Thankfully, his face was never in the picture.

He was pretty sure Jamie had left for Portland without ever knowing about the video, but Carlan lived in fear that someone would recognize her, and that they would realize who her boyfriend had been at the time.

He needed to find Jamie's murderer quickly and shut down the investigation.

There was a flurry of activity, a ripple through the squad room, which usually meant something major had happened. He got to his feet. Mostly likely they'd found the culprit. Half of the department was out looking for him.

"They get him?" he shouted to one of the cops getting up from his desk and putting on his coat.

"What?" Detective Burkett looked confused for a moment. "Oh, no. Sorry, Richard. There's been a stabbing at one of the homeless camps."

Carlan leaned back in his chair, disappointed. And then a little trickle of suspicion entered his mind. Where could the fugitive have fled? He hadn't been seen on any of the main roads; all the motels had been checked. He had to be eating and sleeping and hiding somewhere.

"Wait up!" he shouted. "I'm coming with you."

* * *

The police had found an old service road that ran near the encampment. Floodlights lit up the scene. Two homeless guys were sitting at the edge of the camp, stiff and obviously uncomfortable with all the attention.

"So the guy was dead," one of the uniformed officers was asking when Burkett and Carlan walked up.

Both of the men were nodding vigorously.

"I'll take it from here, Jerry," Burkett said, stepping into the light. He pulled out a recorder. "Tell me what you got."

"Yes, sir. Apparently there was a fight, and one of these gentlemen stabbed another gentleman in the heart. We got a cellphone call that said that the guy who was stabbed got up and walked away. These guys are saying that's impossible."

"All right," Burkett said, and turned to the two homeless men. "Who stabbed who? And why?"

"Well," said the younger of the two men, a big guy, clean-shaven on head and chin except for some stubble. "We had a malcontent in camp, guy named Perry. He pulled out a big honking knife and stabbed the other guy. Just like that."

"What's your name, sir?"

"Mark..." The man trailed off, obviously reluctant to say more.

"Mark who?"

"His ID says Mark Lincoln," the uniformed cop said.

"OK, Mark. What was the fight about?"

"I don't know," Mark said. "Booze? Who owned which tent? Bullshit like that. Like I said, Perry was a malcontent. Right, Harve?"

The other homeless man, a guy with a big, bushy gray beard and a pony-tail, nodded firmly.

"So I'm confused," Burkett said. "Who said he walked away?"

The patrolman shrugged. "We got a phone call. Some kid in a panic, it sounded like."

"That would have been Damien, if I had to guess," Mark said. "I don't doubt he had a cellphone. Not that he ever said anything to us about it."

"All right. Tell me the rest. If the dead body didn't walk off, where is it?" Burkett sounded frustrated. These kinds of cases should be easy to solve. Bodies didn't disappear; the culprit was usually still around. He turned to the other homeless man. "Why don't *you* answer this time, Harve."

"Perry—that's the malcontent—he and his buddy Grime carried the body off. Good riddance to Grime, he *stunk*. Said they were going to bury him and that we'd better not say anything. Or else." He glanced toward Mark, as if looking for confirmation.

There was a hard gleam in the younger man's eyes. He nodded slightly in approval. Carlan was suddenly certain they were being fed a load of bull-shit. He could tell that Burkett thought so too.

Harve continued talking, nervously. "But of course, we're cooperating. We were planning on walking to town in the morning and reporting it. Da-mien ran away; I don't know where he is. Doubt we'll ever see him again. Probably ran home."

Mark spoke up again. "I'm telling you, detective. Perry stabbed the new guy right in the heart. Right up to the hilt. No way he walked away."

Up until then, Carlan had barely been listening. But as soon as he heard the words "new guy," he stepped over to the two men. He pulled the sketch of the suspect out of his pocket. "Were any of them this man?"

"That's the new guy! That's him!" they both exclaimed.

"Where did they go?" Carlan asked. "Where would this Perry and Grime go?"

"I'm betting they're headed for the homeless shelter," Mark said. "It's going to be a cold night. There isn't really anywhere else they could go."

Carlan had heard all he needed hear. As soon as he could get confirmation that his suspect was dead, he was off the hook. It wasn't the best of solutions, there wouldn't be a confession, but it was good enough. He didn't care who had killed whom, only that Jamie's murder was solved.

"Can I take the car?" he asked Burkett.

"Sure, I'll catch a ride with Jerry. I think we'll wrap this up for now and come back tomorrow in full daylight to see if we can't find any new graves dug in the dirt around here."

"Good luck," Carlan said, anxious to get away.

Burkett handed him the keys and waved him off.

Carlan tried not to kick up dust in his rush to drive away. He was trying to be calm, to be professional. He knew exactly where to go: he'd accompanied Jamie to the homeless shelter more than once, dropping her off and picking her up from her volunteer work. Father Harry would know who these men were.

Jamie's murder was all but solved.

Chapter 28

Brosterhouse got the call about the DNA as he was ready to call it a day and head for his motel room. He was sitting in his supply closet of an office, thinking about driving back to Portland if something didn't break soon.

"Thought you might like to hear what we found," the lab tech was saying. "It's really a strange result."

"Go ahead." Brosterhouse got his pen and pad out.

"Most of the blood was the victim's, of course."

"OK."

"But the skin particles came back as 'unknown.'"

"Unknown? You mean you couldn't identify whose they were?"

"No, I mean 'unknown' as in, this isn't human skin. This isn't animal skin. It's something organic, but we don't know what."

Brosterhouse felt a chill. He got up, phone crooked between his chin and neck, and put on his coat. *Bastards sent me to Siberia*, he thought. But even as he thought it, he knew the chill had come from something else. He suddenly had a vision of Harkins, an image he hadn't remembered until now. The man's face had looked strange as he had picked up Brosterhouse and tossed him into the alley, as if the teeth had grown longer inside his mouth and were forcing his chin out farther than ought to be possible.

"But we did find some DNA in the blood besides the victim's," the lab tech was saying. "It came back a match for a Bend cop named Richard Carlan."

"Well, he was the victim's boyfriend. So that figures."

"No, you didn't hear what I said. Some of the *blood* came back as his."

Brosterhouse's weariness fell away. Finally. Now he had a solid lead to pursue. Other than a traffic ticket, there was very little to connect this "Jonathan Evers" to the crime. Sure, it was suspicious that the man had run, but people ran from the police for all kinds of reasons.

Carlan was a much, much better suspect. There was the restraining order, of course, which was a dead giveaway, most of the time. Then there was the way Carlan was pursuing this case, as if he was looking for a patsy. But mostly, it was Brosterhouse's feeling that the Bend cop was dirty, a manipulator, and most of all, a creep. Brosterhouse didn't like him. In his experience, if there was a history of abuse, it was nearly always the boyfriend or the husband who had committed the murder.

The DNA was important, but it wasn't conclusive. He needed more.

"Thanks," he said. "Do me a favor and hold onto those results for now. No need to send them to the Bend police just yet."

"You sure?"

"Yeah, it's my case anyway. I'd rather not let my suspect know that I'm on to him."

"Oh, I get you. I'll email you the paperwork."

Brosterhouse hung up and sat back in the chair, which creaked threateningly as he put his feet up. He quickly put his feet back on the ground, remembering that he wasn't sitting in his custom-made chair. He pondered for a minute, tapping his pencil against the pad.

How had the chain gotten into Jonathan Evers' suitcase? And why would he keep such an incriminating piece of evidence?

Brosterhouse got up and headed down the stairs. The one advantage of him having been exiled was that he could come and go as he pleased, without being observed. But he only made it halfway down before he changed his mind and headed back up.

He was in luck. Patterson was shooting the shit with some of the other uniformed officers in the break room and Carlan was nowhere to be seen.

"May I speak with you for a moment, Officer Patterson?" Brosterhouse said.

The young man scowled. He didn't want to appear too accommodating to an outsider in front of his friends. He casually took a sip of his coffee.

"Now," Brosterhouse said firmly. The patrolman blanched and put his coffee down. The other cops fell silent. Order was restored, the hierarchy between uniform and detective reestablished.

"Sorry," Patterson muttered as they left the room. "I was out all night searching for the suspect in the Howe case."

"That's what I want to talk to you about," Brosterhouse said. He led the other man to the first landing of the stairs, where he could hear anyone opening the doors and approaching. Their voices echoed, but he knew that they wouldn't carry beyond the doors.

"Now," he said. "I need to know what the situation was when you went to the motel."

"It was a righteous bust," Patterson said defensively. "By the book."

"I don't doubt it. Still, I'd like to hear for myself. Maybe you missed something."

Patterson was obviously mulling over the pluses and minuses of helping an outsider. He looked around and realized no one could hear them. "I got the call from Carlan at about nine o'clock," he began.

"Wait—you didn't go out there together?"

"No, sir. Carlan checked to make sure the suspect was registered and then called me."

"Why did he call you? Is it normal for a uniformed officer to take the lead on a murder case?"

"Well, it isn't the usual, but sometimes it happens. Carlan knew the victim, figured it would be better if someone else took the lead."

"But you're a rookie, right?"

Patterson flushed. He stood up straight and looked Brosterhouse in the eye, which meant he was looking up about half a foot. "I was on duty," he said. "Every police officer in this department can take the lead on a case, or they wouldn't have been hired in the first place."

Brosterhouse was sympathetic to the young man. The case had probably seemed like a lucky break for him, and here another cop—and an outsider at that—was implying that he hadn't been prepared. Somewhere in the back of Patterson's mind, he must have been insecure about it, because he was getting flustered.

"But Carlan asked for you specifically, right?" Brosterhouse asked.

"So?" Brosterhouse could see that Patterson was about ready to shut down on him. If that happened, he'd probably get nothing but monosyllabic answers.

"Look, Officer Patterson. Your name's Cam, right?" Brosterhouse said, lightening up for the first time. "I'm not saying you did anything wrong; I'm sure you were more than ready to take on this case. But I need to know all the facts."

"It's all in the reports," Patterson said, sounding somewhat mollified.

"Bear with me," Brosterhouse said quickly. "So you got the call and headed out there. Then what happened?"

"Officer Carlan was waiting with the key. We went in. He went to search the bathroom and I started with the suitcase."

"The suitcase was sitting right on the bed? Carlan passed by it?"

Patterson looked thoughtful, as if he was starting to see how some of what had happened might appear to have been unusual. "He was probably leaving the easy stuff for me," he said.

Brosterhouse nodded. "No doubt. That's all, Patterson. Like I said, you did nothing wrong. But let's keep this conversation between ourselves, OK?" The young cop looked uneasy, and Brosterhouse put the steel back into his words. "I mean it. Not a word."

"Yes, sir." Patterson was completely cowed. He'd stay silent, at least for a few days, and unless he was mistaken, that's all Brosterhouse needed.

* * *

Brosterhouse drove to the Badlands Motel. He was in luck: the same clerk was on duty. The kid looked as though he was nodding off, or playing solitaire on the motel computer, or something equally boring. But he perked right up when Brosterhouse walked in. No doubt the search for a murderer had been one of the most exciting things to happen to him in his whole life.

"When did Carlan arrive?" Brosterhouse asked after he'd warded off several excited questions from the clerk.

"The guy arrived a couple of days ago. Just around dinnertime."

"No, you didn't hear what I said. When did *Officer Carlan* arrive?"

"Oh. The cop?" The kid looked a little confused. "He got here the next night, about an hour after the—the suspect—left."

"He asked for the suspect by name?"

"Yeah, he wanted the room number and the key. After he went in the first time, he came back and asked to use the phone. That's when the other cop arrived and they searched the room."

Brosterhouse tried not to react when the clerk mentioned "the first time." He'd expected it, but it was gratifying to know he was right, and that he had a witness.

"How long did he spend inside the first time?" he said casually.

"Oh, about five minutes or so."

More than enough time to plant evidence, Brosterhouse thought. He'd been right—Carlan was a dirty cop. At the very least, he was a liar, and someone who cut corners. At worst, he was trying to frame another man for a murder he had committed.

Brosterhouse didn't know who the man was who had stayed in this motel room, but he felt sorry for him. Apparently he'd been guilty of nothing more than getting a traffic warning on the same street and day as a murder.

Chapter 29

Terrill and the two homeless guys reached a quiet country road and started walking down it side by side. *Actually, I shouldn't be excluding myself,* Terrill thought. Three *homeless guys.*

Terrill was starting to feel the effects of being stabbed. He was amazed that he didn't fall upon the two humans walking next to him, that he didn't rip them to strips of bloody meat. He could sense their blood flowing through their bodies, just inches away, but somehow, it didn't call to him. Besides, he liked them.

He was weak, but was resigned to staying weak until he could find some other way of replenishing himself.

Blood didn't even sound all that good to him right now. That broth Perry had fed him... he had a hankering for some of that broth, which, according to the Perry, had contained carrots and broccoli and other things Terrill shouldn't have even been able to keep down. That was strange.

"So what's your story, Christian?" Perry said after awhile.

"What?" It took a moment for the name to penetrate.

"Why are you here? Not to put too fine a point on it, why are you homeless?"

Terrill didn't say anything. He felt he owed the man an explanation, but what could he say?

"You don't have to tell me," Perry said quickly. "It's sort of an unwritten rule; no one's supposed to ask, no one's supposed to tell. I never was one for rules, though. Probably why I'm homeless in the first place. Besides, some guys like Grime here can't stop talking about their past, right, Grime?"

Grime grunted.

"See what I mean? Chatter, chatter, chatter..."

Grime grunted again.

Perry continued. "Other guys never say a word, which is OK. Me? I'll tell you anything you want to know. I like the outdoor life, and I like to drink a little too much. That's the whole story of me. But you got to admit, Christian, you're enough to get anyone curious. I never seen anyone with a crucifix burned into his chest before, like some kind of modern Crusader or something."

"I'm anything but that," Terrill said.

They walked in silence for a while longer. There were few cars, and it seemed that Grime, who was walking farthest out into the road, didn't give a damn if there was traffic. He made them pull around him. A couple of cars honked, but Grime hunched his shoulders and dared them to run him over.

Grime said something that Terrill didn't quite catch. Perry laughed. "I agree. Grime here says you seem to get younger the longer we know you. When you first stumbled into camp, you looked, I don't know, fifty? Now you look like you're in your thirties.

"So I'm going to ask again, what's your story?"

"There was a girl," Terrill began.

"Oh, ho!" Perry said. "There always is!" He and Grime both laughed.

"I... I hurt her, and I'm trying to make amends. As soon as I can get back on my feet."

"Yeah, well about that. I've never seen anyone get back on their feet. Once a bum, always a bum."

Grime muttered in agreement.

"I've had a little bad luck," Terrill said, and again, the other men laughed. "No, really. I appreciate all your help, but I'll be moving on pretty soon. I've got resources."

Something in the way he said it must have gotten through. They didn't laugh this time.

"Well, I admit, you're not like most other homeless guys I've met," Perry said. "So, maybe so. Maybe so..."

Grime pulled out the bottle of whiskey that they'd been passing around in camp. It was barely down a quarter.

As they started drawing down on the bottle, Perry couldn't stop laughing.

"Got to hand it to Grime," he said, raising the bottle in salute. "There might be death and destruction, but by God, he manages to keep his eye on the important things."

They were all pretty drunk by the time they reached the outskirts of town. A police car passed by, and Terrill realized he probably should be alarmed, but with the soft glow of alcohol and friendship, he didn't care.

The cop kept going.

They passed several thrift shops on the edge of town, and Perry turned toward one. He was eyeing Terrill shrewdly. "You need a proper Central Oregon coat, Christian," he said. "It can get cold at night around here."

Terrill was still wearing the overcoat he'd driven into town with. It was filthy and torn, which was one reason he didn't match the description of the guy the cops were looking for. Still, it wouldn't hurt to have something that looked completely different.

"The Humane Society Thrift Store stays open later than the others," Perry said. "We might make it in time."

The clerk was just flipping the "Closed" sign when they walked up the steps. Perry banged on the door and the man nearly jumped out of his skin. Then he came over reluctantly and opened the door.

Perry happened to know the guy and talked him into staying open a few minutes longer.

They started rummaging through the racks of clothing. To the surprise of both Perry and Terrill, it was Grime who picked out the winning coat, walking up to Terrill and measuring him.

"...ry ...his," he said.

It fit Terrill perfectly, in both style and size. In fact, it looked like it had been tailor-made for him. It was dark brown with black buttons, came to about mid-waist, and was made of not-too-thick but warm wool.

"Huh," Perry said, giving Grime a strange look. Then he shrugged. "We all have our pasts, don't we? Here, Christian. Let me pay." He pulled a surprisingly large roll of cash out of his pockets and paid at the counter.

"You hear about Dirty John?" the clerk asked as he took Terrill's old coat from him with two fingers and threw it into a huge trash can behind the counter.

"What happened?" Perry asked.

"Someone murdered him. Butchered him, right behind the store. I almost didn't come to work. That's why you scared me so much when you banged on the door."

"Butchered him?"

"Tore his arm clean off. John was nearly dead anyway, but no one should have to go like that."

Terrill headed for the door without looking back. He kept walking and had gone a full block before Grime and Perry caught up to him, both men puffing with exertion.

"What's wrong?" Perry said. "It looked like you'd seen a ghost."

"Leave me alone, Perry. You too, Grime. I'm dangerous to be around."

"Something to do with that girl?"

"That... and other things from my past. I've not been a good man, Perry. I don't deserve your help, believe me. You neither, Grime. You've been friends this past day, the first friends I can remember having in ages. Ages."

"We like you too, Christian," Perry said. "So you aren't running us off."

"No, you don't understand. People who associate with me die. I'm not joking."

Perry and Grime continued to trudge alongside him, undeterred.

"Stop," Perry said a little later. He was breathing hard, and Grime looked like he was on his last legs. Terrill realized he'd been walking so fast that the two shorter men had nearly been trotting to keep up.

"I'm going to tell you this once, and then we talk no more about it," Perry said.

Terrill stopped to listen: he owed Perry that much, at least. But he wasn't going to let these men get killed for his sake.

"I don't have anything in this world," Perry continued. "I don't have family. I don't have possessions. All I got are my friends. So if I can't help my friends and risk my life for my friends, then there is no point to my life, understand? Are you trying to take away all the purpose and meaning in my life, Christian?"

Grime grunted in agreement.

"You'll die," Terrill said bluntly.

"Then we die. They were going to find us on the side of the road someday anyway, with the bottle still in our hands if we were lucky. That's all we got to look forward to."

Terrill had had a long existence, and for most of it he'd been alone and friendless. Something in what the homeless man said struck a chord.

He slowed down, and they walked the rest of the way to the homeless shelter together.

Chapter 30

Horsham was quite taken with his baby vampire. It didn't hurt that newly Turned vampires hungered for sex as well as blood. Sex and blood, blood and sex: it was all mixed up in their ferocious appetites. It was the downfall of many a new vampire.

"Rule number two," he said after a vigorous lovemaking session in his motel room. "Never leave the remains of a kill, or if you must, disguise the cause of death."

"How do I do that?" Jamie asked sleepily.

"Why, you eat the evidence, mostly. Scatter what's left. There are all kinds of ways. Don't worry; I'll teach you."

He kissed her on the forehead. He should've done this years ago: became a Maker, or at the very least, adopted a baby vampire, as he was doing now and as Terrill had done for him. It was very fulfilling.

"Rule number three: Never feed where you live—which, since we aren't going to stick around here much longer, means this whole town is fair game."

"Hmmm," she said, as if contemplating a mouthwatering meal.

"Rule number four: Kill at random. Never leave a pattern." He paused. "Really, when you think about it, rules two through four don't currently matter. We'll be out of here before they know we're here."

She rose up on one elbow and stared into his eyes, fully awake. "Not until Richard Carlan pays for what he did."

"Of course. That goes without saying. And not, I may add, until Terrill pays for what he did as well."

She flopped back down, and he couldn't get a read on her attitude toward the second statement. Did she desire revenge for her Turning? Sometimes they did, sometimes they didn't. Usually, the longer they were vampire, the more their thoughts turned from revenge to gratitude.

"Rule number five: Never kill for the thrill. Kill only to feed," he continued. "Frankly, I've never much liked this rule, though I understand it. But then again, what are we vampires for? To simply exist? To merely survive? In fact, I don't think this rule is valid anymore. I reject it. Terrill created it and Terrill is a traitor."

"What did he do?" she asked.

Horsham told Jamie about the origin of his vendetta, about his love for Mary and their betrayal by Terrill. It took half the night, he was so worked up about it. She seemed indignant for his sake.

"Down with rule number five!" she exclaimed. She was fully awake now and climbing on top of him, demanding the first of her desires. All thoughts of rules left his head for the next hour.

* * *

"I'm hungry," Jamie said when they were done.

Horsham laughed. "You're insatiable."

"Well, it's your fault," she pouted.

"We could call for a pizza," he said. "But if the pizza delivery guy disappears, I'd have to move again, and I just got here."

She jumped out of bed and started getting dressed. "I'm starved."

Horsham sighed and grabbed his clothes. The baby vampire was fun, but she was also demanding.

* * *

The night before, after they had left the neighborhood of her family home, he had led her into the darkness by the side of the river and they had waited for a jogger. There was almost always an early-morning jogger these days, running in the darkness of the predawn hours.

Horsham let Jamie have the middle-aged, overweight woman, taking only a few ounces of blood for himself as refreshment. She tore into the body sloppily. Blood was everywhere. So much for rule number two, he thought fondly. They should have at least dragged the body off the trail.

Jamie consumed all the fleshy parts, and they threw the bones into the rapids of the Deschutes River. They'd be discovered eventually, but it was better than leaving them for the next jogger to find.

The woman had whimpered like a baby, and after it was done, Jamie said, "I only want to kill bad people from now on."

"What's that?"

"Only bad people. From now on."

"Sure," Horsham said. "Plenty of those." Of course, it wasn't so easy. Who was bad and who was good, and who decided which was which? But she'd get over it before he'd have to explain it.

Jamie washed up in the river. She climbed out, the lighter colors of her clothes now a soft pink from the partly rinsed-off blood; then she demanded that they go back to the Hardaway house.

He obliged, intrigued by what she might do. Eat her parents? Try to Turn her sister?

* * *

Jamie ignored her parents, who were staring, stoned-faced, at a television screen, watching a situation comedy.

Jamie quickly climbed to her sister's room. She smashed in the window. Downstairs, her parents continued to watch TV with dull eyes. Jamie came out with her purple diary in hand.

"It isn't enough to just kill Richard," she said when Horsham raised his eyebrows at her. "I've got an idea of how to make him suffer."

"It won't matter if he's dead," he said.

"No, he's going to die, all right. But that doesn't mean he can't suffer first."

It seemed pointless to Horsham, but he didn't say anything.

He looked toward the horizon and saw a small glimmer of light. Checking his internal clock, he calculated that they had just enough time to reach his motel room, if they started now.

"Trust your inner sense of time," he said. "What does it tell you?"

Jamie's eyes widened. "We need to get out of here!"

He smiled. "Best not to attract attention by hurrying. Try to be aware."

In the end, they did have to run the last few blocks, but they made it inside before the sun rose.

* * *

Now, after a day of sleeping and lovemaking, it was dark again. Now that Jamie mentioned it, Horsham was hungry too. This adventure had stimulated his appetite, obviously. He should get out of Europe more often.

Maybe it was time to finally transition to the New World, which by his reckoning was still new.

He looked toward the Walmart parking lot, where the ghost city of RVs still stood. There was a new motor home parked beside them, so it was only a matter of time before the remains of the vacationers were found.

He probably shouldn't have been so hasty, but he'd been sure that he'd find Terrill right away. Now he was risking exposure if he lingered around too long.

And yet, when would he have a better chance? Did he really want to wait decades more for Terrill to slip up again? It made him uneasy to be breaking so many of the Rules, and with an undisciplined baby vampire in tow as well. Perhaps he should cut her loose. She was an unnecessary danger. But damn if she wasn't cute and sexy and adorably naive.

Besides, though he was certain he could defeat Terrill, it didn't hurt to have a little insurance.

Before they left the motel room, Horsham turned on the police scanner one last time, and the room was suddenly filled with urgent voices, speaking in tones that usually meant murder and mayhem. He started listening, and it became clear that there had been a stabbing in a homeless camp off of Empire Road.

"The body isn't here," one of the officers at the scene was reporting. "He was apparently stabbed in the heart, but he supposedly walked away."

Horsham turned to Jamie. "Your breakfast will have to wait for now. But don't worry; we'll eat before the night is through."

She seemed disappointed, but it was gratifying that she was still following his orders.

"Now," he said, "where's Empire Road?"

Chapter 31

The homeless camp off of Empire Road was in the far northern part of town. Jamie, who had worked with the homeless, knew exactly where it was.

"I have to stop somewhere first," she said. The tone of her voice made it clear that she would brook no argument, and Horsham gave in readily.

They had the whole night to get done what they needed to get done. Terrill didn't seem to be trying to leave town, and it wasn't that big of a town in the first place. They'd track him down without too much trouble now that he was in the wind, without resources. There were only so many places he could hide. Horsham knew that all he had to do was follow his own vampire instincts, and they would lead him to his prey.

They were on foot, but both vampires moved fast in the darkness. They'd recently fed, and Jamie was nearly bursting out of her skin with energy, the excitement of being newly vampire. It tickled Horsham; he remembered those early heady, dangerous days before Terrill had taken him under his wing: the sudden exhilaration, the increased strength and energy, the knowledge that existence would extend into an endless nighttime.

They stopped at a subdivision in the northeast part of town, one with cheaply made, bungalow-style houses cheek by jowl, each staring directly into the neighbor's yard. In one cul-de-sac, Jamie quickly walked around to the back of one of the houses, reached under a bird feeder near the sliding doors, and extracted a key.

They entered the home quietly. They didn't need to turn on the lights. The interior of the dark house was clear to them, clearer than it would be to a human in daylight. She went upstairs and into a small den/office. There were certificates on the wall, awards for Richard Carlan's police work.

Jamie pushed some papers off the desk and sat down, extracting a black pen from a jar on the shelf above the desk.

Ignoring Horsham, she started writing in the dark, biting her lower lip in concentration.

Richard has threatened me again, he read over her shoulder.

Horsham left her to it and began wandering around the small house, though there wasn't much to see. He'd almost forgotten that people lived this way: bland furniture, bland decor, bland colors, bland everything. He would rather open the curtains to the sun and burn than exist this way.

Jamie was still writing, so he wandered out into the backyard. He caught a glimpse of movement in the next-door neighbor's upstairs window. Had they been seen? Could the police get here before Jamie was done? He suspected that she was trying to frame her asshole boyfriend for her murder, and she wouldn't want a break-in reported. It would nullify what she was trying to do.

Horsham leaped toward the second-story balcony, his hands catching the edge, and pulled himself up. He made his way to the window. It was open; it probably never occurred to the human that anyone could climb up there without being seen and heard. He could see the man on the other side of the room picking up the phone.

Horsham reached him before he could dial the third digit of the emergency number. The man squealed once before Horsham tore his throat out. Horsham wasn't hungry, but he ate enough to make sure the man wouldn't revive. There were enough baby vampires already in this town.

He dropped what was left of the man's body to the floor with a thump.

"Are you all right, Daddy?" he heard.

There was a teenage girl at the door. She couldn't see him because the room was too dark. Her hand was reaching for the light switch. Horsham was on her before she could flip it.

She, too, was quickly disposed of. Her blood sprayed against the walls, because he was already full and couldn't drink it fast enough.

One way or another, Horsham was going to need to get out of town in the next twenty-four hours. He was still confident he'd find Terrill before then. But in the back of his mind was his exquisite vampiric sense of timing, and it was telling him that he was breaking just about all the Rules of Vampire.

"Did you have to do that?"

Jamie was at the window, looking a little disturbed. She still had a bit of human empathy, Horsham reminded himself. It wasn't her fault.

"He was calling the police," he said.

She was staring at the body of the girl, who was maybe a couple of years younger than Sylvie, her little sister. "Their lives are short," he said curtly. "You'll understand that soon enough."

She must have found a change of clothing in her old boyfriend's house, because she was dressed in some Kmart special of a dress and a bulky coat. He grimaced at the lack of style, then looked down at the blood that covered his magnificent and very expensive suit. He rummaged through the dead man's closet and found some nondescript trousers and dress shirts. Reluctantly, he put on a pair of the pants and one of the shirts.

"Is there a mall around here?" he asked. "I need to get some real clothes."

"Yeah, just north of town. On our way," she said. She perked up, still human enough to be excited by shopping.

* * *

The mall was open until eleven o'clock, and they got there just in time.

The clothing store clerk was by himself; the stores on either side had already closed. He looked annoyed as they walked in, but as both customers began piling up expensive clothing, he started getting excited. Working on commission, Horsham assumed.

He was probably a high school kid. He had a bad complexion and sallow skin, greasy blond hair, and bloodshot eyes. He'd probably been toking a bit in the back of the store on a slow night.

Horsham knew his own sizes exactly and knew what he was looking for. There wasn't much available, but some classic lines never went out of style, and he loaded up with them after first dressing himself in a better outfit.

At first, Jamie tried on a couple of demure dresses, but Horsham sat back on the dressing room bench and shook his head. "You're a beautiful girl. You've got a great body. Show it off!"

He surreptitiously pushed the dressing room door open as she tried on something much more daring. As he expected, the clerk was hovering outside, trying not to look but unable to look away.

Horsham egged Jamie on as she tried on ever more daring clothing, convincing her that the outfits needed to be tighter and more revealing. The young man couldn't hide his interest. Jamie was transforming from a nice-looking small-town girl into someone much more glamorous and sexy, like someone out of a rock video.

When she had picked out enough of a wardrobe to last her for a while, Horsham sent her with the cart to the front desk. She was wearing the sexiest outfit he could convince her to wear: leggings, a short skirt, and a tight blouse.

"Hey, kid. I really appreciate your staying late for us. I'd like to give you a tip." Horsham was still sitting on the dressing room bench, considerately folding the rejected clothing. The clerk didn't suspect a thing.

The vampire had already eaten enough for a month, and this pimple-faced kid simply wasn't appealing. He stabbed into the kid's chest and then twisted, catching the heart with his razor-sharp claws. The kid died looking strangely disappointed, as if he realized he was going to lose out on his big commission.

Horsham searched the clerk's pockets until he found his car keys, then propped the body in the corner of the dressing room and closed the door so that it locked behind him.

Jamie was laying the clothes on the counter, tags up and easily accessible. *So thoughtful,* Horsham mused. He grabbed a couple of bags and started stuffing the clothes inside them.

"Aren't you going to pay?" she asked, looking around for the clerk.

"No need," he said. He dangled the car keys in front of her and smiled.

She looked furious. "I told you!" she shouted. "No more unnecessary killing!"

"Oh, were you planning to pay for this? Because I'm broke at the moment." It wasn't true, but he wanted to wake her up to her new lifestyle.

"I know I have to kill to survive," she said. "But I told you, I want to eat only *bad* people." She was pouting. She was trying to care, but he could tell that it was meaning less and less to her. She'd learn soon enough. She was no longer human; soon they would mean no more to her than hamburgers had meant to her when she was human herself.

"He *was* bad people," Horsham said. "These clothes were *way* overpriced."

Chapter 32

Horsham and Jamie waited just outside the light of the flood lamps, invisible to the naked eye.

The police started loading up around midnight, and an hour later, they were gone. They'd be back in the morning, the vampires overheard them saying to the homeless guys. They cops seemed to know who they were, and their names.

Then it was quiet again. The campfire had been built back up, but Horsham and Jamie were able to get within a few feet of the two remaining men before they were noticed.

"What now?" the taller of the men said when he noticed them, as if tired of all the fuss.

"Sorry to disturb you," Horsham said, stepping fully into the light. Jamie followed demurely.

But she wasn't dressed demurely. Horsham might as well have not been there. She was dressed about as daringly as she could get away with in a small town—maybe a little more so.

Her dark blue skirt barely covered her ass, but she was wearing striped black and white leggings, so technically she was decent. Her white blouse was so tight that her breasts threatened to burst out of it. She wore a black choker and shoes with high enough heels that they put a swing in her step. Over it all, she wore a long black coat. *She's a real vamp*, Horsham thought, delighting in the irony.

Both men stood up upon seeing her. They couldn't keep themselves from eyeballing every inch of her, top to bottom. The bearded guy literally licked his lips.

"We're looking for a friend," she said. "Can you help me out?"

"Anything you want," the taller man with the shaved head said. "Come on over here, baby, and sit your beautiful ass down. My name's Mark."

She walked over, accentuating the swing in her hips a little. Both men were frozen, watching her. She sat down between them and put one hand on each of their knees. "My friend's name is Terrill—a tall guy, not as tall as Horsham here, but slender. Dressed nicely, though a little worse for wear. Handsome."

"Well, we haven't had anyone like that around here," Mark said. "There was a guy, kind of skinny and tall, but he was a mess. Doubt he was the same guy."

"What happened to him?" Jamie asked innocently.

Again, both men froze. Finally, the bearded guy said, "You just missed the cops. The guy was killed in a fight."

They probably expected her to look distressed, but she only smiled. "Where did he go?"

"I just told you, lady. He's dead."

Horsham stepped forward and the two homeless men looked startled, as if they had forgotten he was there. "Was he alone?"

The bearded guy looked down at Jamie's hand on his knee, then up at Horsham's cruel little smile. He stood up, looking behind him into the darkness as though getting ready to run, seeming to sense that something was wrong.

His more belligerent friend didn't seem to notice a thing. "I told you, buddy. He's dead. How's he going to go anywhere?" He waved off into the desert darkness around them. "He's under a couple feet of dirt right about now. The coyotes will be taking him if the cops don't find him first."

"But someone carried him away," Horsham said calmly. "Who is this Perry? Where would he go?"

"Like we told the cops, he and Grime probably headed for the homeless shelter in town. It's too cold to go anywhere else."

Jamie stood up. "I know where that is."

The tall man's hand lingered on her until the last possible second. He sighed.

"Jesus, lady. You're the biggest prick tease I've ever seen."

"Oh, you actually have a prick?" she said, and Horsham winced at her withering tone.

The tall man scowled. He reached into his coat and pulled out a gun. "You know what, lady? I'd have let you go if you hadn't said that. I'm no rapist. I hate rapists. But you can't walk into my home looking like that and insulting me. Take off that stupid coat."

Both of the bums glared at Horsham as if daring him to do something. Now that his friend was holding a gun, the bearded one no longer looked so worried. Horsham decided to watch what Jamie did. His baby vampire was full of surprises.

Jamie's face was impassive. Then she looked straight at Horsham and smiled, as if to say, "These are what bad guys look like." He shrugged in response.

She took off the long black coat. She dangled it from one finger and then let it drop onto the crude wooden picnic table.

In the light of the campfire, her blouse was see-through. She wasn't wearing anything underneath.

"Now the blouse," said the man with the gun.

She took it off slowly, teasingly. Then, without being asked, she dropped her skirt. She was naked except for the striped leggings.

"Come over here, bitch. I'll show you what a prick looks like."

As she walked over, Mark stood up and dropped his pants. He handed the gun over to Harve. "Hold onto this."

Harve lowered the weapon on Horsham, who still hadn't moved and was standing there with an ironic smile on his face. The bearded bum looked as though he was having second thoughts, but managed to mutter, "Save some of that for me, Mark."

Jamie stood in front of Mark. Horsham saw the transformation from behind. There was a slight movement at the back of her head, as if it had changed shape. Her claws extended, reached up, and wrapped around the man's head. Then blood was shooting into the air and the human was screaming.

Horsham leaped forward. Harve managed to get off one shaky shot that hit the vampire in the shoulder, and then his body was dropping to the ground, spouting blood from the gory stump where his head had once been. His head rolled out of the circle of firelight, a surprised expression still on his face.

After feeding, Jamie poured the contents of the white water bottles over her until she was completely clean. Then she put her clothes back on and whirled around in the light of the dying flames.

She laughed. "Good thing they asked me to take my clothes off. I like this outfit."

Chapter 33

After taking the motel clerk's statement, Brosterhouse drove back to the police station. It looked deserted. He made his way to Captain Anderson's office. He was surprised to find the old man was still there.

The door was open, but Brosterhouse knocked on the frame anyway before going in. "What's going on?"

The captain jumped at the sound of Brosterhouse's deep voice. He'd been staring into space. "Wow, you surprised me," he said. He shook his head tiredly. "There was a stabbing out at a homeless camp. We don't have that many murders around here, and it brought out every cop on duty." He checked his watch briskly, as if to say, "This better be important."

"What can I do for you, detective?"

When Brosterhouse detailed what he'd found, Anderson didn't seem very surprised. "It's suspicious, all right," he said. "But I'm not sure there is enough evidence there to pursue it. We're talking about a cop, one of our own. I think we need more evidence than that."

"I agree, captain. But there is enough for a search warrant, surely."

"Ordinarily, I'd say no. But with Carlan? Let me see what I can do." He picked up the phone and dialed. "Judge? This is Captain Anderson. I need a quick search warrant, and I need it to be quiet. It's for a cop. What's that? Well, as a matter of fact it *is* for Richard Carlan... Yes, sir. I'll send Detective Brosterhouse right over."

He hung up and gave Brosterhouse a glum look, as if realizing what an unusual thing they were doing. He scribbled on a notepad and tore off the note. "Judge Parrish will be waiting for you at this address. We're lucky. Carlan is going to be busy this evening, what with the stabbing. Right now would be a good time to make the search."

"Right."

"Oh, and Brosterhouse? If you don't find anything, maybe we could just keep it quiet?"

"I'm not sure," Brosterhouse said. He wasn't about to break the rules for anyone, even a fellow policeman. He left without another word.

On the way out, he poked his head into the squad room. There were only a couple of officers there, but one of them was Patterson.

"Patterson!" he shouted. "With me!"

* * *

Judge Parrish was waiting by the door when Brosterhouse pulled up. "Stay here," he told Patterson, and hurried up to the doorway.

"I've always kind of thought Carlan was dirty," the judge said by way of a greeting. "This doesn't surprise me at all."

He held the warrant out, but held onto it for a second as Brosterhouse reached for it. "I hope you're right about this, or there will be hell to pay."

"Yes, sir," Brosterhouse said, and Parrish let go of the papers.

The detective turned and left without another word.

* * *

When they pulled up to Richard Carlan's house, Patterson looked pale. "What are we doing here?"

"Just what it looks like; we're serving a search warrant."

"Shouldn't we wait until Carlan is home?" Patterson asked, obviously hoping to delay the unpleasant task.

"Well, maybe we can be in and out before anyone knows we were here," Brosterhouse offered. It was bullshit, but the young cop seemed to buy it. Brosterhouse would be leaving a copy of the warrant on the table, as legally required.

The back door was unlocked. They entered and quickly made their way to the office. It was a mess, and Brosterhouse left Patterson to start searching through the mass of papers.

"What are we looking for?" the patrolman asked.

"Anything," Brosterhouse said. "If you see anything that relates to Jamie Lee Howe, let out a holler."

He chose the bedroom, which in his experience was the place most miscreants hid things.

He'd only been searching for a couple of minutes before he found it, tucked under the underwear in the top drawer of the dresser near the bed.

The book was bright purple, hardly the kind of thing a hard-nosed cop would be likely to have. He guessed what it was even before he opened it and started reading.

He flipped to the end of the book and started reading the last few pages.

* * *

"Richard has threatened me again. He beats me if I refuse to have sex with him. He's playing weird little games. He makes me lie on the floor naked, with my arms crossed across my chest as though I'm dead, and he kicks me if I move. Then he has sex with me again...

"Richard has vowed to kill me if I leave. He found out about the abortion and was so angry he beat me. I'm afraid to stay. He's going to kill me one of these days. I'd be better off in Portland or Seattle or someplace like that."

Then, two days later: "I'm leaving. Richard told me to my face that he was going to drain me dry of blood, just like he thinks I've drained him. He's going to leave me lying on the floor, naked to the world, like the 'whore' I am. I can't stay in Bend any longer. He really means it."

* * *

Brosterhouse snapped the book shut. He did a quick search of the rest of the bedroom, but found only what you might expect in the disordered room of a bachelor.

"Find anything?" he asked, making his way back to the office.

"Ten-year-old electric bills," Patterson said. "Taxes from years ago. Crap. Junk. It's a waste of time."

"Not entirely," Brosterhouse said, holding up the purple book. He took his copy of the search warrant and wrote down a description of the diary, and had Patterson witness it. Then he made the same notation on the copy he left on the desk.

Carlan could scream and holler all he wanted. The diary wasn't prima facie evidence, but it was damning, probably enough to shame him off the police force. Certainly no one was going to look at him the same way again.

* * *

119

They held a telephone conference that very night: Captain Anderson; the district attorney, Jim Haller; and Brosterhouse, with Patterson sitting in the corner looking as though he wished he were anywhere else.

"Are you sure it's all Ms. Howe's handwriting?" Haller asked.

"I haven't had it analyzed yet, but I have no reason to doubt it," Brosterhouse said.

"Still, it isn't really evidence, is it?" Captain Anderson interjected. "Not enough for an arrest."

"Not on a murder charge, maybe," the detective admitted. "But tampering with evidence? He broke into a victim's house and stole a diary. He planted the victim's necklace in another man's suitcase. He had a restraining order taken out on him by the victim. It's enough to suspend him, at the least."

"I agree," Haller said.

Anderson nodded. "I agree, too, but I'm not sure everyone is going to see it that way."

"It's enough to make him a suspect," Haller continued. "But it's not enough for a conviction, in my opinion. I think you need one more piece of evidence before you can make an arrest."

Brosterhouse was frustrated, but he knew the district attorney was right. He'd been to enough trials to know that in the age of CSI television shows, they needed a strong preponderance of evidence.

"At least now we know where to look," he said.

Chapter 34

The man stood blocking the doorway of the shelter and wouldn't let them in. He was a round man, round of face and body, but with fine, slender hands and a strangely gaunt face. The door was at the back of the shelter, in a dark alley, with a single light bulb above it.

"You're too late," the man said.

"Come on, Harry," Perry argued. "We were kicked out of our camp. We got nowhere else to go!"

"...t's ...old," Grime said.

"Cold? Yes, it's going to be cold tonight, but maybe you should've thought of that earlier. If you bundle up, you'll be all right."

"Look, we understand the rules," Perry said. "But the new guy, Christian here, he ain't dressed for it; he ain't used to it."

The man looked over Perry's shoulder and saw Terrill for the first time. His eyes widened in sudden fear and then clouded over, as if he was confused by his own reaction. He shook his head. "Well... maybe this once. We'll let Christian's name be the password. Wait!" he held up his hand. "You've been drinking. I can smell it on you."

"Well, hell. When aren't we drinking?" Perry laughed.

"You can't bring any alcohol in here. I won't bend on that rule." The man crossed his arms and stared them down.

Perry sighed. He pulled the bottle out of his pocket. There was only an inch of whiskey in the bottom, but he eyeballed it regretfully. Then he shrugged, walked over to the trash cans lining the other side of the alley, and dropped it into one with the sound of breaking glass. He winced, then walked back.

The man moved aside, and the others filed in. Terrill was last in line, and as he crossed the threshold, he felt as if he'd been thrown into a pit of burning coals. He cried out and fell backward, landing on his rear end in the alley. "What is this place?" he shouted.

"The shelter at St. Francis Church," the man said. "I'm Father Harry Donovan."

"What's wrong, Christian?" Perry said, confused. "Come on, it's cold. Let's get inside!"

Grime came outside and, with surprising strength, pulled Terrill to his feet by the back of his new coat. "...ry ...gain," he muttered.

Expecting the pain this time, Terrill cautiously approached the doorway. He hadn't been on sanctified ground in centuries, not since his Turning. He should have burst into flames, and yet, though he'd fallen backward, that had been more from surprise than anything else—the pain had been endurable.

So he crossed the threshold slowly, gritting his teeth, and found that though the pain didn't go away, it started to recede into the background, like a toothache.

Father Harry was staring at Terrill, and he shook his head, then reached under his sweater and brought out a crucifix on a chain.

"Christian's got that same cross!" Perry exclaimed. "But he don't need no chain. Show him, Christian!"

Terrill shook his head. This conversation was heading in dangerous directions.

"Please," the priest said. "I'd like to see it."

Terrill unbuttoned his shirt. The crucifix gleamed in the soft light of the hallway. The skin around it was pink, nearly healed.

"How did you do that?" Father Harry asked.

"Can we just go to sleep?" Terrill asked. "We can talk about this in the morning." He had already decided that he'd wait until everyone else was sleeping and then get out of there, find a hole somewhere to hide in. This priest seemed entirely too interested in him.

"Of course," said Father Harry. "This way."

He led them to a big room that was full of sleeping men, then shook his head as if changing his mind and went on down the hallway. They passed a small kitchen. It looked as though they'd interrupted Father Harry while he was fixing a pot of stew. There were sliced carrots and potatoes piled on plates atop the counter, and on a cutting board, there was a pile of raw meat. There was a smaller supply room beyond the kitchen, with some disassembled cots leaning against one wall.

"There's blankets and pillows in the wardrobe there," Father Harry said. "Make yourselves at home."

After a lingering glance at Terrill, he left the room.

The alcohol and the long walk sent Grime and Perry instantly to sleep, still in their clothes. Grime was on his back with his mouth wide open, snoring with ladylike little snorts; Perry was curled up to half his size. But Terrill was wide-awake. The pain was one thing, but the awareness that he was in a church was what really scared him.

It should have been impossible. He should have been burned into a crisp by now. He opened his shirt and stared down at the crucifix, touching it. It didn't send a shock through his fingers this time. It was almost cool to the touch.

Terrill put on his shoes and coat, then went to the doorway and looked down the hall. It was quiet. He consulted his internal clock, but it was fuzzy, for some reason. It was about halfway between midnight and dawn, as best he could make out.

He started to make his way to the door, but upon crossing the threshold of the kitchen, he saw that the meat had been left out. *That isn't safe for the humans*, he thought. He entered the kitchen.

Maybe he'd fooled himself into thinking he was just going to cover the raw meat, but it was in his mouth before he knew it. He started gorging on it.

It tasted wrong. Actually, it had no taste at all—it was like sawdust. Terrill kept eating it because he knew he needed to heal, but with every mouthful, the background pain increased and the crucifix seemed to sink deeper into his chest.

He gave up, breathing hard, closing his eyes. *What am I doing? What is happening to me?*

"What are you doing?" he heard someone ask, as if echoing his thoughts. Father Harry was standing there in a bathrobe; perhaps he'd gotten out of bed after remembering that he hadn't put the meat away.

"I... I need it." Terrill stammered.

"You should have said something!" Father Harry exclaimed. "I've got some already-made sandwiches in the fridge."

"No... I need raw meat."

"Look, I don't know what your problem is, but raw meat isn't good for you."

"I'm vampire," Terrill blurted out. "Unholy." He was stunned by his own words, but they had come out before he could stop them.

The priest was unfazed. "Look, son," he said gently. "I know you may think you're a bad person, but I'm sure that's not true. Why don't you sit down and let me get you that sandwich?"

Terrill plopped down into the chair the priest directed him to as if the strength had gone out of his legs.

"You don't understand..." he started to say.

"Listen," Father Harry interrupted. "It doesn't matter what you've done, only what you do from this moment on. Do you repent your sins?"

"You don't know how much," Terrill breathed.

"God will forgive you if you give yourself to Him."

"It isn't that simple."

"It really is that simple. Christ died for your sins."

"But what if..." Terrill tried to think of how to express it. He was still amazed the words "I'm vampire" had come out of his mouth. The consecrated ground must have weakened him, and the cross on his chest had prepared the way. "What if the crimes are so evil, and so many, that they can't be forgiven?"

"Is one sin too many? Two? A hundred?" the priest asked rhetorically. "It is not the number of crimes you have committed. One unrepented sin weighs more than one hundred repented sins. But you must truly repent."

Terrill knew there was no way to explain it. There could be no forgiveness for his actions, no matter how he wished they had never happened.

"God will forgive you," Father Harry said, making the sign of the cross. Then he became brisk and businesslike. "However, I'm afraid the rules of this shelter will not. I caught you stealing food. You'll have to leave—first thing in the morning." Terrill must have looked stricken, because he quickly added; "You can come back in a few weeks if you promise never to do it again."

Terrill shut his mouth. He'd been about to confess to centuries of crimes: murders, slaughters, and massacres. Ridiculous. The priest wouldn't have believed him: but even if he had, by some miracle, he would have found it hard to come up with enough Hail Marys to absolve Terrill of his sins.

"I'm leaving right now," Terrill said, getting up with a new resolve. The pain was endurable again, but morning was fast approaching. The last thing he wanted was to get caught between sunlight and a church.

He hadn't gotten more than a few feet before he heard voices coming down the hallway.

"Where you going?" Perry asked. He and Grime were standing in the kitchen doorway.

"I'm sorry, Perry, Grime. I have to go. Thank you for everything you've done for me."

"I'll go with you," Perry said. When Terrill started to object, he held up his hand. "Look. I have a place nearby—my sister's house. She lets me stay in the basement when I need to. I don't like infringing on her, but... well... this is a special circumstance. Come on, pal. Let me help you."

Terrill tried to think what to do. He was putting all these people in danger. They didn't know what he was. But it was so close to morning that there was a chance he wouldn't find any other shelter in time.

"OK," he said reluctantly.

Grime started to follow them, but Perry shook his head. "Sorry, Grime. You'd stink up the place. My sister keeps a very clean house."

Grime muttered something, then stuck out his hand, as if realizing he might never see Terrill again. Terrill shook the hand, which was black with dirt. He realized that he didn't mind. "Thank you," he said.

"Remember what I said, Christian," Father Harry said from the door of the church. "God will forgive you anything."

Chapter 35

As Richard Carlan drove toward the St. Francis homeless shelter, he had a sudden idea.

He turned on Franklin Avenue and drove through downtown to the west side, pulling up in front of the Hardaway residence. They were still up, though it was nearly midnight.

He knocked on the door. There was that frightened pause on the other side of the door that every homeowner would take when there was a loud knock so late in the evening. Carlan sensed that he was being examined through the spyhole. Then the door was flung open in welcome and Howard Hardaway was beckoning him in.

"Everything all right, officer?" Howard asked.

"Call me Richard, for goodness' sake." He was annoyed that they still seemed to believe he was a virtual stranger. Not for long, if he had anything to do with it. "I just wanted to tell you, I'm on my way to arrest your daughter's killer. I know this is unorthodox, but I wondered if Sylvie would like to be there when it happens."

He craned his neck to look into the living room and saw her huddled under a blanket, watching *The Colbert Report* and ignoring him.

Mrs. Hardaway went over to her and said something over the din of the TV. Sylvie cast off her blanket and swung her feet around to the floor heavily. She got up and walked toward him as if she didn't care about anything or anyone.

"I'll go with you," she said. "Because I want to ask him why."

She was wearing jeans and a T-shirt, looking almost dumpy. But there was no disguising the lithe shape of her body, the sharp contours of her face. Even rumpled, with no makeup, she was more beautiful than most women at their most put-together. Carlan waited for her as she threw on a shapeless parka.

For a moment Carlan thought she was going to get in the backseat, but then she seemed to realize how silly that would look—or how guilty the neighbors might think it looked—and she sat in the passenger seat instead. She had yet to really look at him. She didn't say anything as they drove onto the Galveston Bridge over the Deschutes River and through downtown, which was still bustling even this late at night.

"I've really worked hard to catch him, you know." It sounded peevish, even to him. "I mean, he would've gotten away…"

Sylvie didn't say anything.

"It's possible the murderer is already dead," Carlan said, curious what her reaction would be. "We're getting some conflicting reports."

She certainly didn't seem as happy as she should be to hear this news. In fact, she barely reacted. Personally, he hoped this Terrill fellow, or Evers, or whatever his name was, was still alive so he could march him through the squad room in triumph. *In your face, Detective Brosterhouse!*

"If he killed my sister," Sylvie said, finally, "and I'm not sure I believe that, he was simply the instrument. You were the cause. If you hadn't scared her away to Portland, she never would have been in danger in the first place."

"I didn't force her to leave," he said. Why did this girl hate him? He'd never done anything to her. In fact, he'd been nothing but friendly. She'd just have to come around. He'd just have to figure out a way to make her go on that first date or two. Then she'd see what a great guy he was.

"It wouldn't hurt you to be friendly, you know," he said. "I could really help you out. You don't have Jamie's money coming in anymore, and your parents can barely support themselves. I happen to know they got a notice of foreclosure last month. You'll be working two jobs in fast-food joints if you don't watch out."

"Maybe," she said.

"Look, I've been on your side all along. You know, Jamie made a big mistake over there in Portland. I just found it. Turns out she made a porn video. I'm going to try to keep it out of the trial."

Sylvie turned and looked at him for the first time. The hate in her eyes was dismaying. "Jamie found out before she left," she said. "She told me about it. *You* made that video and *you* put it online."

He didn't say anything. It had probably been a mistake to bring the whole thing up. Nobody could prove it was him that was with her, but it was pretty hard to deny that it was Jamie being screwed on-screen.

"Well, it's Jamie's reputation that will suffer," he said stubbornly. "If you'd just be nice to me, go on a date or something, then I could keep the video out of the evidence, out of the trial."

"And if I don't?"

He shrugged.

"You're the *real* killer," she said, and there was anger in her voice. "Go ahead. Post the video. I don't care. Mom and Dad need to wake up to what happened to their daughter. They need to wake up to why it happened, and I'll make sure they know that *you* made that video, that the flabby man who was having such a hard time keeping a hard-on was you. Go ahead, Richard. Jamie's dead—you can't hurt her anymore."

"Yeah, but I can hurt you." He reached over and grabbed her arm and squeezed. She gritted her teeth but didn't cry out, unlike Jamie, who almost always became very accommodating when he disciplined her. He let go of her with a snort of disgust. "Quit being such a bitch."

"Bastard," she groaned.

Just like that, he was falling out of love with her. He still desired her, but not for a lifetime. He'd screw her and leave her. After that, he didn't care what she thought or what she did. He just had to find the right leverage to get her in bed. But no more romancing...

"I'm a cop, for God's sake," he snarled. "You're a low-life high school dropout. You should be looking to your future."

She didn't say anything for a while, simply stared out the window. He could see tears glittering in her eyes. "What if I ask for a restraining order?" she said, finally. "How will that look for your career? To have two women from the same family swearing you're dangerous?"

Carlan hadn't thought of that. He wanted to grab her again, just to wake her up. But no, she'd only be stoic, which would be irritating. But he knew one thing: he wouldn't—*couldn't*—allow her to file a restraining order. She needed to know that.

"I'll kill you first," he said.

"And find a patsy to blame?" Sylvie said, turning toward him in triumph. "You killed her, didn't you? Not Mr. Terrill."

"Is that the name he gave you? For an innocent man, he sure goes by a lot of names. How did that insurance settlement go?"

She didn't answer.

"I knew it! The check bounced, didn't it? No, Sylvie. He did it, all right. I have no earthly idea why he's here, but he killed Jamie. Maybe he wants to kill you too."

"He cared for her," she said, but she sounded defeated. "I could tell. And he really wanted to help me. Somehow you've twisted all the evidence, haven't you?"

"Like you said, Sylvie," Carlan said with a pinch of satisfaction. "You can ask him yourself, just as soon as I put handcuffs on him and read him his rights."

He pulled into the alley behind the church.

Chapter 36

Sunrise was only a couple of hours away, and Carlan expected to have to bang on the door of the shelter to wake up the priest. But Father Harry was dumping some trash in the cans in the alley as they drove up.

The priest turned and waited expectantly.

Carlan knew Father Harry didn't like him. Once, as he was dropping Jamie off for volunteer work, he'd made the mistake of saying out loud what he really thought: that trying to help these bums was a stupid waste of time. Since then, the holier-than-thou bastard had all but ignored him.

Carlan rolled down the window but didn't get out. He was having momentary doubts. Perhaps he should call for backup. Patterson was the lead in this case, after all. He didn't want any questions later. But then the image returned of him leading the culprit through the squad room to the cheers of his fellow police officers.

"What can I do for you, officer?" the priest asked.

Carlan opened the door and got out of the cruiser. He adjusted his gun belt, trying to think how best to approach the priest. Father Harry was protective of his vagrants.

"We're looking for someone," he said. "A murder suspect."

Father Harry didn't look as surprised as he should have been. "You'd better come inside," he said.

Sylvie got out of the car and stood about as far from Carlan as she could and still stay within the confines of the alley. The priest smiled at her sadly, and as she started to walk inside, he touched her arm. She flinched, and he retracted his hand as quickly as if had been burned. "You OK?" he asked.

She nodded.

"I'm sorry about Jamie. She didn't deserve that. She was a good woman."

"You know she was a prostitute, right?" Carlan said, watching this exchange.

"She was a good woman," the priest repeated, glaring at him.

They passed the big room, which served as both the sleeping quarters and the dining room for the homeless, depending on the time of day. Carlan stood in the doorway, but all he could see were shrouded shapes on cots.

Father Harry kept going, turning into the kitchen. There was a smaller table for smaller meals in the corner.

There was a filthy man sitting at the table who looked up when they walked in the room. He was eating a bowl of Top Ramen. Carlan immediately remembered Mark, the guy at the encampment, mentioning how dirty one of the expelled bums was. Grime, he'd called him.

"You Grime?" he asked.

The man muttered something, then bent down to slurp up some more noodles.

Carlan shuddered as the man's smell assaulted him.

Sylvie sat at the table opposite the Stinker, and they exchanged a look. No doubt they were sharing some miserable commiserating message, Carlan thought. He was so sick of these dirty, pathetic, depressing people!

Carlan and Father Harry sat in the other two chairs.

"I'm looking for a bum called Perry, and unless I'm mistaken, Grime here. They were accompanying a third man, a new guy in town, called Evers or Terrill, or who knows what. A tall, slender man, is the way he's described." Carlan pulled out the police sketch and handed it to the priest, who barely glanced at it before handing it back. Carlan dropped the picture on the table in front of Grime, who ignored it.

"Is he dead?" Carlan asked bluntly, hoping for a reaction. Grime barely budged, but the priest was obviously surprised.

"So he's *not* dead," Carlan said, snagging the picture and proffering it to priest again. "Take a look, Father Harry. This man is a killer. He shouldn't be on the streets. You need to tell me where he is."

"Is this true?" the priest asked Sylvie. "Is this the man who killed Jamie?"

"He's been accused," she said. Then she shrugged. "I don't know."

Father Harry was obviously troubled and struggling with whether to answer. Finally, he said, "Look around you, Officer Carlan. What do you see?"

I see a kitchen with a stinking bum, Carlan thought. *I see a beautiful but pathetic girl. I see a priest who has wasted his life trying to help those who can't be helped, who most often don't want to be helped.*

He didn't know what to say.

"See what's on the far wall there?" the priest said. "It's a crucifix, signifying the sacrifice that our Savior made for all of us—even the less fortunate, the downtrodden. It is not up to me to punish, or to give up for punishment, those who have asked for forgiveness."

"Did he confess?" Carlan demanded.

"Not exactly," the priest said reluctantly.

"He's a murderer, Father Harry. You really shouldn't be protecting him."

But it was obvious the priest wasn't going to give him up.

"It doesn't matter," Carlan said, getting up. "I'm here, and I'm going to find him." Before the priest could get in his way, he was out of the kitchen and heading for the main room. He switched on the lights and shouted, "Everybody up! Out of bed! Line up against that wall!"

There were at least twenty homeless people there, about three-quarters of them men. There was a crude barricade in one corner where the women were sleeping. He ignored them.

Most of the men were fully dressed, a few had on pajamas, and a couple of them were naked, wrapped in blankets.

He examined them, and it quickly became clear that Jonathan Evers was not among them. "Which of you is Perry?"

No one said anything.

"Answer me, dammit!" he shouted, and the man nearest to him jerked. "You, where's Perry?"

"I haven't seen him," the vagrant muttered. "He wasn't here last night when I went to bed."

Carlan was enraged. He'd been so close! They'd been here, he was certain of it!

If Sylvie and the priest hadn't followed him into the big room, he'd have beaten the man senseless right then and there. It was a room full of losers whose word was worthless, every one of them. But he could also tell that the man was telling the truth. All of these men and women had been asleep by the time Evers and Perry and Grime had arrived.

Carlan stalked back to the kitchen, but as soon as he saw and smelled Grime again, he abandoned any thought of arresting the bum. He could tell that Grime wouldn't say anything, and if he did, it wouldn't make any sense. No point in dirtying up his squad car. He knew from experience that the stink would linger for days.

It was time to call in backup and search the neighborhood. They couldn't have gone far. He started toward the patrol car, almost forgetting Sylvie. Almost reluctantly, he turned back and found her. "I'm leaving," he said. "Come on."

"No," she said. "I'm not going with you. I'll find another way home."

"Suit yourself," Carlan said. He strode to the car without a backward glance, got in, and slammed the door. He accelerated down the alley, keeping his eyes out for movement as he picked up the radio to call it in.

Let Patterson take the blame for the fugitive's escape.

Chapter 37

Sylvie and Grime sat companionably at the table in the shelter's kitchen. She wasn't sure if she wanted to walk home or give her dad a call. He would ask what had happened with Richard, and she didn't feel like explaining. Her parents couldn't seem to understand what a creep he was, and the more she tried to point it out, the more they defended him.

She could show them the video to prove her point, but it would break their hearts.

No matter how much she disliked Richard, however, it occurred to her that she should be rooting for him to find Jamie's murderer. She blamed Richard for Jamie's death, but in her gut, she knew he hadn't committed the final act.

She'd heard the tone of pain and regret in Terrill's voice. He'd done it, all right.

So why didn't she hate him? Why did she believe that he was truly sorry? And why did that matter?

None of her friends were religious, and none of her family were, either. Jamie had started volunteering at the shelter because she had empathy and good heart, not because she bought into the sermons that Father Harry gave at every meal.

Sylvie had a classmate who had tricked her into going on a retreat with what turned out to be a cult. But it also turned out that Sylvie was immune to their tricks and blandishments.

Still, it had piqued her interest in spiritual matters. She had stumbled upon her current beliefs by herself one day, riding in Dad's car while picking up Jamie from her volunteer work at the shelter. She'd wandered in and stared at Christ hanging there in the main room, and the iconography had attracted her like nothing else ever had.

She'd started reading up, reading the parts of the Bible that made sense, talking to Father Harry, and it had only seemed natural when she was baptized in the Catholic Church. It had totally amazed everyone, but Sylvie had never regretted it, never looked back.

She was especially interested in the concept of redemption. Now that she was being put to the test, she found that she could forgive, but only if the sinner was repentant.

Richard didn't even think he'd done anything wrong.

Terrill seemed crushed.

* * *

Grime noisily finished his soup. When he was done, he pushed the bowl away with a satisfied sigh. He looked Sylvie in the eye and said something.

"Pardon?" she asked.

He repeated it, and it sounded to her like he'd said "Are you The Girl?"

Was she The Girl? Well, she supposed she probably was. "I think so," she ventured.

He nodded, as if it confirmed what he'd thought.

"What's he like?" she asked. "What's Terrill really like?"

Grime grinned, showing two front teeth and acres of vacant gums. When he started talking again, Sylvie found that she could understand him, her brain supplying the first letters he left off of the words.

"Good man. Very good man. He saved Perry, got stabbed instead. Right in the heart."

"Why isn't he dead?"

Grime shrugged. "He ain't human."

"What?" Until that moment, Sylvie hadn't realized that she'd suspected that very thing, somewhere inside. "Not human?"

"Not a monster, not a human. Something in between. He's *becoming...*"

She didn't question Grime further, realizing that he was only speculating himself. But from what she knew, it sounded right.

Terrill hadn't fought back when attacked. He'd turned the other cheek. He had tried to help Sylvie. Was that enough? Could she truly forgive a man—or whatever he was—who had committed the ultimate sin?

He must be punished. She knew that. He must wholly give himself up. But she couldn't hate him. He had to be given a chance to repent and, through his actions, redeem himself.

Grime was about to say something else, but he was interrupted by a bone-shaking scream from the alley.

* * *

While Sylvie and Grime conversed in the kitchen, Father Harry entered the main church. He knelt in front of the cross and prayed for guidance. He hadn't believed, truly believed, since he'd been at the seminary. Somehow he'd managed to fool everyone.

Oh, he believed in the message of Christ, and he believed in some kind of higher power, which made him a good Unitarian but a lousy Catholic. The girl, Sylvie, was a better Catholic than he was.

But he couldn't disappoint his family or his flock. He could do more good as a priest than he could do outside the church. Or so he told himself.

Day and night, he prayed for forgiveness. Prayed that he might do the right thing. Prayed that no one would see through his hypocrisy.

Terrill had come to him asking for forgiveness. He hadn't said for what, but Father Harry believed it was for something dreadful, most likely the murder he was accused of. But technically, he hadn't confessed. Nor, unless Father Harry was completely mistaken, was the man Catholic. If he was guilty of as horrendous a crime as killing Jamie Lee Howe, than he needed to be taken off the street.

Here the divide between the unbeliever and the believer was widest. The priest should have been able to forgive Terrill, but he was angry that Jamie had been taken from this world. Jamie Howe had had one of the purest hearts he'd ever encountered. He'd heard rumors about her that should have horrified him, but it hadn't changed his opinion of her.

He went to his office and looked through his papers until he found the address he needed.

It was the man, not the priest, who picked up the cellphone and dialed Richard Carlan's number. He left a message. "Officer Carlan? I've thought about what you said. The man you're looking for is at this address: 2965 Williamson Avenue. He's in the basement apart—"

He, too, was interrupted by the scream in the alley.

As Father Harry ran down the hallway, he saw Grime and Sylvie jumping up from the table in the kitchen. The sleeping room, which had settled back down, was in an uproar again. He didn't stop. He threw open the back door and froze on the threshold.

Somehow, he had the presence of mind to hold Grime and Sylvie back when they reached him.

It was as if he understood at a glance what was happening—which should have been impossible, because he simply didn't believe in the supernatural. Yet what other explanation could there be?

After being rousted out of bed by Officer Carlan, a half a dozen of his regulars had taken to the alley to smoke.

One of the men was flying through the air, as if he'd just jumped off the roof of the church. As Father Harry watched, another man was picked up and tossed an impossible distance into the air.

In the center of the alley was the mad juggler of these humans, a huge grin on his face. No… that was not a grin—it was an extension of his mouth, and those weren't teeth, they were fangs. The creature was dressed in a spiffy gray suit and shiny black shoes, like a midtown Manhattan tycoon.

One of the victims had already landed and lay broken and unmoving. It was his cry that had brought them all running. As Father Harry watched, the second man landed on his head and crumpled into an unnatural tangle of limbs. The third man was falling, a look of sheer terror on his face, which was fixated on the monster who had thrown him. He landed flat and writhed in pain, groaning. He was unconscious, but alive.

Grime tried to force his way past, to help his friends, but with a strength he didn't know he possessed, Father Harry held him back. Behind him, the other homeless residents were coming to see what the commotion was all about. There were three other vagrants in the alley, but the monster was between them and the door.

One of them made a break for the end of the alley, but another shape moved out of the shadows. One moment that part of the alley was empty, and then suddenly someone—something—was standing there. A woman, Father Harry thought, but with the same malformation of her face. Against the backdrop, he saw her hands, which were twice as big as normal, with long fingers tapering to claws.

The man cried out and ran back and huddled with the other two.

"Tell me what I want to know and these men will live," the first creature said. As the priest watched, the thing's face flattened, the muzzle became a mouth again and the huge claws became hands. Now that it looked human again, Father Harry could see that there really was a smile on the monster's face after all, but it was a humorless smile.

The creature reminded Father Harry of the man called Christian, though he couldn't exactly say why. "What are you?" he asked.

"I am vampire. Your church and I are old acquaintances, though you priests seemed to have forgotten us. When you report this—if you live—they'll take your report and file it somewhere deep in the Vatican. Where it belongs."

Father Harry had a strange reaction to the vampire's words. He pulled his crucifix from under his vest and touched it with a devotion he hadn't felt in years. Never again would he shamefully hide it under his clothing. It was a small, sophisticated little cross, more Protestant than Catholic in its features. Father Harry would be pulling out the church catalog tomorrow and ordering the biggest crucifix he could find.

If he survived this.

Chapter 38

"What do you want?" Father Harry asked, feeling strangely calm.

"I'm looking for a vampire named Terrill," the creature said. "Tell me where he is and I'll let these men go."

"He isn't here," the priest said.

The vampire laughed. "Of course he isn't here! He's vampire! But some of the men here know where he is and have given him shelter. Tell me where he's hiding, and you can forget I ever existed."

"A man named Terrill was here," Father Harry said. "He entered this sanctuary. I fed him and he went on his way."

"Come, now—such a stupid lie. He could no more cross the threshold of a church than I can."

Father Harry didn't know what to say. Should he play along or tell the truth? If he lied and said Terrill was inside, the vampire would be stymied. But then he might take his anger out on the three hostages.

When in doubt, tell the truth. "He was here, I assure you. But he is gone now."

He could tell that the vampire believed him, and that it enraged him. He transformed in an instant to the monster he really was, his fangs glistening in the moonlight, his claws extended in anger. The vampire grabbed one of the three men and tore into his neck, and the man's head half-detached, flopping onto his back. Blood sprayed upward in a fountain and the monster dropped him. Then he grabbed the second man.

The surviving vagrant started screaming at that point. The men in the hallway began shouting for the door to be closed. Father Harry heard one of the men puking behind him.

Father Harry should have been terrified, but the opposite was happening. He felt a surge of religious devotion such as he hadn't felt since he was a child, and a firm resolve to confront any danger in defense of his flock.

He had always doubted, but it didn't matter. Evil existed; the proof of it was manifest right in front of him. And if evil existed, then so did good. So did God.

The priest felt the church around him, which had been his home for a decade, become a fortress of belief. It was hallowed ground, and he was an ordained priest, and he knew the sacred words. He started chanting:

"Behold the Cross of the Lord; flee, bands of enemies. We drive you from us, whoever you may be: unclean spirits, all satanic powers, all infernal invaders, all wicked legions, assemblies, and sects; in the name and by the power of Our Lord Jesus Christ, may you be snatched away and driven from the Church of God and from the souls made in the image and likeness of..."

The vampire cringed, threw the vagrant he'd been about the bite away from him, and lunged toward Father Harry. But, only inches away, he stopped.

It will be all right, Father Harry thought. The church would protect him, and so would the crucifix, and the Bible, which he had, until this moment, only half believed. They would help him defeat this evil.

But he hadn't counted on Sylvie slipping under his arm and stepping out in the alley.

"Jamie?" the girl said in disbelieving whisper. And then, her voice stronger, "Is that you, Jamie?"

The fool girl was walking toward the other vampire, the one in the shadows.

Father Harry reached for her, and he felt himself losing his balance and stumbling onto the concrete of the alley.

The vampire was on him before he could move another inch. Claws snagged his vestments and pulled him further into the alley, carefully avoiding the priest's small crucifix. Father Harry felt hot breath on his neck and smelled the stink of rotted meat. "Pray all you want, priest," the monster hissed. "You're mine."

Out of the corner of his eye, Father Harry saw Grime run into the alley and drag the wounded man into the church. The two surviving vagrants had beaten him to the doorway, and there were cries of relief from inside the hallway.

"Begone, demon!" Father Harry shouted, grabbing his cross and pressing it against the vampire's wrists. There was a sizzling sound. But the vampire caught the chain with one of his claws and snapped it, flinging the crucifix away. It landed on the muddy concrete with a tinny sound.

The vampire laughed. "What are you now, without your church and your cross? I sense a weakness in you... you, a priest who only half believes."

The vampire turned Father Harry around and brought his face to within inches of the distended, drooling fangs. "I'll ask you one last time. Where is Terrill?"

Father Harry had been ready to turn Terrill in to the authorities, but he wasn't going to tell this monster where he was, no matter what. No matter that it would be his death. He was ready now, secure in his belief in God. Here, in the last moments of his life, he had finally become the priest he had always wanted to be.

As if the vampire could sense the stiffening of his resolve, he turned toward Sylvie, who was standing near the female vampire. "Hold onto her, my baby vampire. I'll need her for leverage."

"No," Jamie said, for Father Harry could see that was who it was, as impossible as it seemed. "You won't touch Sylvie. Not unless you kill me first."

"Then I'll kill the priest instead. Do you understand, girl? Tell me where Terrill is and I'll let your priest go. You have no reason not to tell me— Terrill changed Jamie, made her a vampire. She'll never be your sister again."

Sylvie had a serious look on her face. She wasn't frightened, Harry realized. She had a faith even deeper than his. She looked at Father Harry and said, "Forgive me."

"No need, Sylvie," the priest said. He felt the tightening of the vampire's claws, the drip of fluid down his neck. He closed his eyes and prayed.

As he gave himself to God, Father Harry sensed movement from the direction of the church. Liquid splashed over him, and he tasted it. *Water,* he thought. *What...?*

It was slightly stale-tasting, and with that realization, he knew what it was. He'd tasted it once before, out of curiosity, wondering if holy water would taste any different than normal water.

Grime was standing there with a defiant look on his face, a cup in his hand. Harry noticed that some of the dirt had washed away from the back of the man's hand, and that the skin there looked almost pink. He almost laughed; then he felt himself being lifted into the air and tossed.

The vampire recoiled with an inhuman scream. The creature seemed to be melting, crumpling into itself, until he appeared to be half his former size.

Jamie came to the monster's side, lifted him as if he weighed nothing, and ran.

Within moments, the alley was empty. Father Harry lay on his back, staring into the sky. He thought he could see the glimmer of sunrise. He was alive. It was morning.

It was the dawn of a new day, and God was in his Heaven.

* * *

Horsham came to his senses a few blocks away from the church. He'd fed so much over the past few days that he was already healing. The damage was painful, but it would go away soon.

"Let me down," he said.

Jamie released him and stared at him curiously.

"I'm all right," he said. "That holy water was weak compared to that of my youth. Why did you run?"

"Can you not feel it?" she said urgently. "The sun is only minutes away."

His sense of time rushed back, and he realized what danger they were in. He'd been so focused on finding Terrill that he'd lost track, like some baby vampire. Instead, this baby vampire had saved him.

They started running, and if any humans had been there to observe them, they wouldn't have believed their eyes: two human shapes moving as fast as the swiftest car, flitting from shadow to shadow, showing only the barest outlines in the artificial lights.

They passed the Walmart parking lot, where the abandoned RVs were festooned with yellow crime scene tape. Obviously, the bodies had been found.

It is time to leave, Horsham thought. He'd broken all the Rules: he'd fed where he lived, he hadn't disguised the remains, he hadn't chosen victims at random. They were in great danger.

They should leave that night. Let Terrill get away this time. Horsham would track him down another day. They were immortal, and time stretched on for eternity… as long as they didn't make any stupid mistakes.

But the hate still burned in him. And, unexpectedly, he found that he'd enjoyed the confrontation with the priest. It reminded him of the old days, when vampires and priests had been locked in mortal combat. He'd like a rematch, he realized.

One more night, he thought as they neared the motel. Terrill was close—he could feel it. *One more night to hunt, and then we'll leave.*

The sun came over the horizon, and the two vampires slowed so they could stick to the shadows. The final hundred feet to their room was in direct sunlight. Horsham shrugged at Jamie and started running for the door. The sun burned into his neck and hands and face, turning them black; they were smoking, nearly bursting into flame. And then he was through the door and Jamie was falling into the room behind him.

Half an hour later, a maid made the mistake of checking the room. Her flesh revived the two vampires, and they spent the rest of day in bed, screwing as if it was their last day on Earth.

Chapter 39

Terrill let his new friend, Perry, lead him away from the homeless shelter, but inwardly, he wondered why he bothered. He could keep running and hiding, but eventually Horsham would find him.

And then what? Would he fight his old friend? Over an evil deed that he himself was ashamed of? That he himself thought he deserved to be punished for? Perhaps what had happened to Mary called out for his own end, once and for all. Did he deserve to go on, year after year, not really a man and not really a vampire?

What am I? Even as he thought this, his gorge rose and he found himself on his knees, puking up the red meat he'd gobbled. He looked down. It looked as though the meat was undigested, as though it had been completely rejected.

That was impossible. He needed raw meat to survive. It always came back to his need for blood. Oh, he might nibble at other foods and try to blend in. He'd thought for years that he could survive that way—that he could pretend to be human. But Jamie's death had proven to him that the deadly vampire always lurked underneath, waiting for any chance to emerge. He was a danger to everyone around him.

Even if he chose to fight back against Horsham, what were the chances that he'd win? He'd taught Horsham well, and his disciple had no doubt learned much on his own over the past decades. He would have been motivated enough. Terrill felt his own weakness, his lack of willpower, and his unhealed wounds.

This was going to end only one way. He regretted that he hadn't been able to help Jamie. Even more, he regretted that he'd brought death to this town despite his good intentions.

Perhaps it was time to give Horsham his satisfaction. Let him exact his vengeance.

Terrill looked at Perry, who was looking at the horizon worriedly.

"Don't worry. If the sun catches me, everybody's problems will cease."

"Oh, really?" Perry said. "See, I don't believe that. I don't think anyone should give up." He picked up the pace, and Terrill had to lengthen his stride to keep up. They reached the base of Pilot Butte. Flush against the hillside, there was a two-story house. It had a nautical theme, with a promenade on the second floor and round portholes along the side for windows.

Perry saw Terrill staring and laughed. "I'm only the second weirdest person in my family. But my sister's weirdness made her rich."

There was a turret on one end of the house, and what looked like an eagle or owl's nest on top of it.

"Come on," Perry said. "I have the key to the basement apartment unit. My sister keeps trying to get me to move in."

On the far side of the house, built almost into the hillside, were steps leading downward, with a low, wide door at the bottom of them. As they stood in the dark stairwell, the sun suddenly splashed its light against the ground behind them. Despite himself, Terrill flinched.

Perry unlocked the door and swung it open, and motioned Terrill in. The vampire had to duck to get inside, but once past the doorway, he discovered that the ceilings were high and wide. *It looks like the lounge of an ocean liner,* thought Terrill, who had voyaged on the grand old ships long before airplanes had come along.

"Trudy invested in freightliners, container ships, and then later, luxury cruise ships," Perry explained. "Not because she's so damn smart, but because she absolutely loves ships. She got rich despite her mania."

"Why does she live in Bend, then? Of all places?" The ocean was almost two hundred miles away.

"I told you, she's weird," Perry said. "And she spends most of her time on the ocean. This is her getaway. Make yourself at home."

Terrill made his way to the long couch and sank into it gratefully.

A counter ran along one side of the room, and on the other side of it was what looked for all the world like a ship's galley. Perry said, "You wanted some more of my homemade stew? I'll get some started. It'll settle your stomach."

He went off the kitchen—*the galley*, Terrill corrected himself.

Later, with the bowl of stew in front of him, he took a sample taste. It shouldn't have had any appeal to him whatsoever. Even the meat was wrong, overcooked by his standards. But only minutes later, he'd hungrily eaten all of it, even the carrots, the potatoes, and the greens. He asked for seconds.

Perry smiled. "I made a big pot. I always do."

Terrill checked the state of his body. His wounds weren't healing quickly, like a vampire's, but slowly, like a human's. The strength and speed he'd always possessed had mostly abandoned him. He felt weak, tired, and hungry, and yet he also felt strangely whole.

What was happening to him? He shouldn't be able to eat human foods, or have a cross affixed to his body, and most of all, he shouldn't have been able to enter a holy sanctuary.

He hadn't wanted to hope, but he finally let himself ask the question that had been forming in the back of his mind for days. *Is it possible to become human again? After so many centuries?* Such a thing had never happened, as far as he knew. He remembered how Michael the Maker had been preoccupied with such questions before he'd disappeared, but Terrill had never taken them seriously.

He finished his second bowl of the stew, lay down on the couch, and fell instantly asleep.

Chapter 40

After the vampires fled, everyone congregated back in the church.

It appeared to Sylvie that Father Harry was trying to hold back his exhilaration. The tragedy would make such enthusiasm unseemly. But it was undeniable; the priest was a changed man. He'd always seemed kind of sad and subdued to Sylvie. She'd caught him several times expressing doubts about church doctrine.

Now, all doubt was gone. He was a man in his element.

Grime found Sylvie in the chaos and motioned for her to follow. "Would you like to find Terrill?"

Would she? Now that the question had been put to her, she realized she'd very much like to talk to Terrill. She nodded.

"Follow me," Grime said. They went into the alley and turned to the right. Within a few paces, they were at the scene of her recent confrontation with the vampire who looked like her sister.

* * *

When she saw Jamie, Sylvie didn't hesitate. She ducked under Father Harry's arm, left the sanctuary of the church without looking back, and marched over to the vampire.

The vampire with Jamie's face looked as if she wanted to flee, to be anywhere but in that alley.

Behind them, Father Harry and the other vampire were talking in loud voices, but Sylvie had eyes only for the vampire in the form of her sister.

They stared at each other, half strangers, half intimates.

"Are you still my sister?" Sylvie asked softly. "Do you have a soul?"

The vampire did her the honor of looking as if she was seriously considering her question.

"I don't think so," the vampire said, finally. "I have her memories. But they are already fading."

Sylvie had been holding her crucifix in her hand, and now she brought it up abruptly to the face that looked like Jamie's.

The vampire reared back, her fangs glistening, and hissed.

"I see," Sylvie said. "You aren't Jamie. You are a creature of darkness and of evil."

"Yet God made me too, did he not? How do you explain that?"

"A test," Sylvie said instantly. "Terrill has been trying to break away from his nature. He has been trying to show the way. Perhaps it is possible to redeem yourself, if you try."

"Impossible," the vampire in the shape of Jamie said. "I like what I have become, though the old Jamie would be horrified. You can't imagine how it feels. I'm quicker and stronger than any human. I will live forever. Why would I give that up?"

"Have you killed?"

The vampire looked away, expressionless, and nodded slightly.

"You must leave here," Sylvie said.

"Horsham is my Master. I will do as he asks, not you."

"Do you seek to destroy Terrill? Do you want revenge?"

"Revenge? I'd thank him if I could. If I wanted revenge, it would be on Richard. No, it is Horsham who seeks to exact vengeance on Terrill. I have been vampire long enough to know that Terrill could not resist Turning me. Hell, he even warned me to leave, but I ignored him. Terrill will be destroyed, but it won't be because I want it."

"Perhaps it isn't too late, Jamie," Sylvie urged. "Repent. Give yourself to God. We will find a way."

"No. I'm leaving. Should you ever see me again, don't count on me being sentimental."

Sylvie looked into her sister's eyes and saw something other than Jamie staring back.

"I see. Then you are damned."

"Yes," the vampire said, sounding unconcerned. "I suppose I am."

From behind them came Horsham's voice. "Hold onto her, my baby vampire. I'll need her for leverage."

"No!" Jamie shouted back. "You won't touch Sylvie! Not unless you kill me first!"

She looked at Sylvie, and there was a hint of the old Jamie's spirit there.

"Then I'll kill the priest instead. Do you understand, girl? Tell me where Terrill is and I'll let your priest go. You have no reason not to tell me—Terrill changed Jamie, made her a vampire. She'll never be your sister again."

Sylvie looked Father Harry in the eye. Her faith was, if anything, stronger than ever, and because of that she said, "Forgive me."

"No need, Sylvie," Father Harry said.

It was then that Grime emerged from the church and threw holy water on Horsham. Jamie seemed to disappear from in front of Sylvie. She caught a glimpse of the vampire who had once been her sister picking up her Master and running away down the alley.

* * *

Now, as she followed Grime to Terrill's hiding place, Sylvie regretted her judgmental last words to her sister. She wasn't sure what she would do when she found Terrill. But she had to know: Was it possible to become human again? To regain one's soul through the grace of God, once it was lost?

It was a beautiful morning. There wasn't a cloud in the sky. In the bright sunlight, the vampires seemed like a bad dream. But darkness would come again, and with it, the vampires would return.

Grime led her toward Pilot Butte, taking side roads. He grabbed a newspaper off one of the driveways and glanced at the main headline before tossing it away. She almost said something, and then laughed at herself. *Good girl, Sylvie.* Even a fifty-cent theft disturbed her.

Grime knocked on the door of a basement apartment on the far side of a very strange-looking house. Perry answered and motioned them in.

Terrill was stretched out on the couch. He appeared to be barely breathing. His face was pale and he looked stressed, even though he was asleep.

Sylvie stood over him and tried to think of what to say. Then she turned and walked to the kitchen, and selected the sharpest-looking knife there. She walked back to the couch.

"Hey, what are you doing with that knife?" Perry exclaimed.

She gritted her teeth. *Don't think, just do it!* she told herself. She brought the knife down onto her forearm and sliced.

Blood immediately began welling up along the four-inch cut. Sylvie leaned down and slapped Terrill across the face.

He rose up faster than she'd seen anyone move, and his eyes, when they opened, had an inhuman gleam. Sylvie stuck her bleeding arm in front of Terrill's face.

He tried to turn his head, but she commanded, "Look at it!" and he obeyed.

His face began to distend a little, then receded, then distended, and finally settled back into a human appearance. He stared up at Sylvie, looking hurt and surprised at the same time.

141

"I had to test you," she said.

"You could've died," he said. "Once a vampire sinks his fangs into you, he can't stop until you're dead."

"I wanted to know if you could be trusted—if you have truly changed."

"And you think this is an answer?" he asked sadly. "You need a better test. I am dangerous when I wake up. I'm dangerous when I am hungry."

"Didn't I just wake you?" she asked. "Aren't you hungry?"

Terrill looked amazed as he realized she was right.

"I have to tell you something," he said.

"I know," Sylvie said. "She told me…"

"I killed your sister," he continued, before he could change his mind about confessing. Then her last words seemed to sink in. "Wait, what? She told you? What are you talking about? I killed your sister."

"No, you did something much worse," Sylvie said in a harsh voice. "You took her soul, turned her into something evil."

Terrill stared at her. It was obvious he hadn't known. "She Turned? I never even considered that possibility!"

"I have to know," Sylvie said. "I have to know if my sister can be saved."

"I don't know," he said, dropping his head.

"You created her! You made her a monster!"

"You're right. I have no excuses. It is my nature, no matter how much I try to change it."

Until that moment, Sylvie hadn't been sure if she could or would forgive Terrill. But as she looked down at this defeated man, she realized that was what he was: a man. Not a vampire. She'd seen vampires, and they weren't anything like this.

"I don't agree," Sylvie said. "I think you have changed. Look at you! You've had every reason to strike out, to protect yourself, yet you've turned the other cheek. You've sacrificed your well-being for the sake of others. You've been pushed and tempted, and yet you've resisted feeding as a vampire."

Perry and Grime had been standing nearby, watching their interaction. Now Perry said, "She's right. Show her the cross."

Terrill turned away, shaking his head, but Grime joined in. "Do it."

Resignedly, Terrill opened his shirt. There was Jamie's crucifix, which she had worn every day since Sylvie had given it to her, though Jamie hadn't been a believer. Sylvie couldn't help but contrast this miracle with the other vampires' reaction to the cross.

"You have been in a church and survived," she said. "That should be impossible."

"He's not eating raw meat anymore, either," Perry said. "In fact, he's turning downright vegetarian."

"I wish it were so," Terrill said, not sounding convinced.

"I will help you," Sylvie said. "If you seek redemption, I will help you in every way that I can."

He stood up. He was tall, and he loomed over her, but she didn't feel threatened. *It's going to turn out all right*, she thought.

She'd no sooner thought this than the door to the apartment burst open.

Something exploded, and a bright flash blinded her. Through the smoke and the chaos, she glimpsed police officers in helmets and bulletproof vests, assault rifles at their shoulders, streaming into the apartment.

"Everyone down! Down! Down!" they screamed. One of them reached Sylvie and nearly threw her onto the floor.

"Got him!" she heard someone shouting nearby. She recognized Richard Carlan's voice.

Chapter 41

Even now, Terrill could have escaped. There was live flesh and blood all around him. While the officer who stood above him detached the handcuffs from his belt, Terrill had more than enough time to bring him down.

Swipe at his legs, cutting into them; the man's neck would hit the ground just so, and Terrill would lean over and bite. The blood would course through his veins, and his supernatural strength and speed would return.

Even now, Terrill was tempted.

As the handcuffs were put on him, he looked over a few feet to see Sylvie also on the ground, and, seeing the shocked look in her face, he suddenly realized the implications of his situation. It was broad daylight. When the cops dragged him outside, Terrill would have no cover.

It would be his end. At last. As it should be.

Even now, he could have leaped upon the police officers; with their necks exposed, it would be a simple thing to bring them down. Then all the bullets and blows they could inflict on him would come to nothing. He'd kill and kill, and feed, and stay in the basement until nightfall.

But he let the cops lift him to his feet and push him toward the door.

Perry and Grime were on the floor also. He heard Grime clearly. "NO!" the man was shouting. "You'll kill him! He's a vampire!"

Even if the cops had understood his mangled words, they wouldn't have believed him. They would have laughed.

Perry was the least shocked. He'd already understood the implications—and he'd already understood Terrill's decision to do nothing. He nodded to Terrill, as if wishing him well and saying goodbye.

One cop seemed particularly happy to see him. "I got you, you bastard. Me… Richard Carlan. You hear that, Jamie?" he shouted. He was looking toward the sky. "I got him for you!"

The cops hauled Terrill to the stairs. They stood in the shadow of the stairwell while a police car was brought around, and it gave Terrill a few more moments of existence. A few moments seemed so important, after an almost eternal life. Years had passed that he valued less than those moments.

But this was good. He should have given up years ago. He'd reveled in the vampire life for centuries, but after Mary, it had all seemed pointless. Perhaps his change in attitude had come with age. Michael the Maker had seemed equally conflicted, though Terrill hadn't understood it at the time.

Perhaps the day had come when Michael, too, had decided he wouldn't kill to save himself. Perhaps somewhere in a distant, unnoticed, superstitious hamlet in Europe, he had met his end. Unnoticed. Unmourned. Just like Terrill would be.

"I forgive you, Terrill," he heard Sylvie call out, and it was as if a benediction had been bestowed. He turned his eyes to the light, and he wasn't afraid.

They walked him up the steps, and the first tingling of sunlight landed on his head, pushing down into his hair. *Get it over with!* he thought. He turned his face to the sun.

It was painful, as if his skin was being stripped away. He was blinded. His hearing narrowed to the sound of his labored breathing.

But a minute passed, and then another. He didn't burst into flame, and the pain was starting to recede.

"Jesus, look at this guy!" one of the cops said. "That's the worst sunburn I've ever seen."

"Oh, yes. The bum's life," one of the others said, laughing. "All sunshine and roses."

Terrill stopped thinking about them. He was breathing the daytime air, and it smelled different; he was looking at his surroundings in daylight, feeling the sun on his skin, for the first time since he'd been Turned. It was all different. There was a kind of dull glow, a softening and suffusing of everything around him. The hardened cops seemed like friends, the bright sky like Heaven.

Terrill felt the pain of the handcuffs, the hard metal biting into his flesh. It didn't heal; it wouldn't heal except with time.

And then it hit him. If one of the cops pulled out a gun and shot him in the heart, he'd die.

He was human. Mortal. God had forgiven him.

His eyes filled with tears, and his human blood and human flesh were flooded with joy.

It was a fair trade: God's grace for mortality.

He laughed.

The two cops on either side of him looked at each other in disbelief. Then one of them punched Terrill in the stomach.

"It ain't funny, you murdering creep."

* * *

It was everything Carlan had envisioned. His fellow cops lined the hallway and filled the squad room, clapping and cheering. The only scowling face was that of Brosterhouse, the big hulk in the corner. Even that felt good.

The prisoner was strangely passive. He looked blissed-out or something. Maybe he was on drugs. He was a coward, that was for certain. He hadn't put up the slightest resistance.

The only thing missing from his triumph was Sylvie.

The two bums had been arrested on suspicion of aiding and abetting a fugitive, but he'd convinced the other cops to let Sylvie go. "She was here on a mission of mercy," he'd said. "She's got nothing to do with it."

Not that Sylvie had seemed very grateful. She wouldn't look at him. Instead, her eyes had followed the prisoner. The man who had murdered her sister.

Carlan shook his head. It was some religious impulse, he supposed. He couldn't understand it. He was having second and third thoughts about Sylvie. She was a little too strange. Jamie had seemed grounded in comparison.

Hey, with this triumph, he'd be set for dates for the next year or two. There were some good-looking lady cops who were looking at him pretty admiringly right now.

He booked the prisoner. The man was a basket case: quiet, malleable, probably totally psychotic. He'd seen a look in Terrill's eyes as they were taking him down that had alarmed him. And then it was gone, replaced by this zombie. As he pushed the guy into his cell, he gave him one last kick in the ass.

Then he returned to the break room and the hosannas of his fellow cops.

* * *

Father Harry didn't sleep, and he barely ate, but he'd never had so much energy.

God was in his Heaven.

Even the logical side of his brain was on board. How could it not be? He'd seen real evidence of real evil. He'd seen how his prayer, which he had pulled out of some deep recess of his brain, had hit the vampire like a physical object. He'd seen the sacred earth of the church remain inviolate. He'd seen how the crucifix had burned the flesh of the vampire.

If there was evil, there was holiness.

He dove into the liturgy, looking for prayers to cast out demons, and he memorized them. These chants had always seemed like vestigial remnants of the medieval church, ridiculous and superstitious and irrational, with no more weight than a modern fantasy book.

Now they seemed like battle plans.

The fight wasn't over, he sensed. The vampires would return. And even if they didn't, he now saw that he needed to be prepared. He needed to defend his flock.

He regretted turning Terrill in to the police. The vampire had come to him for help, to confess, and to change. Father Harry had turned him away. Worse, he had betrayed him to the civil authorities.

Father Harry was in full vestments. He'd searched the church for the biggest crucifix he could find. There was one on the wall, a big thing that he'd always been a little embarrassed by. Now he took it down, removed it from the frame that encased it, and put it on a chain around his neck. The weight felt comforting.

He'd be ready for the nighttime.

In the meantime, after he was sure that all the homeless in his care had been taken care of, the wounded taken to the hospital, the others coddled and fed, he decided that he'd go visit Terrill in jail and ask for his forgiveness.

He'd give the man an opportunity to confess, to shed his evil past. Father Harry would be the first priest in a thousand years to turn a vampire from evil. So what if he hadn't even believed in vampires until the night before?

Father Harry looked around the kitchen. There was a clear, empty water bottle on the counter. He rinsed it out, then went to the vestibule, filled it with holy water, and slipped it into his pocket. He'd never be unprepared for evil again.

He bustled off to the jail, singing a hymn to himself.

Chapter 42

Brosterhouse rolled his eyes at the small-town triumphalism of it all. It was like a football player doing a victory dance after a three-yard gain. Solving murders should be treated like it was just part of the job. Apparently, that was not the case in Bend.

He made his way through the cheering crowd to Captain Anderson's office. The older cop wasn't joining in the celebration, he noticed. He closed the door and sat down.

"What are you going to do about it?" Brosterhouse asked.

"Do about what?" Anderson didn't look like he'd slept. He was a couple of years away from retirement, Brosterhouse realized with sudden insight; he didn't want to rock the boat.

"About this phony arrest!" Brosterhouse raised his voice, and Anderson frowned.

"Phony? The guy ran; he was hiding. He was guilty of something."

"Except we now know that the evidence that was used to make the original arrest was planted."

"Do we know that?" Anderson swung his chair around and faced Brosterhouse squarely. "Look, detective. I understand your concern. But for some reason I'll never understand, Carlan is popular around here."

"So he's allowed to make a false arrest?"

"No, of course not. I'm just saying, we'll let a day or two pass, and then quietly release this Terrill fellow. Let them have their little party."

"For God's sake, the real murderer is out there being cheered while an innocent man sits in jail!"

Anderson sat back with a sigh. "Look, in a day or two, I can do something about Terrill. Meanwhile, the DA still wants another piece of evidence before he's willing to do anything about Carlan."

There was a knock at the door. Cam Patterson pushed it open a few inches and stuck his head in. He frowned when he saw Brosterhouse, then decided to ignore him.

"Sylvie Hardaway is outside. She says she has information about her sister's murder."

"Show her in."

Sylvie Hardaway was a beautiful girl, Brosterhouse thought. *No,* he corrected himself after looking into her serious eyes. *A beautiful* woman.

"There is something you need to know," she said, without preamble. "Richard Carlan made a porn video of my sister. He posted it on Girlfriend Hanky Panky."

Anderson stared at her with his mouth open for a moment. Then he swung toward his computer on the other side of the desk. He turned it on and fiddled with it as if he wasn't familiar with it. "I can do Google at least," he muttered. Within seconds, he had the site up. "I hope my computer doesn't get sick from this."

Brosterhouse stood up and leaned over the desk. There it was, in all its sick glory.

"How do we know that's Carlan?" Anderson said, looking away in disgust.

"Of course it is. He's got the same spare tire around the middle, and check it out—there's a birthmark on his thigh."

"I don't know," Anderson said. "Asking him to show his parts is really pushing it."

Brosterhouse threw up his hands. But Sylvie wasn't done.

"He's been harassing me," she said. "He won't leave me alone; he's ingratiated himself with my parents so he's always hanging around. I intend to go for a restraining order tomorrow."

That seemed to be the final straw for Captain Anderson. Apparently sexual harassment was his trigger.

"Arrest Richard Carlan," he said. "I'll clear it with the DA. We'll drop the charges for this Mr. Terrill and the other two vagrants."

* * *

Brosterhouse found Carlan drinking coffee with a couple pals. He had a victorious smirk on his face when the Portland detective walked up to him.

"Richard Carlan, you're under arrest."

"What! What for?" Carlan turned pale. He had that guilty look that Brosterhouse recognized from a thousand arrests, the look that said "They finally found me out."

Brosterhouse found himself spouting off charges, some of which he knew wouldn't stick, but he'd ask for forgiveness later. Meanwhile, the list of felonies was very satisfying. "Tampering with evidence. False arrest. Sexual harassment. And the murder of Jamie Lee Howe."

"What the...?" The dirty cop had winced at each of the first three charges, but seemed totally mystified by the last accusation. Unless Brosterhouse was mistaken, the man didn't think he was guilty of murder.

It didn't matter. Murderers often convinced themselves that it hadn't really been murder. Sometimes they maintained their innocence for so long that they started to believe it themselves.

Perhaps the evidence wouldn't convict Carlan, but his career was done. The lesser charges were enough to get him booted off the force, at the very least.

* * *

The parade was reversed. The squad room fell silent as Brosterhouse led Carlan, handcuffed, through the crowded space.

To fill the silence, he said, "You have the right to remain silent. Anything you say or do may be used against you in a court of law. You have the right to consult an attorney before speaking to the police..."

The words echoed through the room like a prayer.

Chapter 43

The cops put Perry and Grime in the cell next to Terrill. "I'm sure they'll let you go," he said. "As soon as I tell them you didn't know…"

"Never mind about us!" Perry interrupted. "We'll get a couple of free meals out of it, and I always try to get a dental checkup. But what about you, Terrill? You did it! You're human!"

Somehow, hearing Perry say it and Grime agree with a grunt was confirmation that it had really happened. Just being alive should have been proof, but the walk through the sunlight seemed like a dream to Terrill now. But he could feel it. He was mortal. Each minute that passed was a minute closer to his death, but he didn't care.

How ironic that he'd spend the rest of his human life imprisoned. For some reason, the prospect didn't faze him. It was a prison of the flesh, after all, not of the spirit.

As if in answer to that thought, the door at the end of the corridor opened and Father Harry Donovan was ushered in by one of the guards.

"Stay back from the bars," the guard warned.

Father Harry nodded his head solemnly, and then, the minute the guard left, he was sticking his hands through the bars, shaking hands with Perry and Grime, and then Terrill.

The priest stared at Terrill as if he was a revelation. "I still can't believe it. Are you real? Were those really vampires?"

"Yes," Terrill said. "There are such things as vampires. I was one of them. As to whether I am one now, I'm still not sure myself."

"…e's …eal," Grime said firmly.

Father Harry and Terrill laughed.

Once the laughter died down, the priest seemed a little uncomfortable. "I, uh… I'm sorry," he said, finally. "I turned you in."

Terrill shrugged. "You had to."

"No… you tried to confess to me, but I was more worried about a little stolen meat than I was about really listening. Please forgive me for that. I should have taken your words in confidence."

"I am not Catholic," Terrill said. "I'm not sure I was even all that religious, until this afternoon."

Father Harry laughed. "Me neither." He hesitated, then said, "If you're willing, I'd like to listen to your confession now."

"Father, it would take your whole lifetime to hear all my sins. I've got hundreds of years of them."

The priest looked shocked, as if he understood, for the first time, the extent of Terrill's crimes. "How about we do a general amnesty, so to speak," he said. "I'll absolve you as best I can."

"I ask forgiveness, of course," Terrill said. "But you can't grant me that. Only God can."

"I am God's rep—" Father Harry started to say.

Then the doorway at the end of the hallway opened again. "I don't know if I should," the guard was saying.

"They're going to be released anyway," Sylvie said. "What difference does it make?"

The guard looked at Terrill with suspicion, but it appeared that what Sylvie was saying was true, because he nodded reluctantly.

Sylvie came toward them with a smile and was greeted by Grime and Perry as if she was their long-lost girlfriend. Terrill smiled shyly.

"They've arrested Richard Carlan for the murder of my sister," she said.

Everyone else was delighted, but Terrill froze. That wasn't right. As bad as this Richard Carlan was, he hadn't killed Jamie. "I can't let him take the fall for that," he said, breaking through the sounds of celebration.

"You must!" Sylvie exclaimed. "It was Richard who drove her away from here. As far as I'm concerned, he's guilty, guiltier than you."

"I killed her, Sylvie. I killed your sister."

"No you didn't," Perry said. "A vampire killed her, that's what I heard. Sucked her blood right out of her. Are you a vampire, Terrill?"

Terrill wasn't going to have any of that. He'd spent too many years making excuses for his actions, unwilling to pay for them. How could he start his life as a mortal with a lie?

"Can my sister be saved?" Sylvie asked.

"I think perhaps, given enough time," he answered. Best not to tell her that with Michael and him, it had taken centuries. He thought, perhaps, that Horsham had been nearing that point—until Terrill had taken away all hope by Turning Mary.

He looked around at the bare walls, at his future. He deserved this fate, and he would accept it. He had so many crimes and sins to pay for.

* * *

The door to the jail opened one more time, and this time it was Richard Carlan who was led in in handcuffs. A large, bald-headed cop was escorting him. He glanced curiously at the group by the bars. "Having a party?" he asked.

Richard glared at them all, but the sight of Sylvie enraged him. "You bitch!" he screamed. "You told them, didn't you?"

"Told them what?" she asked mildly.

Carlan had enough self-possession left to realize he was on the verge of incriminating himself. "I'll get you for this!" he screamed. "You lying, scheming bitch!"

"I'd say that is confirmation of your harassment charge, Ms. Hardaway." Brosterhouse looked toward the guard at the door. "You heard that, Simmons?"

"Yes, sir. Sounded like a threat."

Carlan sputtered and seethed, but didn't say anything more. They took him to the last cell, where they left him. From the sound of it, he was throwing things around in there, shouting incoherently.

"I still have to confess," Terrill said.

"Oh, for goodness' sake!" Perry exclaimed. "What are you, a saint now? From vampire to saint in one day?"

Brosterhouse came back down the corridor after slamming the door on Richard Carlan. He looked satisfied, like a man who had done his job. He started to walk by them with a nod, then stopped.

The big cop stared at Terrill. He seemed to be examining him, looking for something. Then he said, "We'll be letting you go this afternoon. You may have to come back and answer some questions about why you fled, but they can't keep you in here for fleeing from a crime you didn't commit."

Now is the time to confess, Terrill thought, *if I really mean to atone for my crimes.* "I'm the one wh—" he started to say, but Sylvie interrupted, giving him a warning glance.

"When can they leave?" she asked Brosterhouse.

"Oh, it'll be a few hours. Police officers don't like to admit when they make mistakes, so they'll be dragging their feet through the whole process. But don't worry. You'll be out of here around nightfall."

Terrill had been ready to speak, Sylvie or no Sylvie, but the word "nightfall" brought him up short. Horsham was still out there, still looking for him. He knew who Terrill's friends were now, and he was unlikely to show them mercy simply because Terrill was in jail. Indeed, he might decide to wreak vengeance on those he could reach instead of the real target of his anger.

Night was falling, and these humans were in great danger. *We humans,* Terrill corrected himself. *We are in great danger.* He'd have to confess later, if he was still alive, which he doubted would be the case.

Perhaps it was only right that Horsham exact his final revenge. For Mary's sake.

He let Brosterhouse walk away.

Chapter 44

Horsham awoke as the sun dimmed. He was fully alert, as if he was being hunted, which perhaps he was. He hadn't survived for so long by ignoring those kinds of instincts.

Jamie was draped across him. He pushed her away. Had they had sex last night? After the abysmal failure at the church? He remembered feeling so angry about her disobeying him that he had fondled her neck and began to tighten his grip, ready to rip her head off.

Now he remembered. It had turned her on. She had snuggled up to him, wanting sex, like she had every night, all night. She was insatiable. Her new-found powers of endurance and energy were draining him. But he hadn't resisted. It had been a very long time since he'd had such a willing and eager partner.

It occurred to him that although he'd broken just about every rule on this trip, he hadn't broken the first and most important one. He hadn't trusted a human. Because of that, he might still make it out of this foul town. If he left now... tonight. He should take the baby vampire and run, come back another day, wait for Terrill to make another mistake.

Until last night, Horsham hadn't left a human alive who could recognize him. They thought they had a serial killer in town, one who was a rather spectacular cannibal. It was making the national news, but they couldn't connect any of it to him.

Until last night. That priest had been an unexpected obstacle. It was rare to run across a priest who knew the warding prayers anymore. Even more strange, it was as if, even as he bent down to kill the man, the priest's faith had grown stronger, making Horsham hesitate for a moment, just long enough for that dirty human to come out of nowhere and throw holy water on him.

How had he known to do that? It was almost as if they had been prepared for him. The only way that could have happened was if Terrill had told them what he was—thus breaking Rule 1.

Horsham turned on the police scanner, and the stream of chatter was full of the recent spate of brutal murders. But it was the little comment at the end of one of the messages that caught his attention: *"At least we caught that murdering bastard that Carlan was after. The one who killed his girlfriend in Portland."*

Horsham was enraged. He paced the room in full vampire form; he ran his claws into the walls, tearing out chunks of plaster. He grabbed a chair and threw it across the room, breaking the mirror. That was so satisfying that he broke the rest of the mirrors. Damn the useless things!

He wanted to leave the motel, fall upon the first humans he saw, and devour them in full view of everyone. He wanted to take on the entire town, destroy it, down to the last woman and child.

All this commotion woke Jamie up and she came to him, naked, wanting to drape herself on him, as if sex would calm him down. He threw her across the room, and she crashed against the wall.

"Don't ever do that again," she said in a guttural voice.

He paid no attention to her. He should've been happy, it occurred to him. Under the control of humans, Terrill would be forced into the sunlight sooner or later. He was doomed. Unless—and this was a delicious possibility—Terrill was forced to feed. Unless Terrill gave in to his real nature.

Horsham would like that. It wouldn't save Terrill, but it would be a last humiliation, proof that Terrill couldn't escape his vampire nature no matter how hard he tried. A final little relapse that would make his death all the more painful.

But Terrill was behind bars, with an entire police department surrounding him.

Take on the whole town? Horsham thought. *Why not? Let them try to stop me!*

Screw the Rules of Vampire. They were sniveling, cowardly precepts that been created by a renegade and a traitor. They were as worthless as he was. Without Michael and Terrill, Horsham would be the oldest vampire. The others would do as he said. No more hiding in the shadows. No more pretending to be human. They would become fully vampire and dare the humans to defeat them!

He had twelve hours before dawn came. Let them try to stop him. They'd shoot him, no doubt. They might try to restrain him with pepper spray or electric shocks. None of it would do any good. They wouldn't know what they were up against. They'd be helpless. There weren't a lot of crosses or much holy water in a police station.

He turned to Jamie. She was looking at him with a defiant but uncertain expression. There was no way the humans could stop two vampires. They'd break into the jail, take care of Terrill once and for all, and kill any human who tried to stop them; hell, kill any human who even *saw* them.

Horsham had never felt so strong, so certain.

He threw open the door and marched out into the night. Jamie scrambled to keep up, throwing on clothes as she ran, astonishing the night clerk with a glimpse of her lingerie.

* * *

Horsham started at the front entrance, killing the duty clerk before the woman even knew he was there. He worked his way through the rooms. It wasn't until he got to the second floor that a human finally reacted, shooting him twice. Both bullets would have missed the vital organs of a human. They didn't slow Horsham in the slightest. He took special satisfaction in tearing the limbs off the man and leaving him still living—briefly—on the floor.

Until then, Jamie hadn't had to do a thing. Horsham had directed her to walk in front of him, with her revealing clothes and her sexy stride, as it was confusing to the poor humans.

But after the sound of the first two shots, more humans started producing more weapons, and soon Horsham was being sprayed with bullets. But each time, he fed on the attacker, and whatever damage had been done was instantly healed. Jamie was similarly engaged. He could tell she was reluctant at first, but the more she fed, the more bloodlust she felt. She was going to be a real vampire by the end of the night.

He continued upward. He'd glanced at the directory on the ground floor, and it showed that the jail cells were on the third floor. He took his time, making sure none of the humans got past him. He could almost feel Terrill's presence. At last, he would confront his old friend. His old enemy. The murderer of the one human Horsham had ever loved.

Chapter 45

It had taken all afternoon and into the evening before Terrill was finally released.

Strangely, they let him—the murder suspect—go before they released the two men who had simply tried to hide him. Terrill and Sylvie waited for Perry and Grime together, and Father Harry joined them. They couldn't say much with the police listening, but they had an interesting conversation about religion, and encoded in that terminology, they talked about themselves.

"Your sister is new to… these sins," Terrill said to Sylvie. "It will take a long time before she begins to really think about the meaning of it all."

"How long?"

Centuries? Terrill thought. What he said aloud was, "The good news is, I don't believe I am the only… person like me… who has turned against the darkness. There was another like me. Like Horsham was becoming, before… Anyway, it is possible, but it will take a long time."

"Jamie was a good soul," Father Harry said. "Maybe that will help."

Terrill tried to remember his human self. Had he been good? Had he been bad? What he remembered most was being hungry and tired and beaten down, by both his family and life itself. Maybe Jamie would work her way through to the light faster than he had. "It's possible."

Perry and Grime were being led out of the cellblock, smiling. The others stood up to greet them.

That was when they heard the first two shots.

* * *

Most of the cops ran for the stairwell, toward the shooting. Only the jailer remained, and the big cop from Portland, Brosterhouse, who came into the room a couple of seconds later.

"What the hell is that?" he asked, drawing his gun.

Terrill stared him in the eyes. "Detective Brosterhouse. Will you listen to me for a moment? What I have to say may seem very strange to you, but I assure you it's true. Your gun won't be of any use."

At first the big man frowned, and then he lowered his gun and put it back into its holster. "What do we do?"

Terrill looked about the room. It was all metal, plastic, and plaster: no wood to be seen. "We need wood," he said. "To make stakes."

Brosterhouse laughed. *Well, it was worth a try,* Terrill thought.

Father Harry looked up into the face of the detective. He looked like a child next to the huge man. He was in full vestments, a giant crucifix around his neck. "You must believe him, detective. I have seen it. I believe it."

Brosterhouse didn't move. He didn't go running off; he didn't pull out his gun again. He stood there like a massive statue for a few moments. Then he nodded once. "You know, if it wasn't for something that happened to me in Portland, I'd think you were crazy," he said. "I believe the only wood in this whole station is that old beat-up desk they gave their unwanted visitor. In my office..." he turned and lumbered away, and the others followed him.

In the background, it sounded like a war had broken out. There were hundreds of shots from downstairs; an impossible number. The jailer was turning whiter and whiter, and rather than running down the stairs to join the other cops, he followed the little band. There was a long, narrow corridor on the other side of the squad room, and at the very end, there was a tiny little office, not much bigger than a broom closet.

"Welcome to Siberia," Brosterhouse said.

They squeezed into the little room and slammed the door shut. There was no lock. It was a supply closet; why would there be? Terrill pushed the filing cabinet against the door. It wouldn't do much good, but it might buy them a few seconds. They were packed inside almost on top of each other.

"Listen to me, everyone," Terrill said. "The vampire attacking us is probably the most dangerous vampire who has ever existed. He wants me, but that won't save you. He won't leave anyone alive. First Rule of Vampire: Never trust humans."

"How do we stop him?" Brosterhouse asked.

"A stake in the heart, as you've seen in every movie. But even that won't do it unless it remains there for several seconds. He can remove it and regenerate immediately if he has blood to drink. Almost nothing you can do will kill him, simply because you are all full of the blood he needs."

"Then what's the use?" the jailer exclaimed.

"We must weaken him by any means possible. We must hold him down and stake him. And he must not be allowed to remove the stake."

Brosterhouse pulled out his gun. "I shot him right between the eyes. It seemed to scare him off."

"Only because he was surprised and unprepared. Your gun is of no real use. But by all means, put a couple of bullets in his head."

Terrill examined the desk. It was solid oak, not very splinterable, but the drawers seemed to be made of white pine, and were thinner. He pulled out a drawer and dropped the contents onto the floor: Chapstick, a few sticks of stale gum, and a paperback novel. He handed the empty drawer to Perry.

"You and Grime start making stakes. As many as you can. Even if it doesn't hit his heart, the wood will weaken him a little." *A very little*, he thought, but he smiled encouragingly. Perry threw the drawer onto the floor and started stomping on it.

Father Harry looked resolute. He was holding out a water bottle. "I came prepared. Holy water drove him off last time."

"No, the dawn drove him off last time," Terrill corrected him. "The holy water only kept him at bay long enough for daylight to arrive. But it might delay him a few moments. Try to throw it into his eyes. It might blind him for a time."

Grime held up two pieces of shattered wood in the shape of a cross. He looked questioningly at Terrill.

"Stakes are better. A cross is merely uncomfortable, an inconvenience, something to avoid if possible. But it won't stop him."

Father Harry fingered his giant crucifix doubtfully.

"Now, your cross might do some good," Terrill said. "It's covered with silver, and it comes from a church. It might keep the monster away for a few moments."

Grime and Perry were busy breaking up more drawers. Terrill grabbed one of the pieces that tapered to a point. He went to the door and started moving the filing cabinet out of the way.

"What are you doing?" several voices exclaimed at once.

Terrill turned to Sylvie. "I'm sorry I brought this to your town. I never would have come if I'd known."

"Stay," she said.

"He wants me. Maybe once he's killed me, he'll leave the rest of you alone. Maybe bullets to the head, holy water, inconvenient crosses, and the sight of wooden stakes will be enough to dissuade him. But don't count on it."

Terrill went into the narrow hallway and closed the door firmly behind him.

It occurred to him, as he walked toward the sound of violence, that none of the war preparations had affected in him the least. He hadn't felt discomfited by the closeness of the holy water; the crosses hadn't made him feel queasy.

Ordinarily, he might have been pleased. But just now, he wished he had some of his old strength and quickness back.

It was a temptation. He sensed that, even now, it wasn't too late to turn back. A little blood, a little flesh, and he would start to reverse his progress.

But it didn't matter. Horsham was much stronger than him; he had been for a long time. It was perhaps fortunate for Terrill's soul that he knew this, that he wasn't tempted to fight vampire to vampire to save his friends.

He entered the big room just as bloody, savage-looking Horsham came in, followed by a beautiful and vicious-looking female vampire. Jamie. Looking as though she was enjoying every minute of it.

It was the sight of her savage beauty that gave Terrill peace. He deserved whatever happened to him. He was ready.

Chapter 46

Humans are so easy to kill! Jamie thought. Their bullets would hurt for a moment, and then she'd bite into the nearest flesh, taste the blood running down her throat, and all pain would be replaced by pleasure. She tore the humans apart as if they were meat puppets.

There's a soul inside each of these pieces of meat, someone in the back of her mind said. But the voice was dim and distant, and irrelevant to her current existence. She found she didn't really care.

Horsham seemed to be taking even greater pleasure in feeding. It was cathartic for him, a way to take out his anger and his pain. She watched him kill and maim with abandon. She followed his example, making sure that none of these cops would come back as vampires. She found she was jealous of her new abilities, jealous of Horsham's time—she didn't want to share this existence with anyone or anything.

They reached the third floor and entered, expecting to be confronted by whatever force of cops was left. Perhaps a hail of bullets. Some kind of organized resistance.

The room was empty but for one tall, frail-looking man at the far end. He stood motionless, his eyes fixed on the doorway as if he'd been expected them. He didn't seem frightened. He didn't seem dangerous. With a shock, Jamie realized it was the vampire who had Turned her—Terrill. Except... he wasn't a vampire.

How was that possible? According to Horsham, once a vampire, always a vampire. She'd adapted to this new life with the knowledge that there was no going back. Not that she wanted to. She searched her feelings for this man. She had a memory of liking him, thinking he was a nice guy, but no more than that.

She felt nothing toward her Maker.

So this was the great Terrill, the object of Horsham's obsession? He didn't look like he could put up much of fight.

"I'm going to look for Richard," she said.

"No. Stay here," Horsham ordered.

"Why? You can have him all to yourself. I don't care. I want Richard Carlan dead."

"I told you to stay here!" Horsham screamed. He backhanded her. For some reason, it hurt. She had been shot and bludgeoned by dozens of cops, and she'd been able to shrug it off, but one blow from her Mentor, and she was sent reeling.

She should have been cowed, but instead some of her old memories came back: memories of the Jamie who had been a helpless victim, unable to get away from the men who abused her. Well, she wasn't that Jamie anymore.

"I told you," she hissed. "Never strike me." She turned and left without waiting for Horsham's reaction. Richard Carlan was near. She could smell him.

* * *

Jamie found the back corridor to the jail cells.

Luckily for Richard, she didn't feel like playing anymore. She was going to kill him and be done.

He was at the bars of the cell, obviously alarmed by the sound of gunshots. It must have seemed to him that an army was storming the police station.

It occurred to her that Richard had no idea what was going on. With that thought, she retracted her claws and fangs. She wiped the blood off her face and put on what she thought was a pleasant smile.

From Richard's reaction, the smile was actually anything but pleasant. He didn't recognize her at first. She was simply a blood-drenched woman in skimpy clothing. She stood there with her grimace of a smile until realization dawned on his face.

"Ja... Jamie?" he stuttered.

"Hi, Richard. Miss me?"

He fell back from the bars as her face transformed into that of a vampire, the mouth and jaws pushed outward as if in search of blood. Her fingers turned into claws, her nails into talons, curling to razor-sharp points.

"Get away from me!" he shouted. "You're dead. I saw your body!"

"No, Richard. I believe it's called 'undead,'" Jamie laughed. He was every bit as terrified as she had hoped. She realized that she'd been hoping for this chance for revenge since the moment she'd awoken in the morgue. No matter what happened from now on, she was satisfied.

From the suddenly crafty look in Richard's eyes, it occurred to him that he was safely behind bars. He couldn't get out, but she couldn't get in. He took on a stubborn look. He'd always been a man who got his way by denying what he wanted to deny.

She let him think that for a few moments. Then, with every ounce of vampire strength she possessed, she began to pull on the door. She'd fed on dozens of men and women in the past hour; her body was vibrating with power. The door began to screech and bend outward, and then it came off its hinges.

She tossed it aside. Her smile was now a genuine smile, and no doubt all the more frightening for it.

She stalked him into the corner, until he couldn't retreat any further. He tried to strike her. She could have let him, let him see that he couldn't hurt her. Instead, she reached out and grabbed his hand and squeezed. His bones liquefied, mixed with his flesh, and splattered onto the floor.

It was so satisfying that she did it to his other hand, then his arms and legs. He was screaming at first, she could hear it somewhere in the background, but she was focused on his eyes as he realized he was going to die.

Finally, she raised her claws, making sure that he was looking at them, and then lowered them slowly toward his heart. She dug in, centimeter by centimeter, taking her time, his hoarse final breaths in her ears, until the tip of her sharp talons reached his beating heart. She snipped each of the connecting arteries, one by one.

The light faded slowly from his eyes, then blinked out.

Jamie sucked his blood for a moment, as if by habit, but her memories of him made it taste sour.

She sighed and dropped him.

She looked down at Richard's body. She'd drunk some of his blood, but she was damned—double damned—if she'd eat him too. But she couldn't risk the slightest chance that he would come back.

She reached down and twisted his head, first in one direction with a solid crack, breaking the spine, then back the other way, tearing the muscles and ligaments, and finally back again, peeling the head off along with the skin of the upper back.

She threw the head into the corner. It bounced off the toilet and rolled for a couple of feet.

* * *

After Jamie left, Horsham had eyes only for Terrill.

Terrill stood quietly, waiting for the inevitable. Horsham looked puzzled. The object of his obsessive searching for decades was nothing but a tired, pale man. He walked slowly toward Terrill.

"I imagined this would be a battle for the ages," Horsham said, shaking his head in dismay. "That vampires would talk about it for centuries. I even brought a witness, though she seems to have inconveniently run off."

Terrill waited until Horsham was standing in front of him. He had a wooden stake up his sleeve. He let it slip into his palm and whipped it around as fast as he could manage, directly toward Horsham's heart.

The vampire easily snatched the stake from Terrill's hand, faster than human eyes could perceive.

"How pathetic," Horsham said. "You really have become human. How is this possible?"

"I asked for forgiveness," Terrill said.

"As you should, at least from me. But why become human? Why give up this glorious existence?"

Terrill shook his head. "Look at yourself. Covered in blood and gore. Smelling like a charnel house. Hiding at night, never seeing the light of day. You find that glorious?"

"How quickly you forget. Humans and their short lives and short memories." He stared down at Terrill. *When did he become so much taller than me?* Terrill wondered.

Horsham grimaced in disgust. "This doesn't even feel satisfying."

Nor should it, Terrill thought. But he said nothing.

"Come on, Terrill. Is that it? Is that all the struggle you're going to put up?"

"I'm sorry for what happened to Mary," Terrill said.

"'What happened to?' Something just 'happened?'"

"You're right. Even now, I try to avoid responsibility. I'm sorry for what I did to Mary. I'm sorry for killing her."

"People think that vampires have no heart. But they're wrong. Mary was my heart."

"I'm sorry," Terrill repeated. "I should have understood that. I shouldn't have killed her."

"No, you did something much worse than kill her. You Turned her! Mary could never have been a vampire. She could never have followed your precious Rules. You took a saint and damned her."

"You have to believe that she wasn't damned, Horsham. She never became one of us. She never killed. She gave herself into God's hands."

Horsham paused for a moment, looking thoughtful. Then he shook his head. "It doesn't matter. She's gone, and you took her from me."

"I accept the consequences," Terrill said. "But leave my friends alone. None of this is their fault."

Horsham laughed, sounding delighted. "That's what will make this worthwhile. Killing you right now wouldn't mean a thing. But killing you *after* I have tortured your friends—that will make it all so much better."

"Please, Horsham."

"And you know what makes it even more gratifying? You didn't even *have* any friends until a few days ago, and now you have a whole clutch of them!'

"I didn't have any friends because I was vampire. It was only when I became human that anyone wanted to be friends with me. Horsham. I know you had begun to feel this way also—that you were starting to doubt—before I took Mary from you. Please. For Mary's sake. It isn't too late."

"For Mary's sake?" Horsham's voice rose into a roar. "FOR MARY'S SAKE?"

He picked Terrill up as if he was a dried leaf and slammed him to the floor. Then he reached down and snapped one of Terrill's legs. The femur poked jaggedly through his trousers. The pain seemed to tear through every cell of his body. Terrill screamed and nearly passed out.

"Don't go anywhere while I go take care of your 'friends,'" Horsham sneered. "You should be able to hear their screaming from here. I'll tell you what: I'll bring back their heads so you can say goodbye." He sniffed the air. "I believe I smell them hiding, *that* way..." He walked over to the door to the corridor that led to Brosterhouse's office.

Terrill was in so much pain that he couldn't think. But something impelled him to start dragging himself after Horsham, inch by inch. He couldn't use his legs and had to pull himself with his hands and arms.

He heard the screaming of his friends before he'd crawled more than a few yards.

Chapter 47

No one in the little office had anything to say after Terrill left. The only sounds were the splintering of wood and the huffs of exertion from Grime as he smashed the drawers.

Sylvie had realized she couldn't stop Terrill from trying to protect them, though it was obvious there was little he could do. It was what he had become. For him to run, to hide behind his friends, would be to betray his very being. For him to avoid death would mean he was denying his humanness.

Brosterhouse sat in the chair behind the desk, gun in hand. Father Harry seemed almost happy to be confronted by real, concrete evil. He lifted the water bottle, and Sylvie could almost see an idea bloom behind his eyes. He went to the door and poured a little of the holy water along the bottom. Then he frowned and looked around, as if realizing how inadequate their defenses really were.

Sylvie walked over to the desk and picked up one of the stakes that Perry was laying out in a row. It wasn't much, but it was something.

The jailer had been watching all this from the corner. Now he moved toward the door, and started moving aside the filing cabinet. "There's a rear exit to this building. Who's with me?"

Everyone looked at him without reaction. "You people are crazy!" he exclaimed, and ran out the door. Only seconds later, they heard his scream, cut off in the middle of its crescendo. They stood stock-still as the door began to move.

And then the door flew wide open, and he was there. Brosterhouse stood and shot twice, but the vampire was already leaping through the air toward him, the biggest target in the room. Brosterhouse fell backward against the wall, and Sylvie heard a loud splat, as if his head had split open. He dropped to the floor with a thud.

Father Harry was spraying his water bottle on the vampire, squeezing and waving it back and forth. The vampire screamed and his hands and face began to smoke, but he didn't flee. Then the water was gone, and the priest was holding up his cross and chanting:

"Glorious Saint Michael, Prince of the Heavenly hosts, who fought with the Dragon, the Old Serpent, and cast him out of Heaven, I earnestly entreat you to assist me also, in the painful and dangerous conflict which I sustain against the same formidable foe. Be with me, O mighty Prince! That I may courageously fight and vanquish that proud spirit, whom you, by the Divine Power, gloriously overthrew..."

The vampire advanced on him, and retreated; advanced again, and again fell back. Then he picked Brosterhouse's gun up off the floor and shot Father Harry in the stomach.

While this was happening, both Grime and Perry had leaped toward the vampire, each of them with stakes in both hands. Grime's first stake missed, glancing off of the vampire's coat, but the second sank into the fiend's shoulder. Horsham grunted and smacked Grime across the face, and the man dropped where he stood.

Perry's first stake was headed directly for Horsham's heart, but the vampire turned in less than the blink of an eye, and Perry stumbled past him. The vampire snagged him, turned him around, and began to lower his fangs toward Perry's neck.

Then Horsham, who had been moving so fast that Sylvie could barely take it all in, stood still. There was a moment of silence.

A stake quivered in the vampire's heart, and Perry had a triumphant grin on his face. "Got you, bloodsucker!"

Horsham looked down and, seemingly without a care, plucked the stake from his chest and flung it aside. He struck Perry in the chest, and the homeless man stumbled backward, clutching his heart, and fell on his friend Grime, who was unconscious on the floor.

And then it was just Sylvie and the vampire.

She raised her cross and stake, knowing it was hopeless. She found herself praying out loud, not the martial prayers to ward off evil that Father Harry had been shouting, but comforting prayers about the deity she would soon meet.

Horsham was in no hurry. He seemed to understand that of all the humans, she was the one who mattered most to Terrill. Her pain, and her death, would hurt Terrill the most.

"I told you to leave Sylvie alone!" she heard someone scream. It sounded like her sister, but harsher, louder, and angrier than she'd ever heard Jamie sound.

Horsham turned his head slightly, and at that moment, Jamie wrapped her arms around his chest from behind. "Now, Sylvie! Stake him now!"

Sylvie plunged the stake into the vampire's heart. He seemed to levitate, carrying both Jamie and himself upward and backward. Jamie landed on her back with Horsham on top of her, but she held onto him. The stake stayed in his heart.

But he was thrashing, and it was clear that even mortally wounded, he was stronger than Jamie, and that he'd soon break loose.

Grime and Perry, who had been slowly recovering, exchanged a glance and then threw themselves onto the vampire's legs, holding them down. Sylvie jumped into the fight as well, adding her small strength to her sister's, pinioning the vampire's arms. She landed mere inches from his jaws, and she felt the splash of his drool and the heat of his breath.

But slowly, as their strength began to fade, so did the struggles of the vampire. He was getting hot, and now the humans were scrambling away. Jamie squirmed out from under her former Master, who was starting to glow the red and black of coals, and who was screaming an inhuman scream.

Horsham crumbled into glowing embers, and Perry, with a shout of triumph, kicked the blackening ash into the air.

As Sylvie moved back from the heat, she saw Terrill dragging himself into the room. Jamie was standing over him as if wondering what to do. Her sister took one last look back at Sylvie and smiled her old smile, her kind and wise smile. Then she was gone.

The fire sprinkler went off, raining cold water down on the dead and the living alike. The cloud of ash was washed to the floor, to mingle with the dirt and the dust.

Sylvie made her way to Terrill and nestled his head in her lap.

Together, we'll find a way to save Jamie, she thought.

After all, they had the rest of their lives ahead of them.

Terrill's story continues in *Rule of Vampire,*
the 2nd book from the Vampire Evolution Trilogy.

About the Author:

Duncan McGeary is the owner of the bookstore Pegasus Books of Bend, located in downtown Bend, Oregon. He is the author of the fantasy novels Star Axe, Snowcastles, and Icetowers, and the author of several horror novels, including Led to the Slaughter and the Vampire Evolution Trilogy. His wife Linda is also a writer; together they attend a writer's group in Oregon. Duncan has two children: Todd, an artist, and Toby, a chef.

Available from
Books of the Dead Press

Duncan McGeary - Death of an Immortal:
Vampire Evolution Trilogy #1

The most powerful and feared vampire disappeared at the height of his powers and passed into legend. Most vampires think he's dead. He is not dead. Terrill has gone into hiding to evade his bitter enemy's wrath, and has vowed never to kill another human. But one night his vampire nature reasserts itself, and he kills an innocent young woman.

Duncan McGeary - Rule of Vampire:
Vampire Evolution Trilogy #2

Jamie is on the run. Nobody taught her how to be a vampire; no one told her the Rules of Vampire. How was she supposed to know her limits? Now the vampire hunters want her dead, and the Council of Vampires is looking for her, too.

Duncan McGeary - Blood of Gold:
Vampire Evolution Trilogy #3

Terrill was the most ruthless of vampires, but over the long centuries of his existence he has evolved into a Golden Vampire, renouncing violence, able to walk among humans and in sunlight. What he didn't know—what no one knew—was that the evolution was directed by forces bigger than himself.

Duncan McGeary - Led to the Slaughter

Trapped in the Sierra Nevada without food, The Donner Party are led to the slaughter. After being manipulated into a string of bad decisions, the travelers, frozen and abandoned, are preyed upon by werewolves in their midst--the very people they thought were friends.

Justin Robinson - Undead On Arrival

Glen Novak is a dead man. Unfortunately for the scumbag who killed him, Novak will keep on cracking skulls until he finds the piece of trash that set him up, or is turned into a walking sack of rotten meat. With Undead On Arrival, Justin Robinson gives us a hard boiled zombie tale, and one of the most brutally compellingly examinations of the living dead you'll ever read.

TS Alan - The Romero Strain

New Yorkers are chased into the city's underground by a zombie horde. Along their subterranean journey, they gather survivors while traveling to Grand Central Terminal, searching for help. Their hopes quickly end when they discover Grand Central overrun with the undead, and come face to face with an adversary born from a lab deep below the city.

John F.D. Taff - Kill/Off

When David Benning is blackmailed by a shadowy organization known only as The Group, he's thrust into a world of guns, payoffs, and killing unknown, seemingly ordinary people. As he becomes more enmeshed, he begins to grasp The Group's true motives, and its secrets--secrets that must never be revealed. David can trust no one... not even the one person he has grown to love.

J.C. Michael - Discoredia

As the year draws to a close, a mysterious stranger makes a proposition to club owner Warren Charlton. It's a deal involving a brand-new drug called Pandemonium. The good news: the drug is free. The bad news: it comes at a heavy price, promising much but delivering far more. Euphoria and ecstasy. Death and depravity. All come together at Discoredia.

James Roy Daley - Authors & Publishers Must Die!

From the mouth of author/publisher James Roy Daley comes Authors and Publishers Must Die! No punches are pulled in this nonfiction title, which is filled to the rim with straightforward, practical advice for writers while exploring what it's like to be on the other side of the desk. A must read for every author.

Weston Kincade - A Life of Death 1 - 4

Homicide detective Alex Drummond is confronted with the past through his son's innocent question. Alex's tale of his troubled senior year unfolds revealing loss, drunken abuse, and mysterious visions of murder and demonic children.

Weston Kincade - A Life of Death 5 - 8

Alcohol claims another life close to home. Alex and Paige set out to discover the truth, but who would believe a troubled teenager who claims to have visions?

Weston Kincade - A Life of Death 9 - 12

Struggling to hold onto his suspicions of Irene Harris, Alex heads to the DC Metropolitan Police Department. There, his suspicions are finally put to rest, and Alex is forced to start his search again.

Julie Hutchings - Running Home

Death hovers around Ellie Morgan like the friend nobody wants. She doesn't belong in snow-swept Ossipee, New Hampshire, at a black tie party—but that is where she is, and where he is: Nicholas French, the man who mystifies her with a feeling of home she's been missing, and the impossible knowledge of her troubled soul.

John F.D. Taff - The Bell Witch

A historical horror novel/ghost story based on what is perhaps the most well-documented poltergeist case to occur in the United States. The Bell Witch is, at once, a historical novel, a ghost story, a horror story, and a love story all rolled into one.

Justin Robinson - Everyman

Ian Covey is a doppelganger. A mimic. A shapeshifter. He can replace anyone he wants by becoming a perfect copy; taking the victim's face, his home, his family. His life. No longer a man but a hungry void, Ian Covey is a monster. Virtue has a veil, a mask, and evil has a thousand faces.

James Roy Daley - Terror Town

Hardcore horror at its best: Killer on the warpath. Monsters on the street. Vampires in the night. Zombies on the hunt. Welcome to Terror Town. The place where no one is safe, nothing is sacred, all will die, all will suffer.

Mark Matthews - On the Lips of Children

Meet Macon. Tattoo artist. Athlete. Family man. He's planning to run a marathon, but the event becomes something terrible. Macon falls prey to a bizarre man and his wife who dwell in an underground drug-smuggling tunnel. They raise their twin children in a way Macon couldn't imagine: skinning victims for food and money. And Macon and his family are next.

Bracken MacLeod - Mountain Home

Lyn works at an isolated roadside diner. When a retired combat veteran stages an assault there, her world is turned upside down. Surviving the sniper's bullets is only the beginning of Lyn's nightmare. Navigating hostilities, she establishes herself as the disputed leader of a diverse group that is at odds with the situation. Will she--or anyone else--survive the attack?

Gary Brandner - The Howling

Karyn and Roy went to the peaceful California village of Drago to escape the savagery of the city. On the surface Drago appeared to be like most small rural towns. It was not. The village had an unsavory history. Unexplained disappearances, sudden deaths. People vanished, never to be found.

Gary Brandner - The Howling II

For Karyn, it was the howling. The howling that had heralded the nightmare in Drago… the nightmare that had joined her husband Roy to the she-wolf Marcia and should have ended forever with the fire. But it hadn't. Roy and Marcia were still alive, and deadly… and thirsty for the most horrifying vengeance imaginable…

Gary Brandner - The Howling III

They are man. And they are beast. Once again they stalk the night, eyes aflame, teeth flashing in vengeance. Malcolm is the young one. He must choose between the familiar way of the human and the seductive howling of the wolf. Those who share his blood want to make him one of them. Those who fear him want him dead.

James Roy Daley - Into Hell

Stephenie Page and her daughter Carrie drive down an empty highway. They stop at a gas station that has a restaurant attached to it. Carrie enters the building in need of a bathroom. When Stephenie steps inside, she discovers that the restaurant has become a slaughterhouse. There are dead bodies everywhere. The worst part, Carrie is suddenly missing.

James Roy Daley - The Dead Parade

Within the hour, James will witness the suicide of his closest friend, be responsible for countless murders, and become a fugitive from the police. In the shadow of his mind, a demon lurks. Bloodlust is a virus--it's infecting his logic. James has become a pawn in a game he does not understand, and only one thing is clear: survival is not an option.

Tonia Brown - Badass Zombie Road Trip

Jonah has seven days to find his best friend's soul, or lose his own, dragging a zombie across the country with a stripper who has an agenda of her own, while being pursued for a crime he didn't commit… and dealing with Satan. Two thousand miles. Seven days. Two souls. One zombie. Satan.

John F.D. Taff - Little Deaths

Named the #1 Horror Collection of 2012 by Horror Talk / Named Top 5 books of 2012 by AndyErupts

You think you've got bad dreams? Consider author John F.D. Taff's nightmares. Taff has the kind of nightmares no one really wants. But it's nightmares like these that give him plenty of ideas to explore; ideas that he's turned into the short stories he shares in his new collection.

Matt Hults - Husk

Mallory Wiess is a typical teenage girl... or so it seems. When she moves to rural Minnesota, she discovers her new home won't be as boring as she'd feared. Who is the dark figure watching her from across the street? And why has someone begun digging up graves in the ancient cemetery? In the end, one night will decide if the dead will rise.

Bill Howard - 10 Minutes From Home: Episodes 1 - 4

When a viral outbreak hits Toronto, Denny Collins and his best friend Thom Washington find themselves trapped over 100 km from Denny's home in a town called Pontypool, where his wife and daughter remain. As the streets begin to teem with violence, they must first find safety, then find a way out of the now deadly metropolis.

Bill Howard - 10 Minutes From Home: Episodes 5 - 8

The journey gets bloodier as the group runs into hordes of the infected in a suburban neighborhood. Thom must make some drastic decisions when the survivors encounter a military camp. But does the camp provide safety, or just another hurdle delaying Denny's expedition home?

Tim Lebbon - Berserk

The army had said it was a training accident. But why had the coffin they sent home been sealed? On a dark night, in a deserted field, Tom begins to unearth the mass grave where he hopes--and fears--that he will find his son's remains. Instead, he finds madness: corpses in chains and dead bodies that still move. And one little girl, dead and rotting, who promises to help Tom find what he's looking for...

Best New Zombie Tales - Volume One

Includes Amazing Fiction by: WHC Grand Master Award Winner Ray Garton / New York Times Best Seller Jonathan Maberry / Bram Stoker Award Winner Kealan Patrick Burke / Bram Stoker Award Nominee Jeff Strand / Micro Award Finalist Robert Swartwood / British Fantasy Awards Nominee Gary McMahon / Bram Stoker Award Winner Kim Paffenroth... and so much more.

Best New Zombie Tales - Volume Two

Includes Amazing Fiction by: Bram Stoker Award Winner David Niall Wilson / British Fantasy Award Nominee Rio Youers / Bram Stoker Award Nominee Nate Kenyon / Authorlink New Author Award Winner Tim Waggoner / George Turner Prize Nominee Narrelle M. Harris / Bram Stoker Award Winner John Everson / Pulitzer Prize, Bram Stoker Nominee Mort Castle... and so much more.

Best New Zombie Tales - Volume Three
Includes Amazing Fiction by: Anthony Award Winner Simon Wood / Bram Stoker Award Nominee Joe McKinney / New York Times Best-Selling Author Tim Lebbon / Arthur Ellis Award Winner Nancy Kilpatrick / British Fantasy Award Nominee Paul Kane / Bram Stoker Award Nominee Jeremy C. Shipp... and so much more.

Best New Werewolf Tales - Volume One
Includes Amazing Fiction by: New York Times Best Seller Jonathan Maberry / Bram Stoker Award Winner John Everson / Bram Stoker Award Nominee Michael Laimo / Aurora Award Nominee Douglas Smith / Bram Stoker Award Winner David Niall Wilson / Bram Stoker Award Winner Nina Kiriki Hoffman / Golden Bridge Award Winner David Wesley Hill... and so much more.

Best New Vampire Tales - Volume One
Includes amazing fiction by: Bram Stoker Award Nominee Michael Laimo / Bram Stoker Award Winner David Niall Wilson / Authorlink New Author Award Winner Tim Waggoner / Bram Stoker Award Winner John Everson / International Horror Guild Nominee Don Webb / British Fantasy Award Science Fiction Award Nominee, Jay Caselberg / Arthur Ellis Award Winner Nancy Kilpatrick

James Roy Daley - Zombie Kong
Big. Bad. Heavy. Hungry. While a 50-foot tall zombie gorilla smashes the hell out of a small town, Candice drags her son Jake through the hazardous streets in an attempt to get away from the man who is determined to kill them. She wishes her husband Dale was by her side; he would know what to do. The good news: Dale's alive. Problem is, he was eaten by the gorilla.

John L. French - Paradise Denied
This is one of the best collections you will ever read. There isn't a single story in this collection that feels like filler. Vampires, zombies, tough cops, faeries, heroes, or super-scientists, John French has got a tale for you, and it's amazing. Again and again, readers agree: this is the book you won't be able to put down. A must read.

James Roy Daley - 13 Drops Of Blood
Thirteen tales of horror, suspense, and imagination. Enter the gore-soaked exhibit, the train of terror, the graveyard of the haunted. Meet the scientist of the monsters, the woman with the thing living inside her, the living dead... James Roy Daley unleashes quality horror stories with a flair for the hardcore. Not for the squeamish.

Zombie Kong - Anthology
Zombies are bad, but ZOMBIE KONG is worse. Way worse. Big. Bad. Heavy. Hungry. This is the most original zombie anthology of all time. In the jungles, in the Arctic, in the cities, in the towns--Zombie Kong rules them all. All other zombies must bow to their god... ZOMBIE KONG!

Paul Kane - Pain Cages
Reminiscent of Stephen King's classic best-selling book Different Seasons, Paul Kane gives us an unforgettable collection of four novella-size stories. Each story is refreshingly original and delivers an emotional impact that is rarely seen in today's literature. Dark and moody, clever and well-written, Pain Cages is speculative fiction at its best.

Matt Hults - Anything Can Be Dangerous
Anything Can be Dangerous contains four amazing stories:
Anything Can be Dangerous--the simple things in life can kill.
Through the Valley of Death--a dark vampire story that will make you re-member fear.
The Finger--zombie literature has never been so extraordinary.
Feeding Frenzy--lunchtime in a place called Hell.

Classic - Vampire Tales
Includes: J. Sheridan Lefanu / Bram Stoker / M. R. James / F. Benson / Algernon Blackwood / F. Marion Crawford / Mary E. Wilkins Freeman / James Robinson Planche / Johann Ludwig Tieck

Thank you for reading this book!

CPSIA information can be obtained
at www.ICGtesting.com
Printed in the USA
FSOW02n1639041016
25599FS